KILLING GOLIATH

To John

MIKE RABIN

enjoy

Mike Rabin

REGIS BOOKS

Copyright © 2012 Mike Rabin
All rights reserved.
ISBN-10: 1478187298
ISBN-13: 978-1478187295

For my girls
Teri, Sam and Liv

Acknowledgements:

Frankie Vaughn
Harry Belafonte
Norman Hartnell
The Oscar Rabin Band
Tommy Steele

Film: 'The Bridge on the River Kwai'
Song Title: 'Mary's Boy Child'
Use of lyrics from the song: 'Roll over Beethoven'

Grateful thanks to Iain Banks,
Roger de la Perrelle and Teri Rabin
for their expertise, patience and support.

KILLING GOLIATH

Prologue

His store was situated in the Whitechapel Road that ran through the heart of London's East End. The shopkeeper wrapped the young woman's groceries and handed them to her along with her change. She smiled her thanks, bid him farewell, and left. It was six o'clock in the evening and time to close for the day.

He reached into the pocket of his brown coat and took out a bunch of keys to lock up the shop. It was part of his daily routine. With the premises secured he would then cash up his till, tidy away the merchandise, and make his way home for the night.

Before he could reach the door, three heavily built men entered the store, one carrying a sledgehammer and another, a petrol canister. The shopkeeper's face turned pale. He backed away as they moved towards him. He knew he should have paid them. But it wasn't easy giving away his hard earned money to Bill Haskin's hoodlums.

'No, please wait! I have the payment,' he pleaded. 'I've got it here in the till.'

Two of them grabbed him, one on each arm, and forced him to watch as their accomplice moved around the small shop wielding the sledgehammer. He smashed everything in sight: shelving, light fittings and finally the counter, splintering it into pieces. The thug then emptied the contents of the cash register into his pockets.

'I'll see you two back in the car,' he said, preparing to leave. 'And remember, the boss said to make an example of him.'

The men dragged their terrified victim deeper into the wrecked store, out of sight from inquisitive eyes. The smaller of the two restrained him, while the other savagely punched him repeatedly in the stomach, rupturing his vital organs. He was then released to collapse at their feet where they continued their assault by kicking and stamping on his head, until his face resembled a grisly red mask. Their final job was to sprinkle the contents of the canister around the place.

'This should convince that old bastard in the café to pay up,' said the smaller man.

He flicked open a cheap lighter, thumbed it alight, and tossed the small, flickering flame into the depths of the store…

Chapter 1

The door slammed hard, waking the whole household. No one ever complained, as it would probably invite a mouthful of abuse, or at worst a beating. Andrei saw nothing wrong in playing with his friend, Yakov, who lived at the blacksmith yard; unfortunately his father, Gustav Wolenski, felt differently.

The Wolenskis lived in the ancient town of Kielce in southeast Poland. It was 1946, and the ravaged Jewish population that had managed to survive Hitler's occupation were striving to rebuild their lives, returning to past skills, finding homes wherever they could. Even as a boy, Andrei understood the awful fate that had scourged European Jewry. Most of the Nazi death camps had been situated within his country, and stories of the Holocaust were widespread. What he could not understand was why some of his own countrymen, including his father, still harboured such hatred towards these long suffering people.

Gustav Wolenski had never forgotten the closure of his family's business; a successful cobbler's shop that had stood close to Herbski Railway Station, benefiting from a constant flow of passing trade. He had enjoyed a happy and prosperous existence, until tragedy struck with the death of his mother. His distraught father lost all interest in life, spending most of the shop's income on cheap vodka in the local bars around Kielce, leaving his son to deal with the daily running of the establishment. But the young Gustav's general lack of expertise, and support from his father, saw the customers gradually diminish. The debts increased to such an extent that they were eventually forced to sell out to a Jewish family. In a matter of months the new owners had turned the small premises into a thriving tailoring business.

With an eight-year old daughter and a three-year old son to feed, Gustav Wolenski sought work as a labourer. The hours were long, and the pay miserly. Every time he was forced to pass the tailor's shop a growing resentment would burn inside him. He became obsessed with jealousy, watching these people grow wealthier while he and his family continued to struggle. His wife patiently endeavoured to reason with him, disturbed by his growing hatred of the Jews. She saw no harm in the people, and constantly tried to protect her children from his prejudices. Her efforts were finally dashed with the death of her father-in-law who had eventually drunk himself into an early grave. It was the final push that sent Gustav Wolenski spiralling into a world of drink, hatred and violence.

Later that year, in September 1939, the Germans invaded Poland. Jews were denounced, and the remainder of the Polish population had no choice other than submit to Nazi rule. Heinrich Himmler, Commander of the Schutzstaffel, decreed that the Polish police would come under his jurisdiction.

They became known as the 'Blue Police', and any officers objecting to the transition were spirited away to an unknown fate by Himmler's 'SS'. When it was announced that they were looking to recruit new members, Gustav Wolenski eagerly volunteered. He spent the rest of the occupation vigorously carrying out his orders, rounding up Jews for the Gestapo. His first arrests were made, late one night, at the small tailors shop near the railway station.

Gustav Wolenski's reign of terror eventually came to an end with the allies' liberation of Poland, and like many other collaborators he managed to slip away, unnoticed, into the war's aftermath.

'*Andrei!* Andrei you little brat, what did I tell you about mixing with those bastards.'

The harsh voice was immediately followed by the sound of clumping boots on wooden stairs, shaking the walls of the sparsely furnished home

Shocked from sleep by the commotion, Marta Wolenski stumbled out onto the narrow, gas-lit landing desperate to protect her son.

'Gustav, no…please…I beg you, leave the child alone.'

A powerful hand grabbed her chin, crushing her mouth shut, silencing her pleas. She was thrown to the floor in tears, powerless to stop him.

While his older sister, Maria, cowered in the corner of their room Andrei hid beneath the blankets, praying that the approaching footsteps would cease. They didn't, and as the bedclothes were whipped back he steeled himself for what was to follow.

'Leave me alone,' the boy cried, 'he's my friend. I've done nothing wrong.'

There was no answer, just excruciating pain as he

was pulled from the bed by his long fair hair. His hands went to his face in a pathetic effort to ward off the vicious slap that sent him sprawling across the bedroom floor.

'They're Jews! They're evil!' bellowed the thickset man, his fiery eyes glaring beneath heavy brows. 'I've forbidden you to go near them, but you still disobey me.'

The ten-year-old child curled himself into a protective ball. It did little to prevent the kick in his back from knocking the breath out of him. Grabbed by the collar of his cheap cotton nightshirt, he was heaved upright until his toes barely touched the ground, to stare directly into a face twisted with hate. The stench of stale alcohol from his father's beard made him retch.

Gustav Wolenski shook his son violently. 'If I catch you near that yard again, I'll kill you. I won't tolerate my family being involved with that scum.' He dropped the boy to the floor.

Andrei fought to control his trembling body, hardly daring to breathe, until his tormentor had stormed from the room. The house slipped into an uneasy silence. Rising painfully to his feet, he forced a brave smile towards his weeping sister and limped back to bed. He reached for his comforter, a battered guitar that leant against the nightstand. By softly strumming a few chords, and singing a simple song in his small voice, he made the world go away.

Chapter 2

The man leaned across and gently pulled the heavy rug further over his wife and small son, tucking it more tightly around their sleeping bodies. Inside the makeshift shelter a circle of faintly glowing embers looked comforting, but offered no real warmth. While the fern covered roof and wooden slatted walls were enough to protect them from the driving sleet, they did little to alleviate the freezing temperature. There wasn't much to look forward to. Their one meal a day consisted mostly of watery potato soup and a handful of rye bread.

He fancied he could hear a distant droning. Urgent voices started to disturb the stillness of the Naliboki forest. It had been rumoured that the Germans were intending a strike against them, but that's all they had been, just rumours.

Suddenly they were upon them. JU 87 Stukas roared vertically from the dawn sky, deploying their weapons directly into the encampment. The screaming whistle of a bomb was followed by a blinding flash…

Mikail Bronovitch blinked into consciousness as his wife swept back the curtains, allowing the morning sunshine to flood into the room.

'Morning, my love, breakfast will be ready in

half an hour,' she said, dropping his dressing gown on to the bed. 'And remember you promised Yakov he could help around the yard during the school holiday.'

'How could I forget, he's talked of nothing else for a week,' her husband yawned, rolling onto his back to gaze at the ceiling.

His wife laughed and left the room.

The fragments of his dream lingered. He needed a moment to collect his thoughts, and a few extra minutes in bed would be welcome. His memory began to rewind, dragging him back to the beginning of the war.

After the treacherous invasion of their country, he had been persuaded by his parents to leave the blacksmith yard in Kielce and take his family north as quickly as possible towards the Baltic Sea. Their plan was to board a ship for Denmark where they would seek refuge with his mother's relatives, but the journey had been ill advised. The German Panzer divisions had swept across northern Poland faster than anticipated, cutting off any chance of escape, forcing the Bronovitch family to enter an overcrowded ghetto in Minsk. Their nightmare had begun. Starved of food, and living in atrocious conditions, they were forced into hiding from the storm troopers who would be constantly combing the streets, herding Jews towards the trucks for deportation.

In December 1941 two men stole into the ghetto offering sanctuary to those brave enough to follow them. They were members of a Jewish Partisan unit that had retreated into the forests of northern Poland and made a commitment to fight back against the Germans for as long as their luck would hold. Ironically, they would often join forces with Soviet troops, the very ones who had driven Jews out of Russia in previous anti-Semitic purges, but these events would be conveniently forgotten when attacking Nazis: the common foe. Mikail Bronovitch made the decision to take his family into the depths of the forest and join the defiant Jewish community with a powerful determination to survive the war.

It would be another three gruelling years before their courage was rewarded by the Russian army making a final assault from the east, fighting its way across Poland to the banks of the Vistula River, to hasten the destruction of the Third Reich.

The Bronovitch family returned to Kielce in 1945. Their loved ones had perished, but to their good fortune the blacksmith yard had survived. Others had not been so lucky, finding their properties occupied by local people with no hope of repossession: an unsavoury consequence of war. The sight of their nine-year-old son, Yakov, running excitedly through the broken gates lifted their spirits. Mikail Bronovitch had fallen to his knees amid six years of dilapidation and given thanks to God for their deliverance.

*

Regardless of the warnings, Andrei found himself entering the blacksmith's yard again. It was an unscheduled visit driven by an urgency that could not be ignored. The echoing metallic rings ceased abruptly as the dark haired, muscular man caught sight of his visitor. Mikail

Bronovitch rested his hammer across the anvil and wiped the sweat from his brow. Raising a powerful forearm to shield his eyes from the summer sun, he could not help but notice the boy's face.

'Morning, my young friend, what have you done to yourself?'

'Oh you know me, clumsy as ever,' Andrei said, looking away to hide the bruising on his cheek. 'I fell, running down the stairs.'

'You kids are always in such a hurry. Life is precious. Slow down and enjoy it.' The blacksmith pulled the molten piece of metal from the fire and continued to beat it into shape. 'Yakov is indoors helping his mother,' he boomed cheerfully above the hammering. 'If you're lucky you might get a drink and a biscuit…and don't run.'

'Thanks, Mr Bronovitch,' Andrei shouted, sprinting towards the modest dwelling at the end of the yard.

'Like talking to a brick wall,' the big man laughed, shaking his head.

Andrei was the same age as his friend. They had become inseparable after he had rescued the small boy from a beating in the school playground. Having not yet acquired his father's powerful physique, Yakov made an easy target for the bullies. But despite being subjected to constant ridicule he managed to maintain an insatiable thirst for life, embracing every day as if it were his last. His cheerful optimism never failed to lift Andrei's spirits.

Yakov was wiping a plate dry as Andrei

entered the kitchen. His eyes lit up. 'I didn't think I'd see you today. I shouldn't be *too* long,' he grumbled, breathing a tragic sigh.

Katrina Bronovitch grinned, ruffling Yakov's thick black hair. 'Oh go on with you, I'm sure I'll manage on my own, and don't get up to any mischief. Goodness, that's a nasty bruise, Andrei.'

'It's nothing, honest,' he answered dismissively.

Yakov threw down the tea towel and grabbed his friend by the arm. 'Come on, let's go. We can both help Dad in the yard.'

'Sorry, just a minute,' Andrei said, standing firm, looking intently at Yakov's mother. 'I wanted to make sure you were all at home. I need to tell you something. Do you think Mr Bronovitch would mind joining us?'

Her face creased into a frown. 'What is it? Why so serious?'

'I really *do* need to speak with you all, right away,' the youngster insisted.

'As you wish. Yakov, go and get your father. Tell him it's urgent.'

Once Mr Bronovitch arrived, they all took seats around the kitchen table. 'So, what's all this about?' he asked with a curious smile.

'I've come to warn you,' Andrei said in a trembling voice. 'There's an angry mob outside the Jewish Centre in Planty Street. They're smashing windows, and painting stuff on the walls...they're shouting horrible things at the people inside...'

Mr Bronovitch lost his smile. He spoke softly, trying to calm the boy. 'What sort of things?'

'They're saying some Catholic kid's been taken

by the Jews, who are going to kill him…they're going to use his blood for some terrible ritual …it's not true is it?'

'Good God, no, of course it isn't. They're talking absolute rubbish,' Mr Bronovitch said, looking worried. 'Has anyone called the police?'

'They're already there, but they're doing nothing to stop it,' Andrei replied, fighting back the tears.

A shadow fell across the blacksmith's weathered face. 'I can't believe it's all starting again. We came from Russia to escape persecution, only to be driven into hiding from the Nazis, and now we're turned upon by our neighbours. Are you sure about this, Andrei?'

'I am.' The boy's voice faltered. 'I'm ashamed to say my father is one of them. He would kill me if he knew I was here.'

Yakov watched his friend turn pale at the thought.

Mrs Bronovitch's eyes were drawn to Andrei's swollen cheek: realisation dawned. She reached across and gently clasped his hand. 'You have nothing to be ashamed of, my love. You're a fine, brave boy. I hate to think what you've been through at home.' Her tone became solemn. 'This business could turn ugly, Mikail.'

Defiance flashed in his eyes. 'We've spent our lives running from this evil. The time has come to make a stand. I will remain here, and if necessary, protect our home. Katrina, you must take Yakov and go somewhere safe until this has blown over.'

'Father, let me stay,' Yakov cried, springing to

his feet. 'I can't just leave you on your own.'

Mr Bronovitch smiled sadly at his son. 'It's far too dangerous, and besides, who will look after your mother.' He turned to his wife for support. Instead he was met with a look of stubborn determination; she had no intention of going anywhere.

Suddenly Andrei seemed to possess wisdom beyond his years. Perhaps it was the constant abuse that had stolen his childhood, or simply an overwhelming urge to protect his friend?

'Your father's right, Yakov, what could you do if you stayed, or me for that matter. We're too small. Believe me, I know. We wouldn't stand a chance.'

Yakov shrugged half-heartedly.

Mr Bronovitch laid a hand on his boy's shoulder. 'He's right, son. But where can we send you?'

'I know just the place,' Andrei said, his eyes widening as the thought struck him. 'Yakov, you could stay with my Grandma Anna. You remember, last summer, when we used to visit her cottage. We had a great time.' He spun round to Mr Bronovitch. 'She lives in the village of Bartok, only a few kilometres from here.'

The man was unsure. 'With respect, Andrei, that could be dangerous. How do we know your grandmother doesn't share your father's beliefs?'

'I'm talking about my grandmother on my *mother's* side. She hates my father for the way he treats us. I know she'd be only too happy to look after Yakov. She's a wonderful old lady.'

The blacksmith scratched his close-cropped

beard. 'Bartok, you say?'

Andrei nodded eagerly.

'Very well, that's settled. We have no choice. Yakov, you must leave immediately, there's no time to lose.' Mr Bronovitch stood up to hug his son who looked lost, resigned to his fate. 'Be a good lad, and don't forget to give our thanks to this kind lady. We'll come for you when things have quietened down, I promise.'

Close to tears, Katrina Bronovitch managed a smile of encouragement at her small boy and hurried away to pack what few clothes and possessions he owned into a faded carpetbag. A perfectly happy day had been cruelly destroyed in a matter of minutes. Andrei Wolenski found it hard suppressing his envy at the love this family shared; a stark contrast to the misery suffered by his own.

*

The gates to the yard had been securely bolted. After stowing away his workload for the day, Mr Bronovitch joined his wife in their living room. His strong arms embraced her in gentle reassurance. She wept silently: fearful of what the day might bring.

*

Andrei led his friend through the wrought iron gate to discover Grandma Anna kneeling beside a wicker basket, cutting flowers from her garden. She looked up, pleasantly surprised, and rose to her feet. Dusting her hands together, she swept a few silver hairs back into her tightly combed pleat, before opening her arms to greet them.

Andrei loved everything about his

grandmother. From her favoured high-necked blouse and long grey skirt, to that pervading scent of lavender, she provided the homely reassurance he craved as a child: his emotional shelter from the tempestuous cruelty suffered at the hands of his father.

Her joy at seeing the two boys was quickly dampened after hearing about the developments in Kielce. She happily agreed to take Yakov into safe keeping, suggesting that her grandson might also stay with them. However, Andrei insisted it would be better for him to return without delay. That way his father would be unaware of her involvement and it could remain their secret.

As he prepared to leave, Andrei found it painful returning Yakov's brave smile. But seeing his friend standing in front of Grandma Anna, with her hands crossed protectively across his chest, made him feel confident that he had done the right thing. He gave a cheerful wave and reluctantly set off for the journey home, praying that he hadn't been missed.

He needn't have worried. Gustav Wolenski had become too involved as one of the self-appointed leaders of the mob to concern himself with his son's whereabouts: a mob that was gathered in Planty Street, and growing more hostile by the minute, undeterred by the presence of a few apathetic police officers.

The Jewish Community Centre had become the focus of their attention. Every so often its occupants would appear at the smashed windows, trying to reason with their persecutors, only to be chased from view by another hail of stones. Children's cries could be heard from inside the building during brief lulls between the constant abuse being bellowed from the pavement.

The roar of a large engine turned heads. An army lorry rounded the corner and rumbled down the road to draw up alongside the building. The more moderate onlookers expected the hostilities to cease with the presence of the military. But to their astonishment, a group of soldiers goaded by the baying crowd jumped from the back of the truck and entered the building. Suddenly, and for no apparent reason, they started to open fire indiscriminately. The Jewish occupants, who had not been shot inside the Centre, were dragged into the road to be set upon by the rabble where they were cruelly beaten to death; old men, women and children, it made no difference.

The orgy of violence that followed would become a dark stain on Polish history for years to come as the bloodshed continued with gangs of thugs rampaging through the streets of Kielce, killing and looting in a frenzy of hatred.

*

Mikail Bronovitch waited under a scorching sun, courageously ignoring his fear, with a hammer clenched in his fist. His mouth was dry, and his shirt damp with sweat, as he watched the tall wooden gates shuddering against the relentless battering.

It was not long before the bolts were torn away, allowing the screaming mob to surge into the yard led by Gustav Wolenski.

Chapter 3

Andrei walked briskly away from the bus drawn towards palls of smoke spiralling into the pink evening sky. Local townsfolk hurried passed him in the opposite direction, avoiding his eyes, as if driven by guilt. A sense of foreboding instinctively quickened his pace. He turned the corner towards the Bronovitch home to run headlong into a grey uniformed policeman.

'That's far enough,' the officer ordered, grabbing the boy's sleeve.

'Let me through, my friends are down there!' Andrei protested, trying to pull away.

'I doubt that, only a few Jews. Best keep out the way. Go home to your family. It's not safe out here.'

'Let him through. He's with me,' a guttural voice shouted.

The policeman released his hold, glad to be relieved of the responsibility.

Gustav Wolenski appeared through a haze of smoke and strode up to seize his son's collar. 'Where have you been you little fool? Come, I have something to show you.'

Andrei was dragged along the road and pushed through a set of familiar gates where people were jostling for position to gawp at what appeared to be a large pile of rags lying in a misshapen heap. His father barged a path to the front of the crowd.

Mikail Bronovitch was hardly recognisable from the strong, handsome man he had once been. The bloodied clothes were virtually ripped from his body that lay like a broken, oversized doll at Andrei's feet.

'Now *that* is what I call a good Jew,' Gustav Wolenski announced, with a burst of wild laughter, causing the crowd to shift restlessly. 'The bitch was burnt in the house. We haven't found the boy yet, but he won't get far. A good day's work, I think. I'll see you at home, and don't be late.'

He cuffed his son around the head and wandered off, followed by a handful of cronies. The remaining onlookers quickly melted away, leaving the boy alone.

Andrei knelt down beside the remains of Mikail Bronovitch. His youthful innocence found it hard to comprehend the evil that surrounded him. He saw nothing repulsive about the mutilated body, only the sleeping figure of a much-loved friend. He reached out to lay his hand on the dead man's arm.

'Don't worry, I'll look after Yakov…I promise,' he whispered, almost expecting Mr Bronovitch to speak with him as he had earlier in the day.

A charred beam finally gave up its hold and crashed into the smouldering ruins of the blacksmith's house, shocking Andrei back to his senses. A solitary tear welled in his eye, and slid down his bruised cheek.

*

The pogrom that took place in Kielce on the 4th July 1946 was rumoured to have been instigated by the communists as a callous ploy to divert their western allies' scrutiny from allegations of rigged elections, but it only succeeded in bringing condemnation. Appeasement had to be offered urgently.

At the far end of the spacious oak-panelled office a large red flag, displaying a gold hammer and sickle topped by a red star, hung imperiously above the dapper figure of Boleslaw Bierut, the newly appointed chairman of the State National Council. He sat behind a mahogany desk with a pen poised in his hand, studying several documents. A Polish army officer stood stiffly to attention in front of him, his cap stowed beneath his left arm.

Boleslaw Bierut took a sip from his glass of black tea and produced a folded handkerchief to dab his clipped moustache. 'We have to act quickly,' he said, leaning forward to scribble the required signatures. 'It seems this damn Kielce incident has ruffled our allies' feathers. Who would have thought there'd be so much fuss over a few Jews?'

The soldier grunted in agreement. 'When is the order to be carried out, comrade Bierut?'

'At dawn tomorrow,' said the dark-suited man, holding out the papers. 'And make sure the press are notified. We need them to witness the swift justice meted out by our courts. It should satisfy our critics if nothing else.'

'Very well,' the officer replied, collecting the death warrants with a curt bow.

He saluted, performed an about turn, and marched from the room.

*

A hastily arranged show trial had convicted twelve people as being ring leaders of the riot, nine of whom were sentenced to death by firing squad. Others, who had been involved in the slaughter, fled Kielce in fear of their lives. Gustav Wolenski had been one of them.

Although his disappearance brought a welcome peace to the Wolenski household he had, nevertheless, been the only breadwinner. Andrei's sister had been forced to leave school and work as a seamstress, adding to the meagre income Mrs Wolenski earned by taking in laundry. Andrei remained at his studies to appease his mother who was convinced that one day he would achieve the qualifications necessary to take on a well-paid job. He spent every spare moment playing his guitar. It was his only solace from a drab, impoverished existence.

*

Five months had passed since the Kielce rampage and Yakov Bronovitch was showing few signs of coming to terms with the violent deaths of his parents. He refused to speak of it, and perhaps more disturbingly he never cried. Andrei's shame at his father's involvement in their murders would haunt him for the rest of his life. The family swore an oath never to disclose the truth.

Living with Grandma Anna had helped Yakov settle into a quiet, uncomplicated existence. There was no school in Bartok. Not that it bothered him, having inherited his father's ability to work with his hands he made himself useful helping the old lady with her chores, and acting as a young handyman around the village.

Chapter 4

The bus driver's vision had been reduced to a small arc by the solitary wiper that fought stubbornly to prevent a raging blizzard from blocking the windscreen completely. As the old single-decker slid to a halt, Andrei wiped his gloved hand across the misted window to gaze upon the ghostly white spectre of Bartok village.

He pulled up the collar of his coat, pushed open the door, and jumped into the ankle deep snow. With a scarf thrown across his mouth against the biting wind, he trudged down the lane towards his grandmother's cottage. It was early December, and the Wolenskis were planning to invite Grandma Anna and Yakov over for Christmas, which was the reason for his visit on such a bleak afternoon.

'Come in quickly, poor love, you must be frozen,' the old lady said, pulling her grandson into the welcoming warmth of the tiny hallway. She closed the door swiftly to shut out the blustery snow. 'Yakov, look who's here,' she called out, helping Andrei out of his coat.

A small, serious-faced figure appeared at the entrance to the sitting room. 'It's good to see you. I'm surprised you managed to get through.'

'I must admit the roads were bad,' Andrei said

brightly, rubbing some warmth back into his hands. 'The bus skidded all over the place. It was good fun. So, how are you, Yakov? I bet Grandma's been keeping you busy.'

'There's always something to be fixed,' he replied. The cheerless look in his eyes refused to go away.

Andrei followed his friend into the low beamed, comfortably furnished sitting room. Lace curtains draped across frosted windows completed the cosy scene, making him wish he could stay there forever. He lost no time in extending his mother's invitation. The thought of spending Christmas with her family, without the presence of her despised son-in-law, delighted the old lady. Yakov was genuinely happy for her, but he did not relish the thought of returning to Kielce: there were too many bad memories.

Grandma Anna left the room to return with three mugs of hot chocolate and a plateful of freshly baked cinnamon cakes. She stoked the log fire into life and settled back into her favourite chair, with Yakov sitting at her feet. Andrei experienced a feeling of well-being as he sipped at the chocolate and lounged beside the crackling flames, soaking up the hospitality of his grandmother's home. His eyes were drawn towards the mantelpiece where an oval-framed sepia photograph stood as a constant reminder of happier times. It portrayed Grandma Anna as a younger woman, standing proudly beside the seated figure of her husband: the grandfather he had never known.

Andrei could only recall the brutalities of a

Nazi occupation and the evil deeds perpetrated by his father. He drew some consolation in the close bond formed between Yakov and his grandmother. It helped to ease the shame of the dark secret his conscience struggled to hide.

'*Hello*, remember us,' the old lady cooed, teasing her grandson from his daydream. 'Tell us about your mother, and that sister of yours. Maria must be growing into a beautiful young woman by now.'

'Sorry, Grandma, just thinking,' Andrei said sheepishly. He noticed his friend studying him closely and experienced a sudden rush of guilt, as if his mind had been read.

*

Yakov offered to keep Andrei company while he waited for his bus. Wrapped up against the wintry evening, the two boys embraced Grandma Anna at the front door and shuffled off through the deepening drifts. The blizzard had eased by the time they reached the bus stop where they waited patiently, staring down the darkening lane through the lightly falling snow. Yakov was the first to speak.

'You know I shouldn't really be celebrating Christmas.'

'Oh no,' Andrei gasped, 'I'm *so* sorry, Yakov. I never gave it a thought, how stupid of me.'

Yakov's mouth spread into a mischievous grin. 'It's okay. I'm only joking. Actually, I do remember one Christmas when my parents gave me presents. They didn't want me to feel left out from the other kids. Jewish people celebrated Chanukah at the same time, so Dad said it was no big deal to bend the rules a bit.'

Andrei was heartened by his friend's sudden interest in making conversation. He was desperate to encourage it.

'Was your Dad very strict about religion?'

'No, not really, although he did tell me exciting stories about the Israelite's fighting the Philistines, and stuff like that. I suppose he believed there was more to life than going to the Synagogue. I remember him saying, *"It's no good being too heavenly to be of no earthly use."* He let out a hollow laugh. 'To be honest, he never had much time for praying. Mum would scold him sometimes. But he would just smile, and give her a hug…'

The words choked in his throat. Was it the icy breeze that had caused his eyes to water? There followed an awkward silence while Andrei searched frantically for something to say.

'That's settled then,' he exclaimed, throwing his arm around Yakov's shoulders. 'I will find the best present I can, especially for you to open at Christmas.'

At that moment the floating snowflakes were transformed into a host of glittering stars by the bus's headlights, probing a path up the slippery lane.

Chapter 5

The candles on the small fir tree glowed more brightly every time Andrei's mother swept past, busying herself with final preparations for the festive meal. According to Polish tradition, Christmas Eve was the most significant part of the religious holiday. After fasting all day, people would wait for the first star to appear in the night sky, representing the star of Bethlehem, after which their celebrations would begin.

'Maria, pass me the fish and those dumplings, there's a good girl,' Mrs Wolenski said, taking the heavily laden plates from her daughter.

She placed them on the table and wiped her hands down her apron to smooth out a wrinkle on the crisp white tablecloth, before stepping back to check that everything was in its place. Her handsome face was a picture of contentment, hardly recognisable from the drawn and exhausted woman she had once been. Although it had been a struggle for her family, she cherished every day spent without her husband. It was as if a dark mantle had been lifted from their lives. For so many reasons she wanted to make this a very special Christmas.

'I've never seen so much food in my life,'

Yakov said, amazed by the huge spread as he followed his friend into the room. Mrs Wolenski took great pleasure in her young guest's reaction.

'There are twelve dishes in total, one for each of Christ's Disciples,' Andrei pointed out.

'I see, but why has the table been laid for six people? There are only five of us.'

'Ah, well,' Andrei explained, with an air of importance, 'tradition says we have to do that in case the Holy Spirit should arrive unexpectedly to eat with us.'

'Gosh. He wouldn't be best pleased to find a Jewish boy sitting with him,' Yakov said nervously.

Maria laughed out loud. 'I'm sorry, Yakov, but your face…'

Mrs Wolenski looked down at the dark haired boy, cupping his chin in her hand. 'My dear Yakov, I think He would be honoured. After all Jesus was Jewish, wasn't He?' she smiled.

'I'd never thought of it like that. Thanks, I can enjoy my food now,' he said with childlike relief.

She pinched his cheek affectionately. 'Now, I want you and Andrei to sit by the window with Grandma Anna and keep a look out for that star. I don't know about anyone else, but I'm beginning to feel hungry. Maria, you can help me finish up in the kitchen.'

Much to everyone's amusement, Yakov was the first one to spot a star shining between the smoky dark clouds. They immediately made for the dinner table where Mrs Wolenski was already filling their plates. Laughter and lively chatter accompanied their meal as the food and drink were consumed with relish. Even Yakov made efforts to join in the conversation. He had not experienced anything so enjoyable for a long time.

Leaning back in his chair, and feeling pleasantly full, his attention was drawn to the unoccupied place setting at the end of the table. Its emptiness seemed to reflect his own as painful memories began to claw at his heart. He would never again know the love and comfort that his adored parents had given him. How he wished they could be with him now. Mrs Wolenski was quick to notice the change in Yakov's mood.

'I think we've all had enough to eat,' she said, reaching for the empty plates. 'Boys, how about you sorting out the presents while I get the table cleared.'

The suggestion had the desired effect. Yakov broke into a small grin and slipped from the chair to join his friend beside the brightly adorned tree. Grandma Anna winked knowingly at her daughter.

Andrei was appointed to hand out the colourfully wrapped parcels. Marta and Maria Wolenski had combined their skills and hard earned savings to ensure that everyone would receive a gift. Grandma Anna was presented with a new shawl, while Andrei could scarcely believe his eyes when he opened his small package to reveal a complete set of brand new guitar strings. Mrs Wolenski received an embroidered blouse made by her daughter, who in turn unwrapped a pretty dress bought at the local market by her mother.

'And *this* is for you from all of us,' Andrei announced finally, handing his friend a narrow red box.

Yakov took the gift cautiously, hardly daring to believe this was actually happening: a present especially for him. He carefully untied the gilt ribbon and lifted the lid to reveal a long knife, with an elaborately fashioned ivory handle, secured in a highly polished leather sheath.

'It's *beautiful*,' he breathed. 'How could you afford to buy me something like this?'

'I have a confession to make. That knife belonged to my father,' Mrs Wolenski said, looking towards her elderly mother. 'Grandma Anna has told me how clever you are with your hands. We women would certainly have no use for it, and Andrei is too wrapped up in his guitar.'

Yakov drew the knife from its sheath and held it in front of him, almost reverently, examining every detail in its finely carved handle. Andrei experienced a warm glow of satisfaction as he witnessed the pleasure growing across his friend's face.

'I will treasure this for ever,' Yakov said, getting up to embrace everyone around the table, arriving lastly at Andrei. He clutched his friend's hand. 'I shall carve something special for all of you. You've been so kind to me.'

'Believe me, it's the least we can do after -' Andrei stopped mid-sentence. His cheeks reddened.

'After what?' Yakov asked in the crushing silence.

'Goodness me is *that* the time?' Grandma Anna intervened quickly. 'We had better get ready for church. Am I right in thinking our neighbours will be calling round soon?'

'Yes, that's right,' Mrs Wolenski said, picking up on the initiative. 'You're welcome to come with us, Yakov, or stay here, whatever you wish.'

'Eh? Why yes...of course I'll come,' the youngster said, forgetting his question.

*

They were sitting at the table in their coats, waiting to leave. The three women were talking among themselves, while the boys admired their gifts.

Andrei was carefully inspecting the coiled strings inside their thin paper packets. 'I can't wait to re-string my guitar. It'll sound even better now.'

'It sounds pretty good already,' Yakov said, lovingly running his fingers across the knife's handle. 'You should be a musician when you grow up.'

His friend breathed a gloomy sigh. 'I don't think Mum would approve. She says I've got to study and get a proper job.' He turned to face Yakov. 'So tell me, what are you going to make for me?'

'What would you like me to make?'

Andrei thought for a moment. 'I know, how about a small charm that I could hang around my neck. It would remind me of our friendship.'

'Good idea,' Yakov agreed.

'Done,' said Andrei.

They shook hands playfully.

A sudden knocking on the front door told them it was time to go. Maria started to help Grandma Anna to her feet.

'Come along, boys,' said Mrs Wolenski, 'and no giggling in church.' She waved a threatening finger at her son, trying hard not to smile.

'I won't, I promise,' Andrei said, stuffing the strings into his pocket. 'It's easier said than done,' he hissed. 'Our priest has the funniest high voice you've ever heard. Sounds like a squeaky mouse.'

Yakov's laugh was cut short by a fearful cry.

'*Gustav!* What are you doing here? Go away. You're not welcome.'

Mrs Wolenski had pulled open the door, expecting to see her neighbours. Instead, she was met with the scowling face of her drunken husband.

'Out of my way, woman, it's Christmas, and it's my bloody house,' he roared, shoving his wife aside.

'Run, children! Get out of here,' Marta Wolenski shouted, attempting to shield Grandma Anna from his flaying arms. Maria had immediately shrunk back into the corner of the lobby. The two boys were paralyzed with fear, watching the man lurch towards them. His eyes squinted in recognition at the sight of Yakov.

'You've got that Jew in my house! Come here, you little bastard, thought you'd got away with it, did you?'

The dark haired boy was struck dumb, trying to comprehend what he had done to deserve such abuse.

Andrei sprang into action. 'Quick, this way.'

He dragged Yakov into the living room and threw the door shut, wedging the back of a chair under the handle.

Marta Wolenski tugged frantically at her husband's coat as he shouldered the door. 'Leave them alone, you swine, they're just kids.'

Her bravery was rewarded by a punch to the chest. She clung on stubbornly, until another blow across the cheek sent her crumpling to the floor. Maria flung herself down beside her mother, cradling the unconscious woman in her arms, while Gustav Wolenski continued to batter down the door. Grandma Anna had run into the street shouting for help.

'It won't hold,' Andrei cried, desperately searching for a means of escape. 'The window...we'll climb out the window.'

Yakov experienced an overwhelming urge to defend his Jewish heritage, whatever the cost. His father's words came back to him. *"We've spent our lives running from this evil. The time has come to make a stand..."* There was a sense of quiet resignation about his manner as the fragile door began to splinter under the constant pounding. He would never appreciate the cruel parallels between his father's death and his own deadly predicament.

Andrei was yanking at his friend's sleeve. 'We must jump from the window. It's only a short drop. Yakov, do you hear me. We must go, *now!*'

As the words left his mouth the door flew off its hinges, crashing to the floor, to reveal the terrifying spectacle of a crazed Gustav Wolenski stumbling into the room.

He swayed back against the wall to steady himself, glaring at the small boy. 'Time to finish the job. Your Jew of a father dared stand in my way. He died quickly, just as you will.'

Shocked astonishment flashed across Yakov's small face. His eyes blazed in anger. *This* was the person who had killed his family, and taken away all that he had cherished. This person had destroyed his life.

'No, Father, are you mad? Leave him alone!' Andrei yelled.

The deranged man lunged forward, catching his foot on the broken door. He lost his balance, cursing loudly, to fall heavily at Yakov's feet. He began to push himself up, grunting like some monstrous beast.

Yakov's hand was already raised high above his head. He brought the knife down with all the strength he could find. Gustav Wolenski slumped back to the floor, blood spurting from his neck like a surreal red fountain.

The boy dropped to his knees beside the prone body.

'*This…is…for…my…Father…and…Mother…*' he chanted through clenched teeth, his voice shaking with fury, stabbing again and again, the blade flashing up and down with rhythmic repetition.

Andrei looked on in horror as his mild-mannered friend erupted with unimaginable ferocity. Maria's screams pierced the room.

Finally the carnage ceased.

Yakov rose slowly to his feet, the knife lying loosely in his hand. Exhausted by his act of savagery, he stared blankly at the blood soaked corpse with its head twisted at an impossible angle, having nearly been severed from its body by the sheer force of the attack. Maria averted her eyes, sobbing, still clinging to her mother's limp body. Andrei cautiously approached the traumatised boy, reaching out to touch his back. The youngster turned round to stare at him with vacant eyes.

'I did it for them,' he said with a trembling smile, as if to apologise for some petty misdemeanour.

'I know, Yakov, I know...' Andrei replied tearfully. He cautiously took the knife from his friend, and drew him into a close embrace.

It was then that Grandma Anna returned with the neighbours. The couple insisted she remain in the lobby as they edged around Maria and her mother, fighting to control their revulsion at the gruesome sight beyond the doorway.

'I did it! It was me!' Andrei cried, holding out the blood-drenched knife. 'I had to do it. He was going to kill my friend.'

Maria's head shot up in disbelief. Andrei locked eyes with her instantly, willing her to remain silent. Born out of a necessity to survive their father's brutal regime, the two siblings had developed a bond of understanding that often required no spoken word; this was to be such a moment. His sister said nothing. Yakov had no comprehension of what was going on. His mind had simply shut down.

Distant church bells began to peel across the snow-laden rooftops, calling the people of Kielce to Midnight Mass.

*

The subsequent inquest into the killing of Gustav Wolenski resulted in many harrowing disclosures. The relentless violence carried out against his wife and children, and his personal involvement in the previous year's riots that had led to the murders of Mr and Mrs Bronovitch, helped to bring about a speedy conclusion to the hearing, exonerating Andrei from the charge of patricide that had been brought against him. It was judged to be justifiable self-defence. He had simply panicked and grabbed the knife to protect his friend, Yakov, from certain death.

Mrs Wolenski and her elderly mother remained unaware of the truth that lay behind the Christmas Eve slaying. Despite the huge relief at seeing Andrei walk free, they found it difficult to understand why he had shown no apparent signs of distress after killing his own father. The family doctor assured them that he was going through a predictable period of denial, convinced that time would eventually heal the problem, just as Maria's constant refusal to discuss the events of that night was seen as a natural reluctance to relive such a dreadful experience.

Yakov had become deeply withdrawn, spending his time carving wooden ornaments at Grandma Anna's cottage. His condition had been seen as a direct consequence of supposedly witnessing the bloody attack on Gustav Wolenski so soon after the trauma of his parent's murders. At the end of the trial, Andrei had begged the court's permission for the knife to be returned to his friend, explaining that it had been given as a

Christmas present on the night of the killing, and how much it still meant to him. Considering the circumstances, the magistrates saw no harm in allowing the request. Any gesture that might bring comfort to the distressed boy seemed reasonable.

Chapter 6

Andrei allowed the gate to swing shut and walked the short distance to the front door. He flipped the brass knocker, aware of a pleasant fragrance rising from the flowers nestling close to the stone-walled cottage. He was making one of his regular trips to Bartok in the vain hope of finding his friend released from the dark shroud that had enveloped him for so long. Grandma Anna beckoned him in with a welcoming kiss.

She pushed open the door to the living room. Yakov was sat in his usual place beside the window, hunched over a small piece of wood he was carving with the same knife he had once used to stab a man to death. His hair had grown long, hanging down the side of his face, hiding it from view.

'Yakov, look who's here to see you,' the old lady coaxed, as if addressing an infant.

There was no reply.

'How has he been, Grandma?' Andrei asked quietly.

'Little change I'm afraid. The poor love just sits there all day. He hardly eats anything, and hasn't spoken to me in weeks. I think you might be his only chance. Don't give up on him.'

'Never!' he whispered sharply.

Grandma Anna eased the door shut, allowing the boys their privacy. Andrei pulled up a chair to sit beside his friend.

'It's a beautiful day. Why don't we go out into the garden?' Sunshine streamed through the lace curtains as he spoke. 'Maybe we could walk into the village, or across the fields. It's too nice to be stuck indoors.'

Yakov kept whittling wood shavings into a large basket, seemingly unaware of his visitor.

'Mum sends her love, and my sister keeps asking after you. If I didn't know better I would think she's sweet on you,' Andrei joked, searching for the slightest reaction. 'Maybe I should tell her you don't like older women,' he laughed self-consciously.

The silence was unbearable: almost embarrassing.

'What are you making?' He tried a straight question, hoping to encourage an answer, but there was still no reply. 'Yakov, why won't you talk to me? I promised your Mum and Dad that I'd look after you, but you're not making things easy. Please don't treat me like this. I miss you so much,' He swallowed hard to clear his tightening throat, staring at the curtain of black hair. 'What have I done wrong?' he pleaded in a secretive voice. 'I thought I was helping by taking the blame for my father's death. I would do anything for us to be friends again.'

The slow, methodical carving continued.

Andrei wiped a tear away with the back of his hand. He waited patiently, praying for some reaction. It never came.

*

Travelling home on the bus through the streets of Kielce, Andrei was too pre-occupied to notice the unusually large amount of people converging on the railway station. It was a sight that had become all too familiar over recent weeks.

Despite assurances from the government, the last wave of anti-Semitism had prompted large numbers of the Jewish population to leave Poland and head for the displaced person's camps in Austria and West Germany, from where they would endeavour to seek new lives in another country.

The exodus had begun.

*

Before the war, Grandma Anna's close friends, Mr and Mrs Hurwitz, had run a successful patisserie in Bartok, offering a wide selection of coffees and home made pastries. But after the arrival of the German army their business had immediately been closed down. Like the rest of the Jewish residents, they had been forced to sew yellow stars on their coats, and even walk in the gutters so as not to defile the pavements. Disgusted by their treatment, Grandma Anna had bravely offered them refuge in the cellar beneath her cottage. It was to become their home for the rest of the occupation.

The friends' lives had been fraught with danger. One of the most frightening episodes had taken place on a winter's evening when the old lady's son-in-law had arrived, unannounced, accompanied by another police officer, demanding a hot drink and a seat beside the fire. Gustav Wolenski had been on one of his regular quests to hunt down Jews in Bartok.

Long after that night she would still recall the shame of having to entertain the two men, while being forced to agree with their venomous opinions about Jews, and the righteous cause of the Nazi's *final solution*, in order to protect her friends hiding in the cellar below. Ironically, being the mother-in-law of Gustav Wolenski, who was favoured by the Gestapo for his anti-Semitic beliefs, had helped protect her from any unwanted attention.

She had never regarded herself as a religious person, but their survival during those miserable years had been nothing short of a miracle, which made the present visit all the more painful. Mr and Mrs Hurwitz had called round to inform her of their difficult decision to leave Poland.

'It's so cruel,' Grandma Anna said, re-filling their cups, 'to have survived the war, and now be forced to leave because of our own countrymen. It beggars belief. When will it all end?'

Samuel Hurwitz was a slightly built man in his early sixties with kind eyes and a gentle voice, possessing a compassionate wisdom born from a life of unenviable experiences. He let out a long breath, running fingers through his thinning hair.

'Anna, we love Poland, it's our home, but we live in perilous times. I suppose bad seeds can grow anywhere.'

'Pity they can't grow somewhere else for a change,' his wife remarked bitterly.

Rachel Hurwitz was two years younger than her

husband. Traces of her former beauty were still apparent in her almond shaped eyes and luxuriant dark hair that was now streaked with grey, hastened without doubt by the horrors of a world war. Her thoughts slipped back to the day when her only son, a darkly handsome man in his early-thirties, had been arrested by the Gestapo on his return home after foraging for food. He and his wife, together with their young family, had been bundled onto the back of an open truck and driven away: never to be seen again. The guilt of not being with them, to share their fate, was like an open wound that would never heal.

Grandma Anna noticed the sorrow creep across her friend's face. She looked towards Mr Hurwitz. 'So where will you go, Samuel? Do you have the correct papers to leave the country?' she asked, sounding concerned.

'I'm afraid not, but Rachel has a nephew living in London. He escaped from Poland at the start of the invasion to fight with the Allies. If we can make it to one of the Displacement Camps, he has offered to sponsor us at the British Consulate. To be honest, we're not expecting an easy journey.'

Mr Hurwitz reached across to hold his wife's hand. She acknowledged his gesture with a supportive smile, before turning to her friend.

'Anna, do you not fear for Yakov? Has he any idea of the dangers he faces here?'

'Of course I'm scared for him, but it's difficult to know what he thinks anymore. After all he's been through I couldn't bear the thought of him suffering further at the hands of those wicked people. But what choice does he have? His parents are dead. He has no relatives, and if it weren't for me and my daughter's family the poor child would have no one. Today is one of those rare occasions I've been able to persuade him to put down that wretched knife and go out for some fresh air.'

'You're right, of course, he's so fortunate to have -' Mrs Hurwitz was silenced by the front door banging.

'Yakov, is that you?' Grandma Anna shouted, getting up to hurry from the room.

'Good grief, what happened? Speak to me child!' cried the distant voice.

A sharp gesture from his wife stopped Mr Hurwitz from leaving his chair just as Yakov was led through the door.

'You know my good friends, Samuel and Rachel Hurwitz, don't you,' said Grandma Anna, throwing a look of desperation towards her guests.

Yakov stared at the ground, unwilling to look up, until the old lady placed her fingers lightly beneath his chin to raise his face. Mrs Hurwitz caught her breath. Her husband clamped his eyes shut, sickened by the sight of a vicious gash down the boy's right cheek. His bottom lip was split open, and deep bruising had started to develop across his eyes and forehead. He stared defiantly across the room, showing no hint of pain. His mouth began to move.

Mrs Hurwitz left the couch to kneel down in front of him. 'Who did this to you, my love?'

The anticipation of hearing him speak after so

long was unbearable. His weak voice was barely audible.

'They still hurt me...I don't care...I did it for them...'

After the first tentative words, he raised his right fist and started to pump it up and down much to everyone's bewilderment.

'I don't understand. What are you trying to say?' Mrs Hurwitz asked, attempting to steady his arm, only to have her hand thrown aside as he continued to pump more vigorously, repeating, '*I did it for them*', like some kind of mantra.

'This is getting us nowhere,' she sighed, rising to her feet. 'He's obviously been attacked by those ruffians at the bottom of the village. They've been causing all manner of trouble, daubing the *Star of David* on people's doors, including our own. You see why we must get away from here, Anna. It's far too dangerous to remain.'

'Sadly, I do,' the old lady agreed. She managed to calm the boy and sit him on the couch. 'Please excuse me for a moment while I get something for his wounds, although I fear he'll need stitches in that cheek.' The brief glimmer of devotion in Yakov's eyes went unnoticed as he watched her leave to fetch the medicine box.

Mrs Hurwitz sat down beside the boy, laying a protective arm around his shoulders. 'How could they do this to such a defenceless child? And what on earth was all that fist waving about?'

Her husband looked unsure. 'He seemed to be punching, or stabbing. You can't blame him for that, poor kid. How many times have you felt like hitting back at our enemies?'

Grandma Anna could not help overhearing Mr Hurwitz as she returned to the room. She gently dabbed the blood from Yakov's battered face and looked deep into his eyes. They had lapsed into a torturous stare, fixed upon some unimaginable horror. She experienced an involuntary shiver. Gone was the happy, innocent young soul she had once known.

There were so many reasons why this tragic boy needed to leave Poland.

Chapter 7

London's East End was home to one of the most multi-cultural communities in the United Kingdom. Over many years thousands of refugees had arrived at its docks to seek new lives for their families, most having fled Europe to escape some form of persecution. Rich rewards awaited those who were prepared to work hard.

Behind its steamy windows, Sam's Café was heaving with activity. A heady aroma of cigarette smoke and fried food hung in the air. It was lunchtime in the Whitechapel Road and the place was packed. An elderly couple were working flat out in the kitchen, trying to keep up with the orders being demanded above the clatter of cutlery and the noisy conversations of hungry customers.

A tall, well-built young man hovered over the counter. 'Sausage, egg and chips, and a ham salad, both with rolls and butter,' he shouted urgently.

'The salad's there in front of you, the rest will be ready in two minutes,' came the reply.

The young man wiped a hand down his soiled apron and lifted the salad onto his tray. He held it high above the diner's heads and edged his way across the bustling café to place it in front of an attractive fair-haired girl who was sat by the window, idly fingering a pattern in the condensation. She swung round with a coy smile.

'Thanks, Jack. I'm starving. Same time this evening?' she ventured, trying not to sound too forward.

'Of course,' he answered in a deep, resonant voice. His stiff reply was softened by the trace of a smile. Short-cropped hair and a deep scar across his right cheek intensified his rugged features. He appeared awkward in her company. 'Maybe we'll go up the West End. Anyway, better go, we're real busy. See you later…usual place?'

Her blue eyes blinked briefly in consent. She chewed her lip and broke into a wicked grin, watching his toned body snake away between the tables.

Jack lived with Mr and Mrs Hurwitz in the small flat above the café. The elderly couple had raised him as their own, endeavouring to heal the emotional wounds inflicted during his tragic childhood. He never spoke of those early days, choosing to ignore the horrendous memories that still lurked in the depths of his mind.

After a heartbreaking farewell with Grandma Anna, he had left with the Hurwitz's to undertake the hazardous journey out of Poland. They endured many months of hardship together, eventually managing to bribe their way across the border into West Germany. There followed more weeks of tedious legal wrangling, until they were finally allowed to remain in England where they set up home in the East End of London.

The first thing the couple did was to change the

boy's name from Yakov Bronovitch to Jack Bronson: Jack being the English equivalent of Yakov, and Bronson, simply because it sounded the closest match to his Russian surname. They hoped it would help him become more readily accepted at school. Unfortunately, his pronounced east European accent and Jewish parentage subjected Jack to the same ridicule he had suffered in Poland. As the years passed he matured into a tall, muscular teenager, but his quiet disposition still invited the unwelcome attention of the school bullies who took sadistic pleasure in mocking him at every opportunity.

The day had been no different from any other. It was break time, and Jack was being hounded across the school playground by a group of jeering boys. How many times could a young person endure the vindictive taunts, and humiliating pushes and prods, without hitting back? From a tender age he had suffered traumas that no child should have been subjected to: cowering in sewers to hide from Nazi Storm Troopers, witnessing fellow human beings being herded like cattle through the streets of Minsk, watching the coffins of his murdered parents being lowered into the ground…and the bloodbath on Christmas Eve.

He had almost reached the sanctuary of the main building when a vicious shove sent him sprawling to his knees. At that defining moment years of suppressed fury were unleashed, putting an end to his persecution. Jack leapt to his feet and grabbed the nearest of his tormentors by the throat, forcing him to the ground. After pummelling his fists repeatedly into the boy's face, he straddled his victim's body and began to throttle him. The screams from a gathering crowd of pupils brought two teachers running across the playground. There had been no doubt in anyone's mind that the bully might have been killed had they not intervened to drag his assailant from him.

Jack remembered wondering if his friend, Andrei, would have been proud of him for standing up for himself. But that thought had been quickly banished. The serious assault had left the school hard pressed to justify a reason for allowing the young Polish boy to continue with his education. However, after heartfelt pleas from Mr and Mrs Hurwitz, and much consideration from the school governors, he was allowed to remain.

He went on to become an able student. But despite gaining impressive qualifications, that would have allowed him to seek lucrative employment elsewhere, he had chosen to work in the café with his adoptive parents. They had bought the run-down establishment with money smuggled out of Poland, and over the following ten years had established a thriving small business.

*

The last customer had left by mid-afternoon, allowing them to display the 'CLOSED' sign and take a welcome rest. Mrs Hurwitz appeared from the kitchen with three freshly brewed mugs of tea. She took a seat beside the young man who was sat opposite her husband at one of the tables.

'I see Sandra was in again today,' she remarked casually. 'Such a lovely girl. You seem to be spending a lot of time together.'

Mr Hurwitz cringed at his wife's boldness. '*Rachel*, it's none of our business.'

'I must admit I do like her,' Jack said, reaching for his drink with a bashful smile.

'I don't believe it. Our beautiful boy's going steady. And about time too, such an Adonis shouldn't go to waste. Mind you, she's not Jewish, but I won't tell anyone if you don't,' said Mrs Hurwitz, giving him a playful nudge.

'Rachel, *please* leave him alone. Take no notice, Jack. She's impossible,' Mr Hurwitz grumbled, stirring his tea irritably.

Jack's eyes softened. He reached over to touch her hand. 'Impossible, I agree, but still the best.'

Jack had never found the courage to talk about the dark deed he had committed as a child with anyone. As the years passed the guilt and anger had festered inside him, feeding his insecurities, destroying his confidence. He lived in perpetual fear of erupting into violence. Sandra was special to him: her love was unconditional. She knew there were demons in his past, but never probed, assuming them to be the horrors of surviving a Nazi regime.

Mrs Hurwitz held her tea aloft. 'To Jack and Sandra,' she proclaimed, undeterred, forcing them to chink their mugs together.

The elderly man raised his eyes and took a mouthful of tea, powerless to curb his wife's enthusiasm.

They were interrupted by the small bell jingling

on top of the door. Two men entered the café.

'I'm sorry, we close early on Saturday. You could try the place on the corner of Commercial Street,' Jack offered pleasantly.

'Shut up,' snapped the shorter man, cutting him dead. *'Well?'* he threatened, looking straight at Mr Hurwitz.

Jack tensed and began to slide his chair back from the table. Mrs Hurwitz grabbed his arm with a small shake of her head.

Her husband attempted a feeble smile. 'I've told you before we really can't afford it. Please leave us alone. I'm sure one small café will make no difference to your people.'

'No more excuses, you've had enough time. We'll be back on Monday evening, and if the cash isn't here you'll know what to expect,' said the man who turned round and left without another word. His companion paused to look back with a mocking grin, before closing the door quietly behind him.

Jack could contain himself no longer. 'What the hell was *that* all about? Sam? Rachel? What's going on?'

The couple exchanged a fearful glance. Jack had seen that look many times before back in Poland. He had hoped never to see it again.

'These people want money from us on a weekly basis,' Mr Hurwitz confessed, 'they call it *buying insurance*. So far I've managed to avoid paying them.'

'Insurance against *what?*' Jack demanded.

Mrs Hurwitz stepped in. 'I think it's time to say something, Samuel. Jack's not a child anymore.'

The old man drew a deep breath and started to explain how a gang of criminals were demanding protection money from the local traders. Jack recalled hearing gossip about vicious assaults in the neighbourhood, and an unexplained fire in a local grocer's shop, resulting in the tragic death of its owner. The reasons were becoming apparent.

'I'm afraid we have no choice,' Mr Hurwitz said finally. 'We must pay them, or leave.'

'To hell with them, we're not going anywhere,' Jack argued.

'I wish it were that simple,' said Mrs Hurwitz. 'These people are ruthless. Your father and I are not strong enough to oppose them.' She laid a comforting hand on her husband's arm. Samuel Hurwitz looked crushed.

Jack felt a sudden swell of emotion. It was the first time the elderly couple had ever referred to themselves as his father and mother. Since his youth, they had encouraged him to address them by their first names, fearing it would be a slight to the memory of his murdered parents. In that instant the truth hit him; these two people had taken over that role long ago. The sacrifices they had made for him went far beyond the duties of well-meaning guardians, and this threat to their future was unthinkable. Something had to be done.

*

The October wind gusted fiercely, forcing Sandra Woodman to hug the coat closer to her slender body and break into a run. Her high heels clattered across the road towards a dark figure silhouetted against neon lights glowing from the entrance to Aldgate Tube Station. Jack Bronson swung round at the sound of her approach.

'Sorry I'm late, had to help Mum clear the supper table. I must look a sight,' she breathed heavily, delicately fingering a lock of hair from her eyes.

'You look wonderful,' he said, drawing her close for a lingering kiss. He felt relaxed when they were alone. Her sweet scent scattered his brooding thoughts.

'So what are we doing?' she asked, pulling him into the station, where a comforting stream of warm air blew constantly from the depths of the underground tunnels.

'I thought we'd make for Leicester Square. *The Bridge on the River Kwai* is showing at the Empire. Maybe we could grab a coffee afterwards.'

'Fat chance, Jack, the film's only just come out, we'll never get seats.'

'We will with these.' He reached inside his trench coat and pulled out two tickets, allowing a smile to form in the corner of his mouth.

She gaped in surprise. 'Fantastic! They must have cost you a fortune.'

'Only the best for you, Sandra,' he said, rummaging in his pocket for the train fares.

The tout had not been cheap, but Sandra was worth every penny.

*

They left the cinema and hailed a black cab for the short journey to Soho. Greek Street was at its busiest. The pavements were full of hustlers trying to lure drunken punters into the strip clubs, while heavily made up girls with plunging cleavages lurked in doorways pouting their glossy lips at every man that walked by. Shifty-eyed street hawkers pulled back their sleeves, revealing rows of defective watches strapped to their forearms. Jack loved the raw energy of the place. The clandestine atmosphere was like a forbidden fruit to be savoured whenever he had the chance.

The Café Europa was one of many new espresso bars opening across London in the late 1950s, and had become a regular haunt for Jack and his friends. Its low lit, glitzy décor made it a perfect meeting place after a night on the town. He and Sandra were seated with another couple at a table close to the Wurlitzer Juke Box.

Jack's friend, *Dapper* Doug Levin, was a tough, wiry man in his late-thirties. They had met through the café, and despite their age difference had become firm friends. After working his fruit stall in Petticoat Lane, the suave, sallow-faced Levin would return to his flat in Old Montague Street, and re-appear wearing one of his sharp Italian suits to head for the West End on the prowl for a pretty girl. His thin, carefully trimmed moustache, groomed hair and aromatic aftershave enhanced his dashing looks, ensuring that he would rarely spend the night alone. His latest companion was an attractive redhead called Lucy who was chatting animatedly to Sandra.

Jack chose his moment. 'I think it's time for more coffee. Would you give me a hand, Doug?' he said, inclining his head towards the bar. They left the girls to their conversation and walked over to the counter.

Steam hissed loudly from the Gaggia espresso machine, preventing Jack from being overheard as he recounted the incident at the café earlier that day. Levin's expression turned sour.

'I know those bastards. A bunch of *Johnny Come Latelys* who really fancy their chances. They've just started their scam in the market. A couple of stallholders are already paying them. It'll only be a question of time before they hit on the rest of us.'

'There must be something we can do about it,' Jack insisted. 'What about the police?'

'Waste of time, Jack, they couldn't give a damn. Probably on the payroll too I shouldn't wonder,' Levin said, taking a moment to study his manicured nails. 'No, enough's enough. Maybe it's time to turn things around.'

'Meaning?'

'Meaning that you and I are going to have a chat with some of the lads. There's a bunch of Jewish guys that meet up every Sunday at the snooker hall in Aldgate. To be honest, we're all pissed off at the way we've been treated over the years. It's about time we Jews started to command a little respect in the world.'

'Steady, Doug, we don't want things getting out of hand,' Jack cautioned, despite a strange lack of conviction in his words.

'Sod it. They're already out of hand,' Levin complained loudly. Without warning the hissing machine fell silent, causing his comment to turn a few heads. He smiled at the girl behind the counter. 'Sorry, love, didn't mean to shout. Are those for us?'

She nodded vacantly, looking for payment.

Jack was already handing over the money. 'We don't need to say anything in front of the girls, right?'

'No worries, I've got better things to talk about with that Lucy bird,' Levin grinned, picking up two of the steaming cappuccinos.

*

Mr and Mrs Hurwitz were not used to their son's presence at the breakfast table on a Sunday. His usual lay-in had been abandoned due to an important meeting scheduled for later that morning. The conversation had given way to mundane topics with no mention being made of the racketeers. Jack eventually excused himself, placing a reassuring hand on his father's shoulder before leaving.

*

Lounging on one of the creased leather sofas that lined the walls of the snooker hall, Jack surveyed the figures grouped around brightly lit green baize tables, their murmur of conversation punctuated by the occasional sharp click of cue against ball.

Levin and his three companions finished their final frame, stowed their cues in the rack, and walked over to join him. They seemed friendly enough, but Jack noticed a certain reservation in their manner as the introductions were being made. He was a new face. Would he have the courage to do what might be expected of him?

The information they had gathered was impressive. The extortion racket was fronted by a small time gangster called Bill Haskin, often referred to as *Hammer* due to his fondness for breaking his victim's fingers with a mallet. The practice had proved to be a useful incentive while serving his criminal apprenticeship as a debt collector for loan sharks. He now ran his own lucrative operation from a disused warehouse down by the river, intimidating the local community to such an extent that no one dared stand up to him.

During the meeting, Jack was making his own observations. Three of them were fit, sturdy looking men. Their general lack of finesse suggested a tough working life, possibly on the docks, or in the building trade, whereas the appearance of his pal, *Dapper* Doug Levin, concealed the man's true character. Beneath his slim build and veneer of gentlemanly sophistication there lay an aggressive fighter. Jack recalled, with amusement, when a drunken lout had foolishly tipped a beer over his smartly attired friend expecting an easy target for ridicule. He could still hear the dull crack as Levin's kick dislocated the man's kneecap, swiftly followed by a torrent of ferocious blows, resulting in a hospital stay for his opponent…and a new shirt for Levin.

It was finally agreed that they would confront the *insurance collectors* the following evening. A fine line lay between intimidating these villains and descending to a similar level themselves, but they felt comfortable about their motives. After all, someone had to stand up to these people.

Jack bid his new associates farewell and left for

home. Later in the afternoon he phoned Sandra to apologise for not being able to see her after work the next day, explaining that he had some urgent business to attend to.

Chapter 8

It had started to rain heavily as Samuel Hurwitz locked the shop door, leaving a single light glowing from the kitchen in preparation for his unwanted visitors. The day had gone well enough, with more than the usual amount of covers for a Monday, but what good would it be if he was forced to give the extra business away to these mobsters.

Jack was wiping down the last of the tables having said little about his meeting the previous day, not wishing to worry the old couple more than necessary. He had insisted on handing over the money himself, while his parents were to remain in the safety of the flat until the transaction was completed.

'Leave it, Dad, you look tired. I'll finish up here,' Jack said, taking the shop keys from his father. 'And promise me that you and Mum will stay upstairs no matter what.'

'We will, but *you* must also promise not to try anything stupid with these men. They're like animals, Jack. Believe me, just pay them and let them leave.' He produced a manila envelope from his shapeless cardigan and dropped it on a table close to his son. 'Your life is more precious to us than money.'

Jack scooped up the package and slipped it into his back pocket. 'That might be a hard promise to keep,' he muttered, watching his father shuffle away.

Mr Hurwitz paused at the flat door. 'What was that?'

'I said I love you both, very much.'

The old man smiled back, and started slowly up the stairs.

A black van pulled up outside, briefly illuminating the café walls, before killing its headlights. Jack was comforted by its presence. He snapped the cap off a *Coke* bottle and pulled up a chair at one of the tables.

The current developments were re-awakening old memories. He recalled his childhood friends, Andrei and Maria Wolenski, the only people in the world who had known the truth about his violent act and stood by him so loyally, honouring their vow of secrecy. He still harboured deep regrets for never having thanked them, or bid them farewell. The carved handled knife had been left untouched in the bottom drawer of his bedroom cabinet for many years...

A sharp rapping on glass startled him. Two men stood outside in the darkness. He got up and unlocked the door, allowing them to push past him in their soaking raincoats and swagger into the café.

'Where's Hurwitz?' the short one demanded, settling himself into a chair. His colleague remained standing, wearing the same pointless grin.

Jack turned to face them. '*Mr* Hurwitz to you,' he corrected in a steady voice, 'and he's not available this evening.'

'Whatever, so where's the money?'

'I've got it, but I'm giving it to Bill Haskin, personally,' Jack said, playing for time.

The distant sound of slamming doors could be heard from the black van parked outside.

'You're taking the piss, son,' the seated man sneered. 'He don't talk with the likes of you. That's why we collect for him. That's the way it's done. Now give me the bleedin' money.'

His last words were drowned by the roar of heavy rainfall as the shop door flew open again. Levin walked in accompanied by the same three men from the snooker hall. The last one to enter locked the door behind him, taking time to wipe his feet fastidiously on the threadbare mat, before lining up with the others alongside Jack.

The short man shifted in his chair. 'What's this all about? Who are these comedians?' he said with an unconvincing laugh. His companion's grin disappeared.

'There's no need for rudeness. These *comedians* are my friends, and we're all going to take a drive to see Mr Haskin,' Jack repeated with patronising authority.

The tall man had endured enough smart talk and lunged at Jack: it was a mistake. Jack's reaction was instinctive. He countered the punch and buried his fist into the man's face in one fluid movement, knocking him senseless to the floor.

'You lunatic!' bawled his accomplice. 'You don't sod around with a man like Haskin.'

The fire was raging inside Jack. He grabbed the loud-mouthed man by the hair, wrenching his head back. 'Keep your voice *down*, you bastard. My parents are resting upstairs.'

The man grimaced with pain, shocked into silence. Levin and his colleagues exchanged approving glances, suddenly seeing the young man in a different light, impressed by his command of the situation. They dragged the two men to their feet, stuffed rags into their mouths, and bound their hands behind their backs. Jack walked over to the flat's entrance, bristling with confidence. He lifted his coat from behind the door and called up the stairwell.

'Mum, Dad, I'll be out for a while. Don't wait up.'

*

They ended their journey at the East India Dock, drawing up outside a dilapidated warehouse standing by the quayside. Sodium street lamps glowed orange through the regimented rows of crane gantries, creating a twisted network of black shadows across its walls.

Leaving their driver with the van, Jack pushed the hostages ahead of him through the unguarded entrance. Small windows covered in thick grime prevented what little light there was from entering the place. A damp, fetid smell of disuse greeted his party as he led them into the gloom. Torrential rain hammering against the roof helped to deaden any noise of their approach as they crept between stacks of rough timbered palettes, and rotten tarpaulins, towards a dimly lit office at the back of the cavernous building where the sound of voices grew louder. Jack lifted his hand to halt their progress and looked back at his companions. Their determined faces, barely visible in the colourless glow from the opaque glass panelled door, told him all he needed to know.

He gave a confirmatory nod and kicked the door open. The expression on Bill Haskin's face veered between fear and fury at the sight of his men being propelled unceremoniously towards his desk.

If there had been any question as to how the four of them would deal with a roomful of thugs, the answer came swiftly. Levin's two companions lifted sawn-off shotguns from under their coats aimed directly at the corpulent gangster. His men immediately fell back against the walls, raising their arms in submission.

The situation was escalating, but Jack was undaunted. It felt good bringing fear upon those who would dare to threaten decent, hard-working people. It began to compensate for the oppression that he and his loved ones had suffered for so long.

Haskin heaved his large bulk from the chair, holding out his hands in an attempt to pacify the situation. 'Let's all calm down, lads. No need to get excited. I'm sure we can sort something out.' A bare light bulb hanging from the ceiling cast a grey pallor across his fleshy face.

After a gesture from Jack, the two hostages were untied and the gags pulled from their mouths. Haskin's eyes flashed angrily at them as they were shoved across the room to join the others. He fixed a grin across his face. 'Look, there's obviously been some misunderstanding, Mr…er…'

'My name's Jack Bronson,' said the young man, 'and no, I don't think there's been any misunderstanding. Your men have been demanding money from my family for the *protection* of our cafe, and I'm here to tell you that we don't need it. We're quite capable of looking after things ourselves.'

'Of course you are, Jack, no harm done, eh,' the fat man whined, a film of sweat shining over his face. 'Now, if you'd like to lower the guns I'm sure we can come to some arrangement. How about working for me? You're a big lad, and you've certainly got the guts.' His suggestion was followed by a benevolent smile.

Jack fell silent, ignoring the man. His run of confidence had begun to wane. He was suddenly preoccupied, unsure of everything, wondering what he was doing in the place. Why had he let things go so far? He was becoming a guilt-ridden, insecure child once again.

Haskin was quick to notice how his attempt at flattery had appeared to quieten the young man. He decided to act more boldly. 'You'll make more money with me than you do from that shitty little café,' he said, laughing loudly.

The laughter faded to a weak titter that quickly trailed away, as Jack struggled to make sense of the situation. Where was this leading? There could only be one way to resolve this threat from Haskin. A rigid silence hovered over the room broken by the laboured breathing of the obese gangster who probed the younger man's eyes, searching for a way out of the tense standoff.

'Okay, Jack, let's go, I think he's got the message,' Levin broke in, sensing an unsettling quietness about his friend's manner.

Haskin's mind was racing. *He's backing off. This prat's not worth worrying about.* 'Your mate's right, son, you've made your point. Let's put down the shooters and have a drink. Don't worry. I'll leave your café alone. I know how much you Jew boys love your money,' he sniggered.

Jack came back in an instant. Adrenalin fluttered in his stomach, fuelling his hatred. All he could see was the gangster's sneering face.

'I'm not your damn son, and why would I want to drink with a bastard like you,' he fumed, moving around the desk, driven by an unstoppable urge to confront the villain.

'Now that's out of order. Nobody talks to me like that,' Haskin shouted, his pride getting the better of him. He squared up to the insult, thrusting out his large stomach.

Jack threw up the palm of his hand to strike the man in the chest, knocking him down into his seat.

Bill Haskin lost his temper. Grabbing the arms of the chair, he prised his backside free and hauled himself to his feet. 'Who the *hell* do you think you are? Jewish scum, coming here, throwing your weight around. Now get the fuck out of my office, *before I kill the bloody lot -*'

The bellowing voice was slashed to a low gurgling sound as Jack's right arm swung up towards Haskin's neck with a momentary flash of steel. The heavy man collapsed back into his seat, his plump fingers groping towards the ivory handle that was left protruding from the side of his throat. Jack watched, with macabre fascination, as the man's mouth pumped out pulses of choking blood in an effort to form words. The large body twitched violently for a few moments before coming to rest, slumped across the chair.

Levin fiddled awkwardly with the knot on his tie, unable to believe his eyes. This was Jack. His pleasant, retiring friend, a model of respectability who worked in a café, who rarely spoke out of turn...who had just thrust a knife into a man's neck. 'I think we're all done here. I can't see Mr Haskin bothering us again,' he said, with glaring understatement.

Jack tugged out the knife and proceeded to wipe the blade on the black velvet collar of Haskin's coat. To his own amazement he noticed how steady his hand was. His rage had been quelled by his act of savagery. Those present were all hard men, and bloodshed was no stranger to them, but there was something particularly unnerving in the way this powerfully built young man had quickly, and quietly, dispatched his quarry. The guns were lowered.

The guilt-ridden, insecure child trapped inside Jack for so long had finally been liberated. The slaying of the monster, Gustav Wolenski, all those years ago now seemed like an act of God. Just like the story his father used to tell him about David killing Goliath: fighting oppression, the weak overcoming the strong. Suddenly Jack felt empowered. All remorse and fear had been erased.

He studied the corpse, alone with his thoughts. *I've killed again, and it was so easy. I punished Haskin just as I punished Gustav Wolenski. It was no less than the piece of filth deserved, but the police won't see it that way. Sod them, I managed to stay ahead of the Nazis and survive, so why should they be a problem? From now on I've got to take everything I want in my life. No one's going to give it to me. This moment was meant to be. This is retribution for my family's suffering. Why refuse to accept my destiny?* He began to speak out loud to himself.

'Haskin may have been an ignorant bastard, but he had a point. I have got the guts, and I certainly would make more money than working in the café.'

Levin looked confused. 'I'm sorry, pal, what are you saying?'

Jack swung round to study the faces that were now turned directly towards him. 'Well, it seems a pity to let such a sweet scam go to waste. It might as well be business as usual tomorrow. Who's with me?'

The men hesitated. A long moment passed before Levin broke the silence.

'You're a dark sod,' he said with a slow grin. 'What the hell, I'm up for it.'

He moved forward to shake his friend's hand. One by one the others followed. Jack Bronson had crossed the line.

Chapter 9

Mr and Mrs Hurwitz were delighted, albeit a little surprised, that their son had managed to reason with a man like Bill Haskin. He had not only saved their livelihood, but was now building his own successful wholesale fruit and vegetable business managed by his friend, Doug Levin. They were extremely proud to see their boy doing so well, even though they had never actually been to his warehouse. He had deemed the docks far too rough an area for his parents to visit.

The café continued to flourish. Two women were hired: one to wait table, and the other to help in the kitchen. It was even suggested that Mr and Mrs Hurwitz might consider taking things easier, but they would have none of it.

Jack's outward appearance had changed. Although not as adventurous as his fashionable friend, Doug Levin, his mundane casual clothes had been replaced by conservatively cut, double-breasted dark grey suits, emphasizing his broad shoulders and heavy build. He insisted on wearing white shirts and plain ties, with his only indulgence being a pair of small diamond cufflinks that Sandra had insisted on him buying as a celebration of his newfound affluence.

To his loved ones, Jack Bronson was a successful, caring man, generous to a fault and devoted to his family. But behind that facade of decency he was fast becoming the richest and most feared gangster in London. At present, his *manor* was confined to the East End of London, but his sights were firmly set on new pastures. After committing Bill Haskin's body to the depths of the River Thames, the business at the warehouse proved to be a perfect cover for his rapidly growing organisation.

Jack Bronson's carved handled knife became a symbol of ruthless retribution, with a blade in the throat being his favoured method of killing. The gruesome nature of the deed created a pathological fear among his enemies, and such was his reputation that the ongoing investigations made by the police into the disappearance of Bill Haskin were continually smothered in a blanket of silence: the young gangster was proving to be untouchable.

Jack soon discovered how his tough, self-assured image and newfound wealth began to attract the attention of those bent on furthering their own ambitions. He drew great satisfaction in hosting expensive meals at high-class restaurants, surrounding himself with aspiring talent from the world of sport and entertainment, resulting in his own growing celebrity status. Sandra would see photos of herself appearing regularly in the national papers alongside her successful boyfriend, attending film premieres and important sporting fixtures. Her father, fiercely proud of his working class roots, found the whole concept of his daughter's elevation into such prominent circles difficult to deal with; his wife saw it as a heaven sent blessing.

In the spring of 1958, Jack's proposal of marriage to Sandra was met with the hearty approval of their respective families. He had finally moved out of his parents flat and found a place of his own on the top floor of a newly constructed apartment block in Stepney, commanding spectacular views over London's East End. The stylish penthouse suite was luxuriously appointed, boasting every modern convenience, making it the perfect place to entertain his growing number of influential friends.

A date in August had been set for the wedding. They were to be married in a civil ceremony at the Whitechapel Register Office, followed by a reception at the Dorchester Hotel in Mayfair. It was to be an impressive event, with the guest list reading like a *Who's Who,* boasting names from every spectrum of society, including politicians and local councillors. Jack would stop at nothing to further his business interests, and above all achieve respectability and recognition. Levin was to be his best man.

Chapter 10

The lavish splendour of the Dorchester's Grand Ballroom was complemented by a riot of colourful floral arrangements. Popping corks, chiming glasses and rowdy laughter competed readily with the melodious sounds of the *Oscar Rabin Band* that kept a steady stream of guests heading for the dance floor throughout the evening.

The bride looked stunning in a beautiful gown created by the famous couturier, *Norman Hartnell*, the Royal dress designer. Jack had insisted on the best of everything for Sandra. It was her big day, and no effort or expense had been spared. Most of the arrangements had been left to Levin who had been instructed to ensure that Mr and Mrs Hurwitz were to be treated regally. They were seated at the top table next to Sandra, overawed by the extravagance of the occasion.

'You look so beautiful, Sandra. Jack is a very lucky man,' Mrs Hurwitz said, gently patting the young woman's hand.

Sandra lifted the exquisite veil from her face. 'Thanks, Rachel, but I haven't done so badly myself. I never imagined a day like this in my wildest dreams. I thought fairy tales were only for children.'

She gazed towards the tall, charismatic man sat beside her. Jack Bronson *did* look like a movie star. The sharply tailored morning suit hanging on his perfectly formed physique, and the rare smile that softened his rugged face, drew admiring glances from every woman in the room.

As she spoke, Levin was picking his way down the back of the long table. 'Hi, Sandra, could I have a word with your *husband?*' He grinned at the use of his friend's new title.

She laughed as Jack leaned back, allowing Levin to speak into his ear. After listening for a few seconds he turned to Sandra, brushing her cheek with his lips. 'Please excuse me, sweet heart, I won't be a minute.'

She flashed him a pretty smile. 'Be as long as you like, darling. It's your day too.'

The two friends made slow progress across the crowded ballroom as Jack was forced to acknowledge the accolades from his many well-wishers. After enduring a marathon of hand pumping and back slapping, he finally arrived at a table near the band stand where a portly, middle aged man stood up to greet him.

'It's good of you to see me so promptly, Mr Bronson,' he said, with a practised smile. 'My name's Henry Jameson and I must apologise for taking you away from your gorgeous bride.'

Henry Jameson's burning desire to enter government had forced him to seek whatever avenues were available to achieve his goal. In his youth he had joined the Liberal Party. But after realising their unrealistic prospects of getting into power, he swapped allegiances to the Conservatives when they became the ruling party in 1951. The unexpected, recent death of the Member of Parliament for Stepney provided a perfect opportunity for Jameson to put himself forward as a prospective candidate.

Levin remained standing, while Jack shook hands and sat down. Jameson's fawning manner suggested a shallow opportunist, ripe for exploitation.

'I assume you need money, Henry,' Jack said, dismissing any attempt at pleasantries.

'My God, you don't waste time do you?'

'No I don't. Why else would you want to talk with me?'

Jameson flushed, wafting a warm, flowery scent across the table. 'Well I wouldn't have put it quite like that,' he said, glancing around awkwardly.

'Don't worry, no one can hear us,' Jack said, raising his voice over a loud brass arrangement from the band. 'Great sound isn't it.' He paused briefly to enjoy the music. 'I'm told you're standing as the Conservative candidate for Stepney in the coming by-election, and you need funding. Am I right?'

'Yes, that's correct,' Jameson admitted meekly. He felt cheapened having to appeal to this young villain, but his ambition left little room for self-respect. 'I'm not suggesting anything illegal, you understand, it's just that being a successful businessman from the East End, I thought you might -'

'*Illegal,*' Jack cut in. 'what do you take me for?

As you say, I'm a businessman. Sure, I'll put up the cash, and you know what, I have a feeling you'll get elected. Of course, one favour does deserve another don't you agree?'

'Absolutely,' Jameson gushed, 'I'd be only too happy to accommodate you. I've always believed in supporting local businesses.'

'Good, that's settled then. You can sort out the details with Mr Levin. I wish you a successful campaign. Now, if you'll excuse me.'

Jack broke into a formal grin and rose from the table, leaving the flustered man's outstretched hand unshaken.

*

Their honeymoon was spent cruising the Mediterranean. Jack took great pleasure indulging his wife in the luxuries offered on board the elegant ship. Sandra had a gracious, unpretentious way of appreciating everything; a true East End girl who would never forget her humble beginnings. That's why he loved her so much. She was his shelter from the constant demands of the sinister, violent world he had created. Her innocent belief in him was to be preserved at all cost.

Occasionally, after dinner, he would leave Sandra chatting with newly made friends and slip away to the purser's office on the pretence of drawing foreign currency for their next port of call. The moment would be seized to exchange carefully worded messages with Levin sent through the ship's telegraph, keeping him in touch with developments back in London.

Mr and Mrs Hurwitz proudly displayed their

post cards from the newlyweds on the counter of Sam's Café. The customers were plentiful, and the place was almost as famous as Jack Bronson who was fast becoming a role model for success, earning respect as a generous benefactor to the underprivileged of London's East End. His organisation had financed the opening of a Youth Club, and a Senior Citizens Welfare Centre: a shrewd move to ingratiate himself with the local community.

*

By the winter of that year Jack Bronson's *protection* business had spread further into the West End, financing other interests: nightclubs, coffee bars, gambling and prostitution. Any special licensing requirements, and property acquisitions, were obtained with the influential assistance of the Right Honourable Mr Henry Jameson, the newly elected Conservative MP for Stepney, who enjoyed generous remuneration courtesy of Jack Bronson.

*

The festive strains of *Harry Belafonte's* latest record, *Mary's Boy Child,* spilled into the hallway of the Bronson's spacious apartment where Sandra's parents were preparing to leave.

Mr Woodman was a robust, jovial man who had worked on the docks all his life. He embraced Sandra warmly, before turning to place a hand on his son-in-law's shoulder. 'It's been a good Christmas. Thank you for having us.' His formality betrayed his discomfort at being in such stylish surroundings: he was desperate for the comfort of his modest home.

'I'm glad you could come, and don't worry we'll take good care of this one,' Jack said, gently patting his wife's growing stomach.

Mrs Woodman stopped fussing around her daughter and reached up to kiss Jack on the cheek. 'We couldn't have wished for a better present,' she said with glistening eyes. 'God bless the three of you.'

'Oh go on, Mum, you'll have us all in tears,' Sandra giggled, giving her parents a final hug as she saw them out. 'Jack's car is waiting outside. Phone us when you get in,' she called after them, closing the door.

'Shouldn't take them long to get home,' said Jack. 'I think they enjoyed themselves.' He followed Sandra back into the living room to join their remaining guests. 'More champagne, anyone?' he offered, lifting a bottle from an ice bucket standing on the white marble-topped bar.

Mrs Hurwitz wriggled herself towards the edge of the deep cushioned sofa. 'Your father and I have had enough, Jack. A nice cup of tea would be better.'

'I'll do it, Rachel, stay where you are,' said Sandra. 'It's Christmas Day, for goodness sake, about the only time you and Sam ever take a break.'

She left for the kitchen, stubbornly followed by Mrs Hurwitz who was already lecturing her daughter-in-law on the benefits of rest during pregnancy.

'Does my mother ever do as she's told?' Jack smiled, topping up Doug Levin and Lucy's glasses. 'I have to say, I've never really enjoyed

Christmas. But it has been a nice day.'

'Oh come on, Jack, what about when you were a kid in Poland? I bet you had some great times,' Lucy remarked innocently.

Jack's jaw tightened. Levin threw her an angry look. It bothered him when Jack got upset. She had been told never to ask about his friend's childhood. It was a taboo subject.

Mr Hurwitz intervened quickly. 'Unfortunately they were very difficult times, Lucy. Our lives were spent hiding from the Nazis. A lot of bad things happened. Maybe it's best not to dwell on them.'

Her cheeks went crimson. 'I'm so sorry, Jack, I didn't mean -'

'Forget it, Lucy, you weren't to know,' Jack said in a controlled voice.

'Bloody diplomat you are, darling,' Levin blurted out.

'I *said* forget it, and that goes for you too, Doug,' Jack snapped.

The prickly moment was intensified by a piercing ring tone. Levin leapt up and hurried to the bar. He grabbed the phone, grateful for the interruption. After a few seconds his face dropped.

'Who is it?' Jack demanded. 'What's the problem?'

'Er...nothing to be concerned about,' Levin said, holding the receiver against his chest.

'Out with it, Doug, who the hell is it?'

Levin gave in with a pained expression. 'It's the manager of the snooker room. Apparently some black guy from south of the river is asking for you. He wants to involve himself in our business interests.'

Jack's fight to remain calm was finally lost. 'Tell that idiot *never* to phone me on this number, it's my private bloody line. And tell that black bastard to piss off!' he yelled, oblivious to his guests' embarrassment.

Levin raised a pacifying hand. 'I will, don't worry.'

He muttered into the mouthpiece and hung up just as the two women returned from the kitchen.

'Who was that? Surely Mum and Dad aren't home yet?' asked Sandra.

The music had stopped. But the turntable kept spinning, jarring the tense silence with a repetitive click from the gramophone needle.

Her smile wilted. 'What's going on, Jack? Where's the Christmas spirit gone?'

Sandra's voice seemed to quell her husband's psychotic fury. His wild eyes were pacified, and a spontaneous grin spread across his face as he slipped his arm around her waist. 'It's come back now you're here. I'm just a miserable sod sometimes. Cheers everyone, Happy Christmas!'

He took a carefree swig straight from the neck of the champagne bottle. Strained laughter rippled throughout the apartment.

Chapter 11

A warm July evening made queuing more bearable for the impatient crowd that was shuffling slowly down the length of Wardour Street towards Soho's latest nightspot. Scripted neon lights flashed *'Pink Pelican'* above the elegantly engraved glass doors, illuminating the eager faces of those fortunate enough to be among the first to step inside.

Jack had spent a fortune on the place. He and Levin were standing in the foyer beneath a tented ceiling of golden fabric, enjoying people's reactions to the delicately painted murals of exotic birds, displayed between floor-to-ceiling, peach tinted mirrors. Voluptuous young women, wearing pink feathered costumes and fishnet tights, offered complimentary champagne to the customers as they entered the club. Scarlet carpets and gold flock wallpapered walls greeted them, bathed in the soft glow of crystal chandeliers. Gilt regency style furniture surrounded the brightly lit dance floor where the sophisticated ambiance was enhanced by the rhythmic music of a small Latin American band.

The two men eventually left to join their own party who were seated at a table inside the club. Although heavily pregnant, Sandra had insisted on being present for the opening night, determined to share in her husband's proud moment. She and Lucy were laughing good-naturedly at Mr Hurwitz who was desperately trying to avoid his wife's invitations to dance. Attentive waiters had just served the chilled *Bollinger* under the watchful eye of the club's experienced manager, Steven Bradley, who had been lured from a large entertainment corporation by an extremely generous salary.

'Everything okay, Steve?' asked Levin.

'All under control, sir. I believe the press will be arriving soon. I've reserved the tables around the dance floor for the VIP guests, as you requested, and left instructions that no one is to disturb Mr Bronson this evening unless they are given your express permission.' He glanced respectfully towards his boss who was too engrossed in conversation with Sandra to notice.

'That's good. I'll call you if we need anything. Oh, and Steve.'

'Sir?'

'Tell the doormen to stay alert. This is an important night and I don't want any unwelcome surprises. Know what I mean?'

The manager gave a slight bow and slipped away.

Levin rang his glass with a spoon. 'To the success of the Pink Pelican,' he announced, lifting up his champagne

'I'll drink to that,' Jack said, as their glasses closed together. 'It owes me a lot of money.'

Mrs Hurwitz finally prised her husband from his chair and led him onto the dance floor. They were soon followed by a steady flow of stylishly dressed people leaving their tables to join them.

After dinner, the tables were cleared and drinks were served in preparation for the cabaret. Levin had called in one of many favours and managed to book a popular rock n' roll sensation, *Tommy Steele,* as the main attraction. The young cockney singer proved to be a great success, his lively performance demanding encores long after he had left the stage.

The VIP tables were irresistible targets for the press photographers whose cameras flashed regularly throughout the evening. Much to Jack's amusement, Henry Jameson revelled in the limelight, grasping every opportunity to be photographed. The Stepney MP had proved to be a useful contact, as would many of the other guests present that night.

Another bottle of fine wine was placed in front of Mr Hurwitz. He lifted it closer to examine the label.

'So, now you're a wine expert?' his wife teased. 'Just pour it, Samuel, you wouldn't know the difference anyway.'

'Rachel, that's naughty,' Sandra chuckled. 'Leave him alone. He's enjoying himself.'

Mr Hurwitz pretended to be mortally offended. 'Thank you, my dear. My wife can be very cruel sometimes. Just for that she won't have any,' he said in a superior tone.

As he leaned forward to fill her glass, Sandra's smiling face contorted with pain. She lurched forward, clutching her stomach, knocking the wine across the tablecloth.

Mr Hurwitz instinctively pulled the bottle away. 'Are you alright, Sandra?'

Jack's head shot round. 'What's wrong, darling?'

'I'm sorry, Jack,' she panted, reaching a trembling hand towards him. 'I'm going to spoil the party…our baby's on the way.'

Mrs Hurwitz took charge immediately. 'It's alright, my love, stay calm. Jack, bring your car round. We must get her to the hospital, now.'

'See to it, Doug!' Jack ordered.

Levin was already on his feet, hurrying towards the foyer.

*

The last revellers had left. The house lights had gone up, and the staff were busy stacking chairs and vacuuming carpets. Jack looked at his watch. It was 3.30am. A telephone stood in front of him, disturbingly quiet.

'Another drink?' Levin offered, having remained with his friend after sending Lucy home in a cab.

'No thanks, but you can get me some coffee.'

Levin summoned one of the waiters.

'I suppose no news is good news,' Jack mumbled anxiously. 'I mean if anything was to…you know…not that I'm expecting…'

'I'm sure everything's fine,' said Levin. 'These things take time. If I know Rachel she'll have Sam on the phone as soon as there's any news.'

As he spoke, Steven Bradley approached the table.

'I'm sorry to disturb you, Mr Levin, but there are some people insisting on seeing Mr Bronson,' he said, glancing furtively at his boss.

Jack looked curious. 'Are we expecting anyone?'

'No we're not,' Levin confirmed, eyeing the manager harshly. 'I *said* no uninvited guests. Did they give a name? What do they look like?'

'Three black guys, and they didn't give a name. I've tried to reason with them, but they refuse to leave.'

'Where are the doormen?'

'They've gone, sir, left a while ago.'

'Bloody useless bunch of -'

'Shut it, Doug,' said Jack. 'Send them in, Steve. Let's see what this is all about.'

'That's not a good idea. We've got no back-up,' Levin warned.

His criticism was unwise. Jack threw him an angry look. 'Sod the back-up. Send them in!'

Levin nodded to the manager who didn't need asking twice. He hurried away, beckoning the remaining staff to follow.

Three heavily built men, muscles straining at the seams of their silk suits, sauntered into the club as if they owned the place. Jack was unimpressed by their attempt at intimidation.

'Good morning, gentlemen, please join us,' he said, motioning to a row of chairs standing the other side of his table. 'I understand you wish to speak with me.'

The visitors took their seats. The man in the middle flashed a gold tooth as he spoke. His West Indian voice was deep and menacing. 'You're a little more polite than before. Told me to piss off if I remember correctly.'

Jack's suspicions were confirmed. 'Be fair, I was at home with my family on Christmas Day, not a good time to talk business. Now, would you be so kind as to tell me who you are, and what you want from me?' he asked in a civil tone.

Levin was preparing himself for what could easily follow.

'My name is Clive Remus, and these are two of my associates,' the man answered with a slight wave of his hand, lifting his jacket just enough to reveal the butt of a gun. 'I have profitable business interests south of the river, and soon I intend moving into the West End.'

Jack held a tight smile. 'Then why speak to me?'

'The word on the street is that you own this part of London. I'm here to tell you that you don't. A young man like you mustn't be too ambitious. There's plenty for everyone.' He followed his remark with a condescending grin, baring a row of gleaming white teeth.

'But I *am* ambitious, Mr Remus. I already own London north of the river, and soon I might even move south.'

Jack was deliberately goading the man. The more aggression he drew from his opponents the more brutal he became himself regardless of their size or number. He fed off their violence. It made him feel invincible. That's how he functioned; that's what made him tick. Levin's hand was already clasped around the cold steel of a Webley revolver resting on his lap under the table.

Remus slowly reached beneath his jacket, his grin fading. 'You're telling me to piss off again aren't you, you little prick.'

His two hard-faced companions rose slightly in their seats.

Jack exploded into action. Ramming the table against the men he took them completely off guard, throwing them backwards over their chairs. Levin leapt up with a firm grip on his handgun, aimed at the three prostrate figures.

Jack threw the table aside like a piece of matchwood. 'Get their weapons and cover them. If they move, shoot them,' he commanded with chilling authority,

Levin did what he was told. Jack reached inside his tuxedo and bent forward to grip Remus's tie, dragging him clear of his minders.

'Now, you arrogant black bastard,' he snarled, lifting the man's sweating face towards the glinting blade in his other hand, 'just to make sure you remember who owns this part of London.'

'No, *please!* There's no need for this!' the mobster yelled, grabbing the solid forearm that held him in a vice-like grip.

There followed an agonising shriek as Jack methodically carved a deep, curved line from the bottom of the man's left ear to the tip of his chin, releasing a thick ribbon of blood. Levin remained coldly detached, keeping his gun trained on the other men. Clive Remus lay on the floor, groaning in pain, clasping his bloodied face in his hands.

'Get him out of my sight,' Jack growled, sliding the knife back into its sheath. He had made his point. Remus had been punished for his disrespect. There was no more to be said.

The two men got to their feet and hauled their semi-conscious boss from the club under the baleful eye of Doug Levin, whose gun remained levelled at them until they had disappeared from view. When they were alone, he holstered his weapon and righted the table. As he rescued the phone from the floor it started to ring. He answered it immediately.

'It's for you.'

Jack inhaled a steadying breath before taking the call.

'Hello. Hi, Sam…yeah, I know…sorry it's been engaged, we've been busy. Is that right? That's wonderful news. I'll be right over.'

He slowly replaced the receiver. His face lightened. 'Doug, I have a son.'

'Mazeltov!' Levin grinned.

Chapter 12

He was having difficulty tying his bow, distracted by his wife's reflection in the mirror as she stepped into a shimmering silver evening gown.

'I can see you, Jack Bronson,' Sandra giggled, guiding the zipper over her shapely thighs. 'You'll have to wait until next year now,' she purred, blowing him a provocative kiss, before disappearing into the en-suite bathroom to check her make-up.

They would soon be leaving for their first New Year's celebration at the Pink Pelican. It was 1959, the end of a decade, and it promised to be a special evening. Sandra's parents had offered to stay at home and look after little Marek. Mrs Woodman had welcomed the opportunity of babysitting their five-month old grandson for the night, while her husband looked forward to having a few pints in his local rather than mix with the *"toffs up the smoke"*, as he put it.

Sandra's voice echoed from the bathroom. 'Do you think Marek will be alright? It'll be the first time we've left him anywhere.'

'He isn't just *anywhere*, darling, he's with your Mum and Dad. I've no doubt he'll be ruined rotten,' Jack answered, slipping on his dinner jacket. The slight bulge beneath his breast pocket was barely noticeable. 'Are you ready yet? They'll be here soon. Doug's picking up Sam and Rachel first. It'll be a bit of a squeeze, but we should all get in. I told him about seven o'clock...' his voice trailed away, seeing Sandra re-enter the bedroom. She approached him with a graceful sway of her hips.

'Christ, you look wonderful,' he managed in a throaty whisper.

She looked up into his eyes. 'Thank you, Jack. It's nice to be appreciated.'

He couldn't resist one kiss. Her soft voice and the smoothness of her body aroused him. Sandra felt him harden against her. She lowered her hand to fondle him. He tugged at the zipper, loosening her gown.

'Jack, they'll be here soon,' she giggled.

'Sod them, let them wait,' he said with pressing urgency.

He ripped off his jacket, scooped her up into his arms, and made for the bed. The overwhelming desire for her heightened his protective instincts, reminding him of the filthy business he was in. He hated the thought of it tainting his beautiful family in any way.

*

Two liveried doormen moved forward into the evening drizzle, holding up large umbrellas, as Levin brought Jack's white Rolls-Royce Silver Cloud to a halt.

'I feel like a celebrity,' Rachel Hurwitz chirped, stepping onto the pavement, watched by a growing line of partygoers.

They were all escorted quickly into the club where Steven Bradley was hurrying his staff to attendance.

Mrs Hurwitz allowed her long-suffering husband little respite from the dance floor, while Sandra and Lucy were obliged to partner one another due to the constant flow of people approaching their men throughout the evening. The one time they all spent together was during the cabaret when the chart-topping *Frankie Vaughan* took to the stage, much to the delight of the ladies.

When the singer finished his performance, Jack was forced to raise his voice over the enthusiastic applause. 'How the hell did we manage to get *him* this evening? Must have cost a fortune?'

'Not as bad as you think,' Levin shouted back with a crafty wink, 'down to my friend, Ben Sharmer.'

'Who's Ben Sharmer?'

'The same guy who got us *Tommy Steele* for the opening night.'

'I think I'd like to meet him,' Jack said, as the ovation began to die.

'No problem, he's sat by the bar. Shall I have him come over?'

'No, let's go to him.' Jack was already on his feet. He excused himself to Sandra who replied with a vague smile, trying to stay focussed on Lucy's conversation.

Ben Sharmer's weighty frame was perched on the edge of a bar stool dressed in a garish midnight blue dinner suit, sporting red satin lapels. After a brief introduction, Jack came straight to the point.

'I'm impressed by your contacts, Mr Sharmer. Who do you work for?'

Sharmer was struggling to maintain the air of a show business grandee, but the directness of this heavyset young man unsettled him. Levin was amused by the reaction. He had seen it in others many times before.

'I work for myself, Mr Bronson. It's easier that way. No ties if you know what I mean,' the agent said, chewing on a cigar.

'Good…that's good,' Jack enthused. 'I see a big future in the music business with all this rock n' roll stuff hitting the charts. I want a piece of the action.'

'Sure, why not, but it takes money. If you find a good artist you've got to exploit them, grease a few palms. Then you need offices and equipment.'

Jack liked the man's attitude. *Greasing palms,* and *exploiting,* were precisely what he wanted to hear. 'You get me the artists, and I'll get you the money. I think we're both reading from the same script.'

The light banter seemed out of character. The agent sensed it.

'Maybe I should think about it, Mr Bronson,' Sharmer suggested, nervously running a finger around the inside of his shirt collar. It was all happening too fast.

Jack dropped a powerful hand on the man's shoulder, dislodging him from the stool. The gesture felt too violent to be friendly. 'What's to think about? And please, call me Jack.'

'I suppose you're right, Mr...er, Jack,' Sharmer spluttered.

'The offer won't wait, Ben. Make your mind up, or it'll be gone, just like that!' Jack clicked his fingers in the man's face. Sharmer jumped. Levin smothered a laugh.

'You're right, of course. What was I thinking? I shall look forward to working with you,' the agent said, forced into submission.

'Working *for* me, Ben,' Jack corrected. 'We'll call it the Diamond Agency, because I like the name. I've no doubt that with your skills, and my backing, we'll make a lot of money. As usual, Mr Levin will be representing my interests. Good to meet you.' He left without another word.

'I'll phone you tomorrow,' Levin called out, as the crowd began the countdown to midnight.

Sharmer attempted a sick smile. He had bitten through the end of his cigar.

*

'How did we finish up, Steve?' Levin asked, entering the office.

Steven Bradley looked up from behind neat piles of bank notes lying on his desk. 'We did extremely well, and the punters loved it. We're already booked for the next three months.'

'Excellent. Shove that lot in the safe, and have someone bring the Rolls round.'

'Right away. Good night, Mr Levin...and a happy new year!'

Levin waved a reply and stepped back into the foyer. He walked across to join the others. 'I've called for the car.'

'Fine, we'll wait outside, I need some air,' Jack

replied, buttoning his coat. A commissionaire pulled open one of the heavy glass doors, allowing Jack and Sandra to step out into the sharp night air followed by Levin. Mr and Mrs Hurwitz remained inside talking with Lucy.

Levin tucked in his silk scarf. 'By the way, I just spoke with Steve. The club had a very successful night.'

'I'm pleased. You know I think 1960 is going to be a great year for us,' Jack said, hugging Sandra closer against the cold. Their eyes were drawn to the neon sign flashing across the deserted street. The sound of a car engine grew louder.

It could only have been a few seconds, but it seemed much longer. Levin saw Jack push Sandra to the ground. Before his brain could register what was happening, gunfire shattered the early morning peace followed by the sound of crashing glass and screeching rubber. A hot, searing pain took Levin's leg from under him, sending him down to crack his skull heavily on the damp pavement.

He rolled onto his side, slowly losing his fight to focus on the pink light fading into blackness…

*

'New Year's Eve shooting outside Soho Night Club'

The morning papers all bore a similar headline. Rumours of Jack Bronson's involvement with the London underworld were emphatically denied by the club's management, leading to much speculation as to why anyone would want to kill a successful businessman and his wife.

Jack had saved Sandra's life by pushing her to

the ground, but in doing so, had taken a bullet to his left shoulder. Levin's right leg had been shattered by the gunfire, leaving him with a permanent disability.

Mr and Mrs Hurwitz had been left deeply distressed by the incident. They spent most of their time fending off reporters who relentlessly pursued them at the café with expectations of a big story. Sandra chose to remain at her parent's house with Marek, not daring to venture outside. The shock of that night was an experience she would never forget.

Two of Levin's closest associates took it upon themselves to oversee the organisation's business activities, and provide discreet twenty-four hour protection for Jack's family. Secret hospital visits were arranged for Sandra and Lucy away from the prying eyes of the press. The young women had arrived at a mutual understanding: they would never discuss, or question their men about the source of wealth that provided their affluent lifestyles.

*

Jack discharged himself from the hospital after two days. He had his driver take him straight to his in-law's house. The sight of his small son in Sandra's arms provided a much-needed boost to his morale. But it soon became apparent how ill at ease Mr and Mrs Woodman were in his company, anxious to avoid any mention of the shooting. They were simply grateful that their daughter had survived. After an hour of stilted conversation, Jack and his family left for the Whitechapel Road.

When they arrived at the flat, Sandra insisted that her child remain on the sofa with the elderly couple and made straight for the kitchen to prepare a hot drink, giving her husband and his parents a moment to themselves.

Jack slipped the coat from his shoulders and fell back into an armchair. 'It's good to see you,' he said, wincing slightly as he eased his wounded arm from the sling. 'How have you been?'

'Better than you,' his father replied in a flat voice.

'Hey, I'm fine, it could have been worse,' Jack said, sensing the mood. He stole a glance at his mother who avoided his eyes.

'*Could have been worse,*' the old man shouted.

'Shush, Samuel please, you'll upset the little one,' Mrs Hurwitz pleaded. 'I'm sorry, Jack, you must forgive your father. He's been very upset by the whole business.'

'Of course, I understand,' Jack said, instantly alert. He had never underestimated his parents, and often wondered how much they really knew about his activities. He would try to appease them: dispel any concerns they might have. 'I've already spoken to the police. They seem to think that a bunch of hoodlums are trying to take over some of the successful clubs by intimidating the owners, and -'

'Intimidating is one thing, they tried to *kill* you, Jack,' Mr Hurwitz interrupted angrily. 'God forbid, it could have been Sandra, or your mother. Supposing we'd followed you outside?'

'But you didn't, and you're alright, and so is Sandra,' Jack said calmly, trying to counter the old man's attack. 'Come on, Dad, there's no point in getting upset about it, we're all fine. It won't happen again, I promise.'

'Oh, *you* promise, just like that. I suppose these...these killers will go away because you tell them to. Jack Bronson says go away, and they will. What bullshit is this anyway?'

Mrs Hurwitz placed a restraining hand on her husband's arm. Jack had never seen his father like this. The sarcasm and bad language were completely out of character. Sandra entered the room, drawn by the raised voices.

Mr Hurwitz would not let it rest. 'You'd have us believe that all this wealth, this sudden success, is simply down to good luck and a clever business brain?'

'*Yes* I would. I've worked hard to achieve what I've got,' Jack argued.

'Jack, you're talking to *me*, Samuel, your father. What am I, *chopped liver?* I've never heard such rubbish in my life.' He brushed his wife's hand aside and jumped to his feet. 'You're twenty-four years of age. Sure, you're a big guy, but you're still a kid. It's not possible to achieve what you have without...' The accusation hung.

'Without *what?*' Jack challenged, rising slowly from the armchair. He was losing patience rapidly. The whole conversation was getting out of hand. 'What are you trying to say?'

Mr Hurwitz looked sadly comical in the way he squared up to his strapping son. He glared up into the young man's face, waving an outraged finger.

'You're a *gangster*, Jack. You're a murderer. I've

seen the way people look at you in the street. They're terrified of you. I've refused to believe it up until now, all the rumours and whispers, but the shooting...the shooting says it all,' he shouted in a trembling voice. The colour flared in his cheeks; his blood pressure was soaring.

Mrs Hurwitz leaned forward to grab his sleeve. 'Samuel, enough already. Sit down, *now!*' she yelled. The little boy started to cry.

Sandra released a timid laugh. 'Jack, tell Sam it's not true, for goodness sake.'

Jack silenced her with a wave of his hand and spoke directly at his father, measuring his words. 'Alright, I admit to having made a few enemies. It's inevitable when you're successful. You can't make an omelette without breaking eggs.'

The cliché was lost on his father, who had fallen back onto the sofa, breathing heavily from the exertion of his outburst.

'Look, this is ridiculous, I've never killed anyone,' Jack lied shamelessly. 'Dad, I don't know where you've got this nonsense from, but you must forget it. I love you all. You're my family. I don't want to hear anymore about it. Come, Sandra, it's been a long day.'

Chapter 13

A shrill ringing penetrated the darkness, jolting Jack from a deep sleep. He turned over and fumbled for the light switch. Sandra stirred at the sudden brightness as he lent on his elbow to squint at the clock. It was two in the morning. He lifted the handset.

'Hello?'

'Jack, its Rachel.'

'Hi, Mum. What's the matter?'

'It's Samuel.'

'What about him?'

'He's dead, Jack…he's *dead*…'

His mother's voice was cut short by a soft click, followed by the mournful hum of a dialling tone. He sat up in bed, ashen faced, staring at the phone still clutched in his hand.

Sandra looked up from her pillow, suddenly awake. 'What is it? What's happened?'

Jack shook his head, tight lipped, and replaced the receiver. He left the bed and walked over to the window. Staring out across the East End's moonlit skyline, he began to reflect on the vagaries of his life, a life that seemed destined to witness the destruction of everything held dear to him. Sandra's hand rested softly on his shoulder, touching a deep-rooted emotion that refused to be stirred.

*

Samuel Hurwitz died at the age of seventy-four, and was buried on a raw January afternoon at Willesden Cemetery. The interment was a Spartan affair, customary with Jewish funerals, followed by a reception at the King David's Suite in Kilburn. A large number of mourners attended, mostly from the East End of London, people who had got to know Mr and Mrs Hurwitz over the years.

There were fellow traders, and members of the local Synagogue, as well as regular customers who remembered the tea and conversations that often lasted long after the café's official closing time. Jack's childhood friends also arrived to pay their respects, cherishing fond memories of the kindly old man who had given them free drinks and ice creams after school.

Then there were Jack's business associates: club managers, loan sharks, drug dealers, pimps, and others that worked for the organisation, all hoping to curry favour with the young gangster by attending his father's funeral.

Sandra had remained at her husband's side throughout the day, ignoring his unsavoury company and the gossip surrounding him. She would not allow anything to destroy her world. As long as he came home at night, and kissed their child before bedtime, she was content. He was a good man who cared and provided for his family. Nothing, and no one, would ever convince her differently.

The same could not be said for Mrs Hurwitz. It

was generally accepted that her husband's heart had simply failed him after a lifetime of adversity. But there had been no doubt in her mind that his suspicions about their son's criminal activities had contributed directly to his death. He had died of a broken heart; it was a heavy burden for her to bear.

*

The shooting outside the Pink Pelican was traced back to Clive Remus who, not unsurprisingly, had gone to ground. On Jack's orders, Levin would occasionally send men south of the river to firebomb a club, or indiscriminately murder known associates of the mobster. The message was clear. No one was to set foot in Jack's *manor* again.

His extortion racket had expanded, targeting successful businesses around the capital. Together with his growing number of brothels, clubs and casinos, Jack was becoming a wealthy man. The Diamond Agency, under the direction of Ben Sharmer, was also making successful inroads into the growing pop industry, and as the money continued to pour in the organisation grew progressively more powerful and sophisticated.

Jack now employed a shrewd accountant, and a solicitor who was well versed in manipulating the law to his clients' advantage. He also invested in a light aircraft: invaluable for transporting large amounts of cash to tax-efficient havens abroad. Doug Levin moved away from the East End and took possession of a comfortable mansion flat in Maida Vale, overlooking the

Edgware Road, from where he would be able to supervise their upmarket West London establishments more conveniently.

In the autumn of 1960 Jack gained the respectability he craved by buying an expansive eight bed-roomed property in St Georges Hill, Weybridge, considered to be the heartland of the Surrey stockbroker belt. Although their families would want for nothing, Sandra's parents chose to remain in the East End of London, as did Mrs Hurwitz who continued to run the café surrounded by memories of her beloved husband.

Jack's people were under strict instructions to watch out for her wellbeing at all times.

Chapter 14

The wooden talisman flew around Andrei's neck on a thin length of twine as he swung his screaming guitar downwards, bringing the band to a shuddering finale. Cheers and whoops of appreciation erupted from the packed, dimly lit cellar.

'We're back in ten,' he shouted to three musicians, before jumping from the small stage into a rush of girls who clamoured for the tall, blue eyed man's attention. His shoulder length fair hair was tied back into a ponytail, allowing the perspiration to run freely down his boyishly handsome face. He hastily scrawled a few autographs and fought his way towards the bar.

The band had been fortunate to find work at the Mojo Club, one of the more popular venues that lay in the basements of Hamburg's Reeperbahn, an area considered to be the heart of new wave beat music. The gruelling hours and low pay were accepted without complaint when a gig was offered in that famous street.

Andrei Wolenski had left home at the age of eighteen. His mother, finally accepting her son's desire to be a musician, encouraged him to follow his heart, hoping it would heal the sorrow that still plagued him after the sudden departure of his childhood friend. Andrei had been deeply touched that Yakov had remembered his promise to carve the talisman, and had worn it ever since as a constant reminder of their lost friendship

He spent a few years improving his musicianship, playing in the bars and cafes across Poland, gradually making his way towards West Germany. Once across the border, he found regular work performing on the US Air Force Bases. The generosity of the American servicemen allowed him to send a modest amount of money back home to his family. During this time he managed to perfect his English, spoken with the hint of an American accent.

In the spring of 1961 he arrived in Hamburg, drawn by its flourishing club scene, where he met up with many young British musicians. Within weeks he had formed his own band. The first to join him was a bass player, called Mark Jacobs, who shared the same enthusiasm for rock and blues music.

Andrei pulled up a stool at the bar. He was obliged to discourage the advances of yet another female admirer, and was soon joined by a dark haired, stocky young man, wearing tight jeans and a sweat stained T-shirt, who promptly ordered two lagers.

'It's my shout, you got the last round,' Mark Jacobs said, flicking a long, damp fringe from his eyes. 'What a gig, the crowd's really cooking tonight.' He looked longingly at the amber liquid being poured in front of them.

Andrei reached for his glass. 'Cooking is right. It's hotter than hell in here. Thanks for the drink.'

'Any idea where we'll be playing after this?' Mark Jacobs asked, taking a generous gulp of the ice-cold lager.

Their four-week residency had won them a big following, but the tenure was coming to a close and they desperately needed another job.

Andrei wiped a line of froth from his lips. 'Afraid not, although the manager's told me that some English guy's heard about us. Reckons he's a big agent looking for new talent. Apparently he's supposed to be here this evening, but I've seen no sign of him.'

'No kidding? That would be cool. I'm nearly skint. Don't really want to wait tables again.' Mark Jacobs' eyes started to roam the darkened cellar, hoping to catch a glimpse of anyone that might look remotely important.

Andrei was fired by his friend's optimism. 'Okay, when we get back we'll kick off with some solid rock n' roll, full blast. That should impress him, always assuming he arrives in the first place.'

'Good idea. So what will it be?'

'How about *Roll over Beethoven?*'

'Nice one,' Mark Jacobs said, downing his drink. 'Gotta take a leak. See you on stage.'

Andrei was left alone, staring into the bottom of his glass. He wondered how much longer he could justify his pursuit of musical success while his mother and sister still struggled to get by. His conscience kept telling him it was time to return home and get a job, any job, to help support them.

A hand slapped his back. He swung round, spilling the remnants of his drink down his worn leather jacket. A plump individual, wearing a camel hair coat slung loosely from his shoulders, stood directly behind him accompanied by a hefty man wearing a dark brown suit.

'Steady, son. Didn't mean to startle you,' said the plump man, whose mouth expanded into a broad grin that still managed to clamp a cigar between yellow stained teeth.

Andrei slid his glass onto the counter, irritably wiping damp fingers down the leg of his jeans. 'Do I know you?'

'You do now. Andrei Wolenski isn't it?' the man said, grabbing Andrei's hand. 'My name's Ben Sharmer. I run the Diamond Agency in London. I understand you're looking for representation.'

Andrei retrieved his hand, wishing Mark Jacobs was still with him. 'Well, we need work that's for sure, but as for a manager, I don't think -'

'That's right, son, don't think,' Sharmer interjected. 'I'll do that for you. Just play your guitar. That's what I've come to hear.'

Sharmer's colleague stared impassively at Andrei, displaying a total lack of interest in his surroundings. His presence seemed out of place in such a youthful atmosphere.

The agent's diamond ring glinted in the dim light as he pointed a stubby finger towards the bandstand. 'By the way, I think you're wanted over there.'

Mark Jacobs could be seen slipping a guitar

strap over his head, signalling urgently from the stage. The drummer was flicking his sticks at the snare drum, loosening his wrists, while the keyboard player fired up the Hammond organ. The crowd had begun to stamp their feet, chanting, 'Blues Knights! Blues Knights! Blues Knights!' Andrei excused himself and hurried away.

When the group steamed into the opening twelve bar riff their audience went wild, almost drowning out the music. Above a sea of waving arms, Andrei could just make out two shadowy figures looking towards the stage. He quickly put them out of his mind and leaned into the microphone, giving it his all.

'I'm gonna write a letter, gonna mail it to my local DJ...'

*

One evening they were playing in a Hamburg cellar; a fortnight later they were sitting in the plush offices of the Diamond Agency in London.

Andrei's initial concerns over their whirlwind signing by Ben Sharmer were quickly dispelled by the smooth talk and generous money paid to them as an advance against their future earnings. Four hungry musicians were not about to turn down such an opportunity over a few niggling doubts. The agent's chubby hands were busy shuffling the newly signed contracts together on his desk.

'Welcome to London, boys,' he drawled, with the ever-present cigar bobbing from the corner of his mouth. 'Now listen up. We've organised a bed-sit for you in Earls Court as a temporary measure. The Abbey Road Studios are booked for tomorrow morning at ten o'clock, where you've got exactly four hours to get a couple of tracks down, so don't be late. You're back here in the afternoon for a photo shoot, and then over to the Pink Pelican club in Wardour Street for your first London gig.'

'Bloody hell, you don't mess around do you?' Mark Jacobs laughed. 'What about our gear?'

'A road crew will drive your stuff around and set it up for you. All you've got to do is turn up and play. You can manage that can't you?'

Mark Jacobs shrugged off the sarcasm.

'I'm Polish. Won't I need a work permit or something?' Andrei said, looking concerned.

'It's being sorted as we speak by a man called Mr Levin.' Sharmer seemed to attach importance to the name. 'He's got friends in high places. Oh yeah, and that reminds me, you're no longer Andrei Wolenski.'

Andrei looked puzzled.

'From now on the band will be called Andy Rivers and the Blues Knights. Much more appropriate for a pop star, don't you think? That was my idea. Mr Levin thought it was great.'

'Who the hell *is* this Mr Levin?' Andrei demanded.

'A very influential man, and that's all you need to know.'

Mark Jacobs sensed his friend's irritation. 'Forget it, Andrei. It's just a name. Maybe Mr Sharmer's right.'

'I'm always right, son.' Sharmer's arrogant comment closed the conversation. He got up and moved away from the desk to pull open the office door. 'Now it's time to earn your money. You can start by sorting out those songs for tomorrow's recording session. There's a rehearsal room in the basement, and if you need anything else give me a shout.'

*

The country's youth were hungry for new groups. When *Evil Love*, written by Andrei Wolenski and Mark Jacobs, was released in the August of 1961 it flew right to the top of the British pop charts. The record company had been forced to release a follow-up single immediately. Andy Rivers and the Blues Knights were in huge demand. Everything happened so fast that the four of them had difficulty in coming to terms with their rollercoaster success.

The bed-sit in Earls Court was continually besieged by screaming girls, making it impossible for them to remain there, but with the money they were now earning it wasn't long before they had acquired their own homes around London. Andrei and Mark Jacobs shared a large apartment in Bayswater, while Mick Brightman, the keyboard player, and the drummer, Jerry Wilson, found places in St John's Wood close to the recording studios.

The Blues Knights became the Diamond Agency's biggest signing. Sharmer was quick to arrange a tour around the country to establish their popularity, and increase record sales, always ensuring that once a month they would return to London for an appearance at the Pink Pelican. The group soon established the club as a popular shop window for every new artist signed by the agency.

Andrei came to an arrangement with Sharmer to have a generous proportion of his substantial earnings set aside for his family. Under the ruling communists, it would not be easy to get such large amounts of money to them, but the agent knew people who still managed to trade with Poland. He promised it would be done when the opportunities arose. Andrei was determined that his family would never again suffer the privation they had endured for so long.

Chapter 15

The housemaid paused beside the breakfast table. 'More coffee, Mrs Bronson?'

Sandra looked up from her magazine. 'No thanks, Ellie, I'm fine, but you could ask Nanny to get Marek dressed. I think we'll go for a stroll later.'

'Of course,' the girl said, leaving the dining room.

Sandra especially enjoyed Sundays. It was the one day they could all spend time together as a family. Greystone Manor was a large property, boasting fifteen acres of well-maintained gardens, an outdoor swimming pool, and an ornamental lake. Jack had employed a nanny, a cook, and a housemaid to assist his wife with the running of the house, as well as two full-time groundsmen. Her life was everything she could have wished for, but there were still moments of solitude when she would seek solace in the company of her handsome little son.

She went back to an editorial about the Blues Knights. The press loved printing stories about the group's sell-out gigs and the frenzied disruption caused by their thousands of fans. Sandra knew they were represented by the Diamond Agency, one of her husband's many businesses, and found it frustrating that the only interest he had in the music business was how much money it brought in. She finished reading.

'Can we go and see them?'

'Who?' Jack mumbled from behind his newspaper.

'The Blues Knights, who else?'

'Sure, why not, I think Sharmer puts them in the Pink Pelican every so often.'

'You always say that, but we never go,' she sulked.

He lowered the paper. 'You really like this group?'

'Well yes, I do actually,' she said, latching on to the sudden interest. 'They have a great sound, and that Andy Rivers guy is *very* dishy.'

'Perhaps I should grow my hair and buy a pair of those tight leather trousers,' he suggested, straight-faced.

Sandra giggled. The thought of her burly man dressed as a trendy pop star conjured up an amusing image. 'I don't think so, darling. I love you just the way you are. But I really would like to see them at some time.'

'Very well, I'll get Doug to organise something.'

'When?'

'When what?'

'When will you speak to Doug?'

'Sweetheart, you're driving me nuts. I'll speak with him today, alright,' he smiled, returning to the paper.

His respite was short lived.

'Won't you come with me?' she asked, nibbling at a slice of toast.

'Not my scene,' Jack grunted. 'But you go and enjoy yourself. Why don't you take Lucy with you?'

'Perhaps I will.' Her shoulders slumped in disappointment.

He peered over the page. 'And do me a favour?'

'What's that?'

'Get me his autograph.'

He managed to deflect the flying toast with his paper.

*

Later that morning a black Vanden-Plas Princess swung through the electronic gates of Greystone Manor and coasted up the gravel driveway, its tyres crunching to a halt beside the sweeping stone steps that climbed to the entrance of the house. A chauffeur hurried to open the rear door, allowing Henry Jameson to step from the car.

'Morning, Henry,' Jack called out, emerging from the tall oak doors into the afternoon sunshine to greet the recently appointed Junior Cabinet Minister.

Jameson was short of breath when he reached the top of the steps, his Savile Row suit fitting a little too snugly: a sure sign of his newly acquired affluence. He entered the house and was led across the entrance hall's black and gold terrazzo floor. His voice echoed around the high domed ceiling.

'Good of you to see me, especially on a weekend.'

'My pleasure,' Jack said, showing Jameson into the study. He offered his guest a seat, gesturing to a silk upholstered armchair, and walked over to the corner bar to pour two whiskies. The scenario amused him: a senior member of the government putting himself under further obligation by begging favours from a young Polish immigrant. He gained huge satisfaction, reflecting on his rise from a life of poverty and persecution to one of affluence and respect. The knowledge gleaned from Jameson was invaluable, and knowledge meant power. He took a seat opposite the minister, placing the cut glass tumblers on an exquisitely inlaid table standing between them.

'So, how can I help you, Henry?'

'It's a delicate matter really. You see, I'm fortunate enough to be invited to the occasional party at this country house owned by an extremely influential man. He holds them for his close friends, business people, government ministers and the like. He's made it known that he would like to introduce a little entertainment into the proceedings, perhaps one of those celebrity pop groups, and maybe a few uninhibited, pretty girls. I rather impulsively suggested that I might be of some use in the matter, ingratiate myself with him, you know the kind of thing.'

'I get the drift,' Jack said, picking up his drink.

'Well I thought that you, with your many contacts, might be able to point me in the right direction…so to speak.'

Jameson was starting to feel uncomfortable. He hated being beholden to the young man, but like it or not he owed everything to him. Not only had his campaign been heavily financed by

Bronson, but the opposition candidates had also fallen into disrepute as a result of damaging smears brought against them. Even their meetings had been constantly disrupted by hooligan elements. Jameson was under no illusions as to who had been responsible for these occurrences. If it hadn't been for the gangster he would not be in government, let alone the cabinet.

'The girls won't be a problem, they're two a penny,' Jack said, watching the politician visibly relax. 'And as for a group, contact a guy called Ben Sharmer at the Diamond Agency, and don't forget to mention my name. It's one of my business interests. Why don't you ask him about the Blues Knights? That Andy Rivers guy is huge at the moment.'

'I will, thank you. Even I've heard of him.' Jameson said, pleased to appear conversant with youthful trends. 'A very good looking young man I believe?'

'I wouldn't know,' Jack replied. 'But he makes a load of money for the agency. By the way, who is this friend of yours, the one with the country house?'

'I'm sorry, I should have mentioned it. His name is Lord Fanthorpe. He's a Peer of the Realm.'

Chapter 16

The fading afternoon sun had turned the furrowed fields to a soft brown and the surrounding woodlands into a blaze of autumnal reds and golds, painting a picturesque backdrop to the grey walled Tudor mansion. The newly erected grand marquee looked oddly inappropriate attached to the ancient building, resembling a gigantic white bag lying across a green expanse of tailored lawns.

Inside its canvas walls the caterers and florists were putting the final touches to their arrangements, serenaded by a discordant mix of sounds being requested by the road crew who were balancing the band's equipment. Mick Brightman held a single note on the keyboard, allowing Mark Jacobs and Andrei to tune their guitars, while Jerry Wilson checked the positioning of his drum kit. Musicians generally disliked playing in 'tents', as they called them, but this evening was to be very different. They were performing at Redwing House, the Berkshire estate of Lord Fanthorpe, whose guests included some of the most powerful men in the country.

Andrei noticed Ben Sharmer trying to attract his attention from the side of the newly laid dance floor. He put down his guitar and walked over to join him. The agent's loud check suit and garish tie cut an almost comical figure in contrast to the conservatively dressed man standing alongside him.

'Mr Jameson, this is my discovery, Andy Rivers, one of the biggest stars in the music business,' the agent boasted as Andrei approached.

'Andy, I've heard so much about you, mostly from my young secretary. It's nice to meet you,' said the politician, shaking hands.

'My pleasure, Mr Jameson.'

'Please, call me Henry.'

'As you wish, Henry,' said Andrei, noticing how the man's handshake lingered.

'Mr Jameson has just been appointed to the Cabinet,' Sharmer announced importantly. 'Means he's an important sod now.'

Jameson was unable to hide his distaste at the remark. 'That's one way of putting it I suppose.' He turned his attention back to the fair-haired singer. 'We really should have a drink some time?'

'Sure, why not,' Andrei replied, with an indifferent shrug.

'Well, we mustn't keep you, Andy,' Sharmer butted in, 'just wanted to make the introduction. You'd better get back to your boys, and tell them to keep their grubby hands off the women. They're here for the guests.'

'Oh I'm sure Andy must get tired of all those girls swooning over him,' the Cabinet Minister said, dismissing the agent's vulgarity with a polite smile.

Andrei inclined his head silently towards Jameson and returned to the bandstand, watched closely by Mark Jacobs.

*

The group took to the stage at midnight. As the music progressed, and the champagne flowed, the dinner-suited partygoers were virtually staggering around the dance floor with their attractive escorts.

After their performance, the musicians met up at the bar where refreshments had been provided for them. Andrei was drinking far more than usual. It helped to ease the dull conversations he was forced to endure with a few of the more inquisitive guests who enjoyed the kudos of socialising with the pop celebrities. It took a while for the novelty to wane, before they were eventually left in peace.

'Some of these blokes are as famous as we are. I see most of them in the papers every week,' Jerry Wilson said, scanning the marquee.

'Bloody politicians, can't stand them,' Mick Brightman grumbled.

'Maybe, but the pay's good,' Mark Jacobs was quick to remind him.

'Can't argue with that,' he said, finishing his drink. 'Well, I don't know about you lot, but I'm out of here.'

'You go ahead, guys. I think I'll hang around for a while,' said Andrei.

Mark Jacobs suddenly rounded on him. '*Great!* How the bloody hell am I supposed to get home? I came in your car. I can't drive, remember?'

Andrei looked startled by the reaction. 'What's

your problem, Mark? It's no big deal. You're welcome to stay with me if you want?'

'Forget it. I've had enough of this place anyway,' he grumbled, avoiding Andrei's eyes.

Jerry Wilson laid a hand on Mark Jacobs' shoulder. 'Don't worry, pal, I'll drop you off. Let him mix with the bluebloods if he wants to,' he joked with a good-natured wink.

Andrei watched the three of them leave. He emptied the remnants of the whisky bottle into his glass, mystified by his friend's aggressive outburst. One of the girls noticed him sitting alone at the bar. The striking blonde sashayed over, wearing a figure hugging, gold lame evening gown. She introduced herself as Janine Devonshire and presented him with a book of matches to autograph. The effect of the alcohol was beginning to blur Andrei's vision. He squinted at the cover, surprised to see *'The Pink Pelican'* printed across it.

He took the pen from her with a curious smile. 'You must have seen me before?'

'Of course I have.'

'Then how come we've never met?' he said, scribbling across the back of the matches.

'Because I'm usually working, like you,' she grinned, caressing her thighs.

'Are you're working tonight?' he asked.

She tilted her head towards the rowdy guests. 'If you call *this* working, playing nursemaid to a bunch of dirty old men, half of them can't even get it up,' she snorted.

Andrei's burst of drunken laughter drew a look of disapproval from the grey haired figure of

Lord Fanthorpe whose bulging waistline and florid complexion bore witness to his over indulged lifestyle. The Earl eventually returned to his conversation with a group of men surrounding him.

'Shush, darling,' she giggled, raising a finger to her lips, 'you'll get us thrown out.'

'I doubt that. I'm too famous, and you're too beautiful,' he answered loudly. 'Why don't you show me around the place? You've obviously been here before.'

The glamorous woman playfully dragged Andrei from the marquee, relieved to get him away; he was in no fit state to socialise with anyone

The red-carpeted stairs creaked softly under their feet as they climbed towards the first floor landing. They continued along a warren of oak panelled corridors hung with musty tapestries and darkly faded paintings. Tarnished suits of armour stood against the walls like lifeless sentries, oblivious to the girlish shrieks and rowdy laughter that disturbed the dignified tranquillity of the stately home. Andrei marvelled at the ancient building, wondering if it had ever experienced the same wanton immorality in its past.

Their journey finally brought them to a recently constructed indoor swimming pool where the squeals and splashes of naked bathers forced them out onto a cobbled courtyard. The woman found a bench and pulled her handsome companion down beside her.

Andrei shook his head in amazement. 'The

press could have a ball with the sights we've seen here this evening.'

'They could, but who would dare say anything? These people are among the elite. I think even the famous Andy Rivers should bear that in mind,' she teased, fondling his thigh.

As Andrei looked towards her she snaked an arm around his neck, drawing him into a sensual kiss. It wasn't every day a girl could make out with a famous pop star, and Janine Devonshire was not about to let the chance slip by. Andrei was unresponsive. He had always associated a woman's embrace with his mother's maternal gestures of comfort against his father's brutality. Anything else seemed distasteful to him. His mind shot back to a previous encounter with a young waitress back in Poland who had been smitten by his guitar playing and good looks. He experienced a small shudder as he recalled her mouthful of saliva and the reek of cheap perfume.

'Well, well, what's going on here?' cried a familiar voice.

Andrei was grateful to break away from the girl. He saw Henry Jameson approaching from the pool area, dressed in a white towelling robe.

'Hi, Henry,' he called back, with a carefree wave.

'Good to see you, Andy,' Jameson said, casting a critical look at the girl. 'I think *you* should be entertaining our guests, my dear. Why don't you run a long like a good girl?'

Janine Devonshire blushed guiltily, worried about losing a lucrative job. She nodded submissively, stealing a glance at Andrei, before hurrying away.

'Maybe some other time?' he slurred.

Jameson was quick to notice Andrei's condition. 'Why don't we go inside and have that drink we spoke about?' he suggested. 'I'm sure we can find something more comfortable than a bench to sit on.'

Andrei got to his feet unsteadily, with a foolish smile, and followed Jameson back to the indoor pool. He was amused by the sights that greeted him. A chubby man, wearing a euphoric smile, was sprawled naked across a canvas lounger, with a young woman's face buried in his crotch. Two other women, clad only in bikini bottoms, were tugging a towel from another man's waist before toppling into the pool with him amid shrieks of laughter, forcing Andrei to quicken his pace to avoid a soaking.

He was eventually ushered into a softly lit room furnished with comfortable seating and a fully stocked bar. He heard the sound of a key turn in a lock behind him. Before he could comment, Jameson was already behind the counter pouring two large whiskies. Andrei walked over and downed his glass, which was immediately refilled.

The minister smiled. 'You certainly have a thirst tonight. Why don't we make ourselves more comfortable?' he said, gesturing to a black leather sofa standing a short distance from the bar.

Jameson sat down, inviting his guest to join him. Andrei placed his glass on a side table. The whisky had taken its toll. As he turned to sit down he stumbled forward, landing clumsily on top of Jameson.

'Whoa, steady, Andy,' he laughed, tugging the robe open to reveal his nakedness.

Before Andrei could protest, the minister threw an arm around his shoulder, pinning their bodies together in a close embrace. Andrei's hand was immediately guided firmly into the man's groin. Jameson's fingers began yanking at Andrei's belt buckle. Within moments, Andrei felt a hand slip under his slackened waistband to grasp his bare buttocks. A surge of sexual arousal washed over him. He succumbed to a frenzied grappling of animal passion. Andrei's mind was drifting in a surreal, alcoholic haze. He experienced the scent of a male, without the stench of sweat and stale vodka. He felt the gentle strength of a masculine embrace, instead of painful blows striking his body ...

*

The place was deserted. Andrei woke up, dressed only in his shirt, naked from the waist down. It took him a moment to get his bearings. He panicked and sprang to his feet. The sudden move caused the room to spin, forcing him to steady himself against the sofa. His head began to pound. He pulled on his jeans, tucked in his shirt, and hunted around for his shoes. Soon he was hurrying from the building to find his car that was still parked where he had left it the night before.

Driving back towards London, memories of the previous night began to filter slowly back into his mind. His homosexual desires had been liberated, but remembering his intimacy with Henry Jameson sent a shiver of revulsion through his body. It had been a senseless, drunken moment of unbridled lust. The thought of facing Jameson again was hugely embarrassing, but he had no choice; the band was simply too popular to avoid any future gigs at Redwing House.

*

Whenever their busy schedule allowed, the Blues Knights became the exclusive entertainment at Lord Fanthorpe's Berkshire estate. They were paid handsomely for their services, despite the obscene amounts of commission skimmed off by Ben Sharmer.

Andrei became addicted to the decadence of Lord Fanthorpe's parties. The hidden wounds from his abused childhood were somehow soothed by the freedom to indulge in whatever licentious activities he pleased, with no fear of punishment or criticism, except for the one thing he genuinely hated: drugs. The other members of his group enjoyed their own particular diversions, taking little notice of their front man's behaviour, apart from Mark Jacobs, who had become increasingly withdrawn.

Chapter 17

To follow up their fourth hit single, Andrei and Mark Jacobs were putting the finishing touches to their first album scheduled for release on 1st March 1962. All the songs had been co-written by them, and judging by the projected sales they would far exceed their current earnings to become extremely rich young men.

Their tour bus was travelling through South London heading for a gig at the Wimbledon Palais. The ballroom had hosted every popular group in the country, making it the most prestigious and largest pop venue in London. The Blues Knights appearance had been widely advertised on thousands of bill posters distributed across the capital, and with the addition of countless articles in all the popular teenage magazines it was guaranteed to be a sell-out performance.

The roadies were laughing noisily, passing a few beers around, chatting animatedly with the driver. The band had taken up their regular seats a few rows behind them. Jerry Wilson did what he always did: as soon as the vehicle hit the road, he slept. Mick Brightman settled down to a book. He had a thing about Westerns, and would drag one from his shoulder bag at every opportunity.

It helped relieve the tedium of the incessant travelling. Most of their time seemed to be spent trawling across the country from one gig to another; the demands of agents and record companies were unrelenting. Andrei usually commandeered the seats at the back of the coach. It allowed more room for him and Mark Jacobs to take out their guitars and concentrate on writing new material for the band. Andrei's love of rock and blues music combined well with Mark Jacobs' talent for lyrics, resulting in a successful creative partnership. However, much to Andrei's bewilderment, the last few trips had been spent with Mark Jacobs staring sullenly through the window, ignoring any attempts at conversation.

*

The group looked out across a sea of faces disappearing into the darkening depths of the ballroom. The stage at the Palais had been raised high above the dance floor and surrounded by metal mesh barriers as protection against over-zealous fans. The music was barely audible above the incessant screaming. Every time Andrei flung his ponytail around his shoulders, or raised his guitar, the crowd went wild. He announced their latest hit as the final song of the first set, and started to count it in above the expectant roar.

'Andrei! It's Mark. What the hell's he doing?' Jerry Wilson shouted from behind his drums.

Mark Jacobs had leant his guitar against an amplifier and was stumbling unsteadily towards the side of the stage. Andrei moved across to grab his friend's arm and was immediately forced to dodge a clumsy punch aimed at his face, sending the audience into a mystified hush. An MC, dressed in an ill-fitting dinner suit, leapt from the wings, babbling some excuse into his microphone about problems with the equipment.

The other two group members rushed to Andrei's assistance, helping to manhandle their bass player from the stage. Boos and jeers followed the four musicians as they hurried through a hastily assembled corridor of security men towards the refuge of their dressing room situated above the 'Long Bar' at the end of the ballroom. The support group finally struck up, restoring a temporary calm to the disgruntled dance hall.

Sharmer's panicking outburst greeted them as they fell through the door. 'What the hell's going on out there?'

'Shut up, Ben, we don't need this right now,' Andrei said, allowing Mark Jacobs to slump into a chair. He lightly slapped his friend's pale face. 'Mark, speak to me. What the matter with you for God's sake?'

Mick Brightman answered the question. 'Just look at him, Andrei, he's high as a kite,'

'He's right. Shit, that's all we need,' Jerry Wilson groaned, helping Andrei lift the man to his feet. 'We must keep him walking around. Mick, get the roadies to fetch black coffee…gallons of it!'

*

The support group's courageous efforts were soon being drowned by the impatient fans that were becoming increasingly more hostile, chanting loudly for Andy Rivers to the rhythm of slow handclaps. Mercifully, the coffee began to take effect; Mark Jacobs slowly regained his faculties.

Andrei shook his friend by the shoulders. 'What the hell were you thinking of, Mark? You never told me you were on that crap.'

Sharmer's tolerance was exhausted. 'Never mind the bloody hearts and flowers. Get back out there before we have a riot on our hands.' *A superstar walking off stage at the Wimbledon Palais, the biggest London venue for pop music, what would the press make of it?* The thought was too painful to contemplate.

The Blues Knights finally returned to finish their performance and appease their boisterous fans. A potential disaster had been avoided, but there were questions to be asked.

*

Sharmer was shocked by his prodigy storming into the office. 'It's customary to knock before you come in, Andy. Can't you see I'm busy?'

A stylishly dressed man was sitting in front of the desk.

'Not too busy to see *me* I hope,' Andrei fumed, ignoring the visitor.

'Just a minute, before you go any further, I think it only polite to introduce you to *Mr Levin*,' Sharmer said, attaching great emphasis to the name.

The last thing he needed was any inference that he might have upset their lucrative celebrity. Doug Levin would not be impressed.

'Mr Levin? Yeah, I've heard about you. But I need to talk with my agent, urgently,' Andrei demanded.

'No problem, you go ahead, we're finished here anyway,' Levin smiled, appearing untroubled by the interruption. *Cheeky little sod. Still, I admire his balls*, he thought rising to his feet, extending his hand. 'I'm a big fan, Andy. You write great songs. It's good to meet you at last.' He looked towards the agent. 'Don't get up, Ben. We'll speak later.'

Andrei noticed the man's pronounced limp as he left.

Sharmer's syrupy smile disappeared the minute they were alone. 'That wasn't clever, barging in here like that? Mr Levin is a very important guy. You owe a lot to that man.'

'I don't owe *anything* to anyone,' Andrei raged. 'I've put you and your agency on the map, and you thank me by feeding drugs to my best friend.'

Sharmer shook his head in despair. 'So this is what it's all about. Before you go shouting your mouth off, did he tell you *why* he took them? He was pissed off at you for sleeping around on those Redwing House gigs, and I'm not talking about the tart. You had it off with that creep, Jameson, didn't you?'

The accusation struck hard. Andrei flushed, consumed with shame. He had deeply regretted his drunken moment of lunacy, and now his sordid secret had been laid bare.

'How the hell did he find out?' he asked in a restrained voice.

Sharmer sighed. 'Give me a break. You walk through an indoor swimming pool with Jameson, in front of a bunch of naked people, straight into a room where the door is immediately locked. You and Jameson were the talk of Redwing House for weeks. Mark Jacobs *has* got ears, he's not bloody deaf.'

'But I don't understand,' Andrei frowned, 'why the hell should he get pissed off at me? Unless...'

Sharmer raised an eyebrow. 'The penny dropped has it? Jacobs came to me in tears, told me he loved you and felt betrayed. He begged me for drugs, something to get him through the gigs. How was I to know the stupid sod couldn't handle it?'

'I had no idea Mark felt that way about me. And anyway, my private life is none of your damn business,' Andrei retaliated. His excuse sounded lame, and as genuine as it was how could he expect Sharmer to understand.

'None of my business,' Sharmer cried. 'I'm your agent. After that bloody fiasco at the Palais, have you any idea what could happen if the press got hold of it? If all this got out it could ruin everything.'

Andrei wished he had never entered the office. He fell into a chair, his brain in turmoil. It was all becoming clear. The incident in the marquee, his friend's mood swings: they had all been motivated by jealousy.

'And what about the thousands of horny little girls out there,' Sharmer ranted on, 'how do you think they'd feel if they found out their macho rock star was...'

The agent clammed up. Although livid with Rivers, he still had to keep the man happy. Had he gone too far?

'You watch your mouth, Sharmer,' Andrei threatened. 'I don't need this, especially from the likes of you.' The infuriated musician got up to leave.

'Hey, just a moment, Andy, I'm sorry. I didn't mean to be rude. Hell, whatever your thing is that's your business. But if your friend, Mark, is getting hacked off at you maybe you need to speak with him? We've got too much going on here to screw things up.' Sharmer begged. He could imagine Bronson's rage if the Blues Knights were to leave the agency.

Andrei calmed down. 'Yeah, you're right. I need to talk to Mark. But this is strictly between you and me, right?'

'Agreed', Sharmer said readily: greatly relieved.

*

Andrei guided his gold Mercedes 300SL into its parking bay. There was nothing he could do about the irresponsible incident with Jameson, but things needed to be resolved with Mark Jacobs urgently. He hadn't appreciated how much he really cared for the man.

He entered the apartment and found his flatmate slumped on the couch, racked with guilt.

'I don't know about you, but I need a scotch,' Andrei said immediately, walking straight to the drinks cabinet.

He poured himself a shot of whisky, and another for his friend.

Mark Jacobs took the glass. 'I'm really sorry about all this, Andrei,' he said, looking dejected.

Andrei sat down beside him, laying a hand on his shoulder, determined to state his case. 'Don't be. If anything, I'm more to blame for this mess than you. How could I have been so blind? I'm deeply fond of you, Mark. We must never be ashamed of what we are.'

'Do you really mean that?

'Of course, we're both creative people, and so alike in many ways. I confess that I doubted my own sexuality for years until that bastard, Jameson, accosted me. I was drunk, out of my head. If I could turn the clock back I would.'

Mark Jacobs looked reassured. 'You've just made me a very happy man. Can we forget about Jameson and move on?'

'That's fine by me,' Andrei replied.

There followed a brief silence while the two of them took in the significance of the moment.

'Oh, and before I forget, this came for you today,' Mark Jacobs said, moving the conversation on. He reached for an envelope lying on the coffee table, and handed it to Andrei who tore it open immediately.

'It's from my sister, Maria. Says she wants to talk with me urgently. But apparently it's nothing to worry about.'

'Well that's something at least,' said Mark Jacobs. 'We're not working for the next few days, so why don't you fly to Poland? I'm sure your family would be thrilled to see you.'

'I might just do that. God, how I'd like to get them out of that country. Even with all the money I send them, they still can't get a phone installed. Only for the privileged few, apparently? Sodding communists,' Andrei grumbled.

'Yeah, well moaning won't change anything,' Mark Jacobs laughed. 'If you're going, you'd better get organised.'

'Christ, you make us sound like an old married couple already,' Andrei grinned. 'Okay, I'll pack some stuff. And remember, when I get back from this trip things are going to be different. I swear.'

Chapter 18

The powerful locomotive had finally come to rest after the long haul from Krakow. Its passengers spilled out on to the platform and swarmed towards the ticket barriers to be engulfed by exhausted sighs of steam billowing from beneath its motionless wheels.

Andrei emerged from Herbski Station clutching his case and hurried towards the first in a queue of blue painted taxis waiting beside the pavement. He tapped impatiently on the window to wake the dozing occupant who stirred reluctantly and sat up. After the flight from London, and a dreary train journey, the excitement of seeing his family after so long was becoming difficult to contain. He jumped into the back seat, gave the address, and slammed the door shut.

The driver pulled a cloth cap lower over his unshaven face and slouched across the wheel to fire up the engine. He made no apology for the shabby, nicotine stained interior of his rusting Moskvitch. Cars were still a luxury in Poland, and to some, Andrei's trip might be considered an extravagance that few could afford. The taxi made a u-turn and headed away from the station.

Andrei gazed upwards at the post-war apartments, towering like ugly concrete monoliths above the old town of Kielce. A grey February sky did nothing to soften the austerity of his homeland. His pulse quickened when they passed Planty Street, close to the road where a blacksmith yard had once stood. A sense of relief washed over him as they left the area and headed east towards the more affluent suburbs, where his family had moved to a small terraced house.

The vehicle trundled on. Andrei sat back and let his mind drift. He pictured himself enjoying the tranquillity of Grandma Anna's cottage, and playing in the snow with his friend. He smiled, remembering the laughter during their Christmas meal and the wonder in Yakov's face after opening his present. Suddenly, a pale-faced boy was standing in front of him, holding a knife dripping with blood...

Rasping brakes fragmented the gruesome apparition.

'There it is, number sixty seven, the house with the green door,' the driver announced, bringing the vehicle to a halt.

Andrei's heart raced as he paid the fare and stepped from the car.

Marta Wolenski stood in the doorway lost for words at the sight of her son's smiling face. Maria flew past her mother, throwing both arms around the upturned collar of his leather coat.

'*Andrei!*' she cried. 'My baby brother's home at last.'

Andrei hugged her tightly with tears in his eyes.

'Hey, you'll squeeze me skinny,' she gasped. 'Save some for Mum.'

*

'Nothing to worry about, Mr Levin, honestly.'

Sharmer was mentally cursing himself for having answered the phone, which was now awkwardly cradled beneath his ample chin as he struggled to replace the Blues Knights' contract back into its folder. He had been checking that there were no legal loopholes for Andy Rivers to exploit, just as a precaution, not totally convinced of Rivers' loyalty to the agency after their recent spat.

'I'm glad to hear it,' said Levin. 'That guy seemed pretty pissed off when he came into the office. What was it about anyway?'

'Oh you know these pop stars, damn prima donnas. They weren't happy about their dressing room on the last gig.'

Sharmer cringed at his own feeble lie.

'Don't sod me around, Ben. I'm not bloody stupid. That guy was not happy.'

Sharmer swallowed hard. He was forced to come clean.

'I'm sorry, Mr Levin. It's just that I wasn't sure how to tell you.'

'Tell me what?'

'Andy Rivers has had an affair with that minister, Henry Jameson. He's a bloody queer.'

There was a short silence.

'Is he now?' Levin said in a quiet voice.

'Yeah, but I've managed to hold things together. Didn't make a big deal out of it. Just hope the press don't get wind of it.'

'That might prove awkward,' Levin agreed. 'But I'm sure you'll keep things under control. Meanwhile, queer or not, he's a valuable asset. Andy Rivers makes a fortune for us, and he's also popular with some of Jack's important friends.'

'He's not going anywhere.' the agent said, taking the phone back in his hand. 'The contract's tight as a drum.'

'Contracts aren't worth the paper they're written on, Ben, you know that.'

'Possibly, but he wouldn't dare cross you, Mr Levin,' Sharmer grovelled.

'That's as maybe. The last thing we need is any problems with this boy.'

'Of course, you can tell the boss there's nothing to worry about. I've got everything under control. Andy Rivers is eating out of my hand.'

'Good.'

The phone went dead.

Sharmer replaced the receiver with a shuddering sigh. Just the thought of upsetting Jack Bronson had left beads of perspiration prickling his forehead.

*

Mrs Wolenski hurried in and out of the kitchen, preparing refreshments, loathe to leave her son's side for a precious second. She and her daughter now enjoyed a degree of celebrity status in the wake of Andrei's enormous success. Although pop music was frowned upon by the ruling communists, who believed it to be steeped in Western decadence, his recordings regularly reached the young Polish population through the foreign radio stations.

Andrei was relaxing in the sitting room hardly able to believe the reality of being with his family again. He settled back with a coffee and looked across at his sister who was sitting on a couch next to her mother.

'Well I'm here, Maria. What's this urgent business you wanted to see me about?'

Maria glanced coyly at her mother.

Mrs Wolenski smiled at her son. 'Maria has been seeing this man. A Polish-speaking Russian, called Stefan Petrov. She's in love with him.'

'*Mother!*' Maria's pink cheeks spoke volumes.

Andrei laughed. 'That's wonderful, I'm very happy for you. So tell me about it?'

His sister explained how she had met the man at one of the local cafes. There seemed to have been a mutual attraction between them from their first meeting. He showed genuine affection for her, unlike most of the young men in Kielce who knew that her brother was the famous pop star, Andy Rivers, and would be constantly vying for her attention. In fact, one of the bonuses of being seen regularly with Stefan was not being pestered by them anymore.

'Are you engaged to him?' Andrei asked.

'No, not yet, he's a really old fashioned guy,' Maria said, with a dreamy look in her eye. 'He's determined to put some money away before he proposes to me. He's working as a salesman for a clothing company, which means he spends a lot of time travelling. The poor love never stops.'

'It can't be easy out there,' Andrei sympathised.

'That's why I need to talk with you,' said Maria. 'Please don't be cross with me, but I want to ask a huge favour of you.'

'Try me,' he said, with a curious frown.

Mrs Wolenski squeezed her daughter's hand in encouragement.

'It's something that Stefan mentioned a while back, when we first discussed getting married. I think it was probably meant as a joke. Frankly, I can understand where he was coming from. He's desperate for money. When I said I would ask you, he became unsure and backed off, telling me to forget about it, saying it would be discourteous, and an imposition.'

'Saying *what* would be an imposition?' Andrei asked, wondering where this was leading.

'He's a salesman, so he's used to talking with people,' Maria continued. 'He's confident, and he works hard. He simply wondered if there was any possibility of you helping him, like maybe a job in the music business in England. His work takes him there occasionally, so he has a valid visa. At least he would stand a chance of earning some decent money. And if it worked out, Mum and I could come to England, Stefan and I could get married, and we could all be together again. What do you think?'

Andrei pondered his sister's words. *How wonderful would that be?* It might prove difficult obtaining visas for his mother and sister, but if he could establish Petrov in a job it would be easier for the man to remain in the country, and for Maria to join him as his wife. He knew there were ways around such things. With Sharmer's shady contacts, and his own considerable wealth, anything was possible.

'I think it's about time you introduced me to your boyfriend,' Andrei smiled.

Maria squealed with excitement. She leapt to her feet and threw her arms around her brother. Mrs Wolenski looked at her son with grateful tears in her eyes.

*

Andrei's first impression of Stefan Petrov did not fill him with much expectation. He looked to be in his late thirties, prematurely balding, with a pasty complexion. The man's high cheekbones and square jaw emphasised his Slavic origin. A shapeless grey suit was draped over his angular body, giving him the air of a dull civil servant. Maria was not an unattractive girl, and Andrei wondered why his sister might be drawn towards such a man. He suspected it was some deep-rooted need for a father figure. Not surprising, considering her own troubled youth.

'Stefan, this is my brother, Andrei, or should I say, Andy…Andy Rivers.' Maria corrected herself as she led Petrov into the living room.

Andrei stood up to greet the tall man, noticing his surprisingly firm handshake and ready smile.

'The pleasure is all mine, it's good to meet you at last,' Petrov said in perfect English.

They sat down opposite one another. Maria brought over a bottle of locally distilled *Siwucha* and two small glasses. She joined her boyfriend on the sofa, affectionately threading her arm through his.

Petrov poured the neat vodka and pushed a glass across the table towards Andrei. They tapped their drinks together and downed them in a single swallow.

'This is indeed a privilege, Andy. It's not every day I get to shake hands with such a celebrity,' Petrov began.

'I guess not,' Andrei replied, sensing hidden depths about the man. 'And I suppose you'd better call me Andrei, seeing as we're almost family. But only in private, you understand,' he added, with a half-smile. He dropped back into Polish for his sister's benefit. 'Maria tells me you'd like a job in the music business?'

'I'd give my right arm for the chance,' said Petrov.

'A little radical,' Andrei laughed. 'But it's not all that glamorous. It involves a great deal of travelling, and long hours. You'll have to deal with a lot of shallow, two faced idiots all out to make a quick buck.'

'I do that already, selling clothes,' he replied.

Andrei ignored the wisecrack and looked at Petrov with a grave expression. 'There's something I have to ask you, Stefan?'

'Of course, anything.'

'Do you *really* love my sister? Enough to spend the rest of your life with her?'

'She means everything to me. She's my world,' he replied without hesitation, stealing a look at Maria who hugged his arm tightly, drawing him into a tender kiss.

There seemed no point in pursuing that particular subject. But Andrei was also old fashioned and protective where his sister was concerned. He liked the idea of Maria settling down, and was keen to encourage it. But although he respected Petrov's desire to provide for her with his own efforts, he knew nothing about the man. It was time to move things on.

'Maria, would you excuse us for a moment. I need to talk with Stefan, privately,' Andrei said, reflecting on how deceptive appearances could be. Petrov was coming across as an extremely confident and assertive individual: necessary qualities for survival in the music industry.

The request was honoured without protest. Maria got up and left the room, hardly able to contain herself, knowing that her brother was about to grant her wish.

When they were alone, Andrei adopted a business-like manner. 'Stefan, you strike me as a worldly person. As it happens, I would like someone I could trust to act as a personal manager to me. And what could be better than my future brother-in-law?'

Petrov leaned forward attentively.

'I have a proposal that might appeal to you,' Andrei said, coming straight to the point. 'I'll tell my agent, Ben Sharmer, that I want you to become my personal manager. I'll have to give him a financial sweetener, but I'm offering you ten percent of my personal earnings, and I can assure you that when my new album is released that will amount to good money.'

Petrov appeared thrilled at the opportunity. 'That would be incredible, but what about this guy, Sharmer?'

'He's a greedy bastard. He'll get big money in his pocket with no questions asked. And with you looking after my interests he knows I'll be less inclined to leave the agency. The ten percent I pay you from my own money won't affect him at all. Quite frankly I think he'll jump at it.'

'Sorry, Andrei, what do you mean *leave the agency?*' Petrov queried. 'Have you had some kind of trouble with them?'

'You don't miss a trick do you? Okay, you may as well know. I have a boyfriend back in England.' He threw the fact in deliberately to shock the Russian, draw out any prejudice he might have.

Petrov shrugged. 'Why should that bother me?'

'Because it seems to bother a lot of other people,' said Andrei. *Either this guy is refreshingly tolerant, or a bloody good liar*, he thought, before continuing. 'I was involved in a stupid incident with some slimy politician called Henry Jameson, and had a run-in with my agent over it. He was terrified of it ruining my career and started to get a bit mouthy. I think he was frightened I'd walk out on the agency. It's no big deal. Being a pop star has great advantages, but it can also be a bitch at times. It would be good to have someone to look after my welfare.'

'I'm your man, Andrei. It will be a privilege and an honour. As they say in English, I think we'll make sweet music together,' Petrov said excitedly, holding out his hand.

Andrei shook it with a guarded smile. *What the hell, I know nothing about this guy, but at least I can keep an eye on him. If things worked out it could mean a new beginning for me and my family in England.*

Chapter 19

Stefan Petrov spent most of the flight back to London gazing silently through the small oval window of the Douglas DC9. After take-off, his travelling companion had reclined his seat and closed his eyes, grateful for a moment to reflect upon recent developments.

After so brief a visit, Andrei had found it difficult saying goodbye to his loved ones, but the chance of them all being together again as a family was a heartening prospect.

Mark Jacobs drifted into his thoughts. He could not have wished for a kinder, more dependable partner. Andrei suspected that his mother and sister had always been aware of his sexuality, but he saw no point in concerning himself about it. Why even discuss it, and risk embarrassing them unnecessarily? It was a stigma that was not generally tolerated by others. He would always be grateful for their love and discretion.

The incessant hum of the aircraft eventually soothed him into a deep sleep.

*

The two Pratt & Whitney engines roared as the plane started to bank steeply, signalling their descent. The red *'Fasten Seatbelt'* sign flickered into life. Andrei stirred and adjusted his seat to the upright position.

After clearing *Arrivals* at Heathrow Airport, they hired a black cab to take them into London. Andrei called in at a local letting agent and managed to rent a small bedsit for Petrov, just a short distance from his Bayswater apartment. He paid the required deposit and gave the Russian some money to shop for a few supplies, before leaving him to settle in.

When he arrived home, Andrei found a message from Mark Jacobs saying that he would be back from the studio later that evening after overseeing a few minor adjustments to the new album. It was time to make that call.

Sharmer had listened to Andrei's intentions of hiring a personal manager with growing apprehension, until the mention of money changed his manner as if by magic. The agent agreed to everything subject to the cash being handed over. A meeting was arranged for the following morning to be attended by Sharmer, Andrei and Petrov.

*

'Hi, Andy, great to see you, my son,' Sharmer said, welcoming the two men into his office. His two-faced blathering and phoney smile oozed insincerity. Petrov took an instant dislike to the man.

The agent settled himself behind his desk, and showed his palm to a couple of waiting chairs. 'Please take a seat, gentleman. So, you must be the Russian guy, the new personal manager?'

'My name is Stefan Petrov, and yes, Andy has

asked me to look after his affairs,' Petrov answered stiffly.

'Seems a decent bloke, eh Andy?' said Sharmer.

'Yeah, he better be,' Andrei joked. 'He's going to marry my sister.'

'No kidding, keeping it in the family, that's nice,' Sharmer said, smiling at Petrov.

Petrov smiled back coolly, not taking his eyes off the agent.

Sharmer's smile dimmed. Something about the Russian's stare made him feel uncomfortable. 'I trust you brought the money?' he said to Andrei, returning to more important matters.

'I have,' Andrei replied, motioning to Petrov who slid a briefcase onto the desk. 'You'll get half now, and the rest after a lawyer's looked over the contract, and it's signed.'

'Fair enough,' Sharmer said, pulling open a drawer to retrieve a bound document. He dropped it in front of Andrei. 'I've had the necessary papers prepared. Ten percent of your personal income, am I right?'

'That's correct,' said Andrei.

Sharmer snapped open the briefcase and tipped out its contents. 'I'll need to check it, no offence.'

'None taken, but we're not waiting around while you count that lot,' Andrei said, picking up the contract. 'I'll send this back with Stefan after my lawyer's looked it over and it's signed,' he added, waving the document in the air. 'See you later, Ben.'

'Yeah, see you later,' the agent called back. He paused and looked up to catch Petrov still staring at him as he left the office.

Weird fucking foreigners, Sharmer thought, going back to his counting.

*

Two days later Petrov was back in the offices of the Diamond Agency. He tossed a large brown envelope across the desk towards Sharmer.

'It appears to be in order. It only requires your signature to finalise the agreement.'

His curt manner irritated the agent.

'Have I done something bad to you in another life?' Sharmer said, beginning to feel a growing resentment for the man.

Petrov looked quizzical. 'Is that supposed to be a joke?'

'Look fella', you better start lightening up. Maybe you Russians don't have a sense of humour, but frankly I couldn't give a shit. There's a lot of stuff you're going to need to know about Andy Rivers. Being a personal manager is no easy ride. I've drawn up a list of forthcoming dates.' He flourished a fanfold of papers in front of Petrov. 'The band's first album is being released next week, and they begin touring a month later. Apart from the gigs, there are TV interviews, photo shoots, promotional dates, in fact a whole bunch of stuff that you'll need to know about.'

Petrov leaned forward to take them from the agent. 'I will study them immediately. I'm sorry if I've offended you, but I treat business very seriously. Maybe we Russians do have a different approach to life. I have a lot to learn.'

'Yeah you have. Like it or not, we'll be working close together from now on,' Sharmer said, reaching for the envelope that Petrov had returned.

He pulled out the contract, balanced a pair of heavily framed spectacles on the end of his nose, and picked up a pen.

'Welcome to the party, Stefan,' he said, leaning forward to add his signature. 'I'll send you a copy of this in a few days. And talking about parties, the week before their tour the Blues Knights have been booked for an exclusive preview concert at Lord Fanthorpe's country house, as a special treat for his guests. It's an important job, so make sure you're there.'

Petrov nodded obediently.

*

The Blues Knights debut album enjoyed rave reviews, creating huge interest before its release. The orders outstripped the supplies. All the major department stores and small independent record shops struggled to keep up with the demand. By the end of the first week in March sales had rocketed.

Petrov gradually settled into his role as a personal manager. He wrote to Maria, telling her of his new experiences, and the money he would be able to save. She was thrilled by his letter and looked forward to regular news of his progress.

*

Stefan Petrov craned his neck to peer through the windscreen at the castellated turrets of Redwing House reaching towards the evening sky. In the failing light, an impressive array of Bentleys and Rolls-Royce limousines could be seen parked in neat formation across the far side of the courtyard. Liveried chauffeurs lounged against the highly polished vehicles, enjoying a chat and a cigarette.

Andrei stepped from his car and lobbed the keys to an approaching member of staff who deftly slid behind the wheel to park it up.

'This way, I'll show you around,' he said to Petrov who appeared to experience some difficulty in hiding his distaste at the spectacle of wealth and privilege represented by the stately home and its rowdy guests.

Andrei led his manager through the impressive arched entrance and spent the next half hour following the same route that Janine Devonshire had used. The Russian endeavoured to memorise the layout of the faintly lit corridors and echoing halls as Andrei's enthusiasm swept him through the old building.

*

The Blues Knights powered through their repertoire. It was a perfect opportunity to run through the album's new tracks in front of a live audience, an audience that bore no resemblance to the thousands of youngsters who had bought up every ticket for the nationwide tour.

Mark Jacobs had taken lead vocal, giving Andrei an opportunity to cast his eyes around the flower-decked marquee. He was sickened by the sight of purple-faced men cavorting around the dance floor, with shirttails flapping over their sagging stomachs. It made him wonder at the desperation of their vivacious companions. What could induce these pretty girls to suffer such indignities? His own moment of stupidity with

Henry Jameson sprung to mind…

'*Andy Rivers!*' Mark Jacobs announced through the PA, rapidly directing his front man's attention to the approaching solo.

Grateful for the cue, Andrei braced himself into a wide legged stance and swung his guitar upwards, his fingers flying across the fret board to deliver a spectacular solo.

Janine Devonshire was sitting next to Petrov at a table close to the bandstand. She watched, spellbound, her chin resting in the palm of her hand. 'He's brilliant isn't he,' she sighed. 'I can't wait to get his new album.'

Petrov had been quick to befriend the woman after Andrei's introduction. 'No problem, leave it to me,' he promised nonchalantly, revelling in his position of familiarity with the famous star. 'Would you like Andy to sign it?'

'That would be fabulous. Maybe he could write a personal message to me on the cover. What do you think?' she said, unable to take her eyes off the handsome star.

Petrov wasn't listening anymore. He was thinking about the person he had seen her with earlier that evening, descending the baronial staircase from the first floor bedrooms. They had appeared to be on intimate terms. The man in question was a senior member of the British cabinet. It had not escaped Petrov's notice how Henry Jameson, the very person with whom Andy Rivers had been fleetingly involved, was constantly pampering to every shameless whim demanded by the important guests present that evening. The place was a hotbed of immorality.

'Mind you,' the woman rambled on, 'I wouldn't want him thinking I was some kind of stage struck teenager that...' she looked round to catch the Russian lost in a world of his own. 'Stefan! Are you listening to me?' she nagged, giving him a sharp prod across the table.

He came back in an instant. 'Of course I am,' he lied, pawing her hand brazenly. 'In fact how about joining me at one of the gigs? A friendly face is always welcome.'

She dipped her eyebrows suspiciously. 'Are you serious, I thought it was a sell-out?'

'It is, but I'm sure I could arrange something,' he said, with a roguish grin.

What the hell, she thought. *I've done a lot more, for a lot less.*

Chapter 20

The small boy had been hoisted onto his father's shoulders for a better view. He saw three bound men, with nooses around their necks, being hauled onto an empty hay cart that stood beneath the branches of an ancient tree growing in the centre of the town square. When the whip cracked the horse lunged forward. As a child, Stefan Petrov had found the men's frantic efforts to avoid falling strangely entertaining. It had taken a few seconds for their kicking legs to become still.

Born into a family of impoverished peasants, Petrov had witnessed his parents scratch a meagre living from the land, until the Soviets' new leader, Josef Stalin, introduced the creation of collective farms, bringing welcome food to their table. His early memories had been forged against a background of terror involving mass executions of Kulaks, prosperous farmers in the Ukraine whose lands were systematically destroyed, or confiscated by the communists. As he grew older, he refused to acknowledge the wickedness of Stalin's murderous regime as being anything other than a righteous cause for the re-distribution of wealth, and the prevention of greed and profiteering by subversive, anti-communist zealots.

In October 1941 Petrov willingly volunteered, as a boy soldier, to help defend Moscow against the German Wehrmacht in the sub-zero temperatures of the Russian winter. His pride at being personally involved in one of the most decisive battles of the war finally embedded his deep devotion to the communist ideal.

After leaving the army, he successfully applied to join the Soviet Security and Intelligence Organisation, rising through the ranks to become a Colonel in the KGB. His deceptively pleasant disposition masked a brutality that would claim the lives of many people, relentlessly hunted down as enemies of the State. He became feared and respected by his peers, while devoting his life to the advancement of his beloved Mother Russia.

The KGB's main directives were to forewarn the Soviet Leadership of any impending military threats, and obtain state secrets from their enemies. By the use of blackmail, subversion, and high profile scandals, they would endeavour to spread discord among their despised adversaries in the Western World.

With ruthless planning Stefan Petrov had managed to secure a position as personal manager to Andy Rivers, a celebrity revered by London's high society that would guarantee access to some of the most senior politicians in the country. The KGB would supply him with the money and information required to carry out his duties.

He returned to his bedsit in the early hours of

the morning. Throwing off his jacket, he slackened his tie and grabbed a bottle from the sideboard. After taking a shot of vodka he lay back on the sofa to tear open a large envelope he had collected from the Soviet Embassy. Before leaving Poland, Petrov had been quick to request assistance from the KGB Intelligence Service for as much information possible concerning the Junior Cabinet Minister, Henry Jameson, after Andrei's disclosure of having had a brief affair with the man; it made interesting reading.

Jameson had been elected as a member of parliament with the financial assistance of a young, Russian-born immigrant called Jack Bronson, a hugely successful gangster who had managed to remain hidden behind a carefully maintained cloak of respectability. The report contained evidence of Jameson's continuing association with Jack Bronson. In return for large deposits to his bank account, Jameson had used his position to provide Bronson with privileged information, allowing him, among other things, to procure valuable property assets. Occasionally, he had also used his influence to thwart police investigations into the gangster's activities.

Petrov had achieved far more than he could have imagined by using Maria Wolenski to get close to her brother. His newly acquired position as personal manager to the pop star, Andy Rivers, gaining him access to the Redwing House parties, would prove to be invaluable. He poured another drink, reflecting on his encounter with Janine Devonshire. The sex had been good, but even better were the revelations made by the woman concerning certain senior ministers, and their various penchants for deviant sexual practices. It brought a malicious gleam to his eyes; it was all ripe for exploitation. Character assassination and blackmail would prove to be effective weapons against the British Establishment. Very soon he would be in a position to strike.

As for a man like Bronson, he would be far too involved with his criminal empire to worry about a lowly music agent. Petrov tossed the report onto the coffee table and toasted himself with another drink.

His eyelids grew heavy, lulling him into a restless sleep.

Chapter 21

Andrei and Mark Jacobs were unwinding in the privacy of their apartment, sharing a bottle of wine, appreciating the rare opportunity of a relaxed conversation. Discretion about their relationship had become a way of life. But they saw it as a small sacrifice to make in preparation for the day when they would eventually retire from public scrutiny and live an idyllic life together in some remote, foreign hideaway. Their fanciful ramblings were cut short by the phone. When Andrei answered it, the look on his face shattered the convivial atmosphere.

'Andy. It's Henry Jameson, please don't hang up,' pleaded the urgent voice.

'Look, that whole damn business is dead and buried as far as I'm concerned. I wish it had never happened,' Andrei said, mouthing *'Jameson'* to Mark Jacobs who rolled his eyes and reached for a magazine.

'This has nothing to do with that,' Jameson replied sharply. 'I'm concerned about your new personal manager. Petrov, isn't it?'

Andrei was suddenly alert. 'What about him?'

'Surely you must have noticed him with that Devonshire girl the other night?'

'Of course, I introduced him to her. She's been driving me nuts for a signed album, and wants to come to one of our gigs. I asked him to sort things out for her.'

'Well he's sorting her out alright,' said Jameson.

'What's that supposed to mean?' Andrei demanded, irritated by Jameson's innuendo.

'The pair of them disappeared upstairs to one of the bedrooms,' said Jameson. 'Lord Fanthorpe brought it to my attention. He's not amused I can tell you. The girls are there for his guests, not your bloody manager. The fact that he's a Russian doesn't help matters either. This is not good, Andy. For Christ's sake, that little tart has slept with some senior members of the government. Do you get my drift?'

Andrei's heart missed a beat. *Jameson must be wrong. Petrov wouldn't do such a thing. He's in love with Maria.*

'Are you listening to me?' Jameson cried impatiently.

'Yeah, I hear you,' Andrei said, coming back to the conversation. 'Leave it with me. I need to find out what's going on.'

'Well make it quick,' Jameson snapped. 'And if he can't behave himself, I want him kept away from Redwing House. Do I make myself clear?'

'Crystal,' Andrei said, replacing the receiver.

Mark Jacobs frowned. 'What the hell was that all about?'

Andrei had to play the incident down: he needed to keep this to himself. Apart from the blatant insult to Maria, if there was anything sinister about Petrov's motives it could prove disastrous for the Blues Knights.

'It seems Petrov's been making a nuisance of himself, chatting up some bird at Redwing House,' he said, with as much indifference as he could. 'The stupid sod should know better, very unprofessional.'

'That's putting it mildly. Especially as he's supposed to be marrying your sister,' said Mark Jacobs.

'*Exactly*. I think I need a word, and it can't wait,' Andrei said, getting to his feet. 'See you later, Mark.'

*

Petrov was surprised by Andrei's unannounced visit and brusque behaviour. He invited him into the bed-sit, offering him a drink. They took seats opposite one another. Dispensing with any niceties, Andrei swallowed his vodka and looked accusingly at the Russian.

'Okay, Stefan, what's this I hear about you and Janine Devonshire?'

A faint smile flickered across Petrov's face. He took a moment to finish his drink before answering.

'Hey, we're both men of the world, Andrei. So I had a little fun. What's the big deal?'

'You bastard,' Andrei seethed. 'You profess to love my sister, ask for my help, and repay me by screwing a woman as soon as my back is turned.'

'Maria doesn't have to know,' he said, with a dismissive shrug. 'What the eyes don't see, the heart won't -'

'Enough, Stefan,' Andrei cut in angrily. 'I don't

believe what I'm hearing. My sister is very special to me. If you honestly think I can just let this go, you're more bloody stupid than I thought. You're fired. You can piss off back to Poland, or wherever the hell you came from.'

'You're being very naïve, Andrei,' the Russian replied calmly. 'If you honestly believe that I'm simply going to walk away from such a golden opportunity, I'm not the only one being bloody stupid. And I'm *not* talking about playing manager to some prima donna pop star.'

A golden opportunity? Andrei felt a chill of realisation ripple through him.

'Your working for the Soviets aren't you?' he said, searching Petrov's eyes. 'What are you, a bloody spy or something?'

Petrov knew he had handled the situation badly, allowing his arrogance to get the better of him. Now he would have to front it out.

'Grow up, Andrei. All you need to know is that I'll be an attentive personal manager to you.'

'I'm telling you, Petrov, you get the hell out of this country, or I'll be forced to -'

'Do *what*, exactly?' Petrov interrupted quietly.

Andrei desperately hunted for an answer.

'You will say nothing,' the Russian continued. 'You're a successful pop star, making an obscene amount of money. Just take a moment to consider what the press would make of your homosexual affair with that cabinet minister, Henry Jameson, let alone the debauchery at Lord Fanthorpe's parties involving all those senior members of parliament. Imagine the damage it would cause the government, and what it would do to your reputation being involved with a Russian spy, a spy that *you* brought into the country?'

Andrei let out a scornful laugh. 'But you would only incriminate yourself, you idiot.'

'What difference would that make? By the time my dirty work was done I would be long gone. It's what I do, Andrei. I would be posted elsewhere, and you and Jameson would be ruined.'

Andrei was speechless.

'We'll speak of it no more,' Petrov concluded. 'You will continue with your music, and I'll carry on with my duties as your manager. Nobody need know any different. And as for Maria, don't worry. I'll let her down gently when the time is right. I think our conversation is at an end, don't you?' he said finally, inviting Andrei to leave.

*

Jameson had been devastated by Andrei's telephone call. Everything he had managed to achieve in his life was in danger of ruin. He convinced Andrei to say nothing and maintain his composure as there was little either of them could do about the situation, insisting that the matter would be dealt by the proper authorities. Andrei had no choice but to leave it in the minister's hands and pray that the problem would be resolved; they both had too much to lose.

Chapter 22

Jack Bronson stood in front of the oak doors bidding his guests farewell. The presence of two bodyguards confirmed that it had been a formal business meeting. He no longer took any chances after the drive by shooting outside the Pink Pelican. They had been extremely lucky to survive, and the matter was never discussed again. However, Mrs Hurwitz remained deeply disturbed over the chilling accusations made by her late husband. She still blamed her son for his death, and found it difficult to trust him anymore.

'We look forward to working with you, Mr Bronson,' said Luis Fernando whose immaculate suit, handsome face and soft Hispanic accent, suggested a well-bred young man from a wealthy family.

But Jack was under no such illusion as he shook hands and watched the stylish Colombian descend the steps to the waiting car, accompanied by two similarly dressed men, one of whom quickened his pace to open the door for his boss.

Cocaine was now becoming the fastest growing commodity in the country. But despite consolidating most of the London suppliers and dealers, Jack was not satisfied. Simply by cutting out the middlemen, and dealing direct with those who produced the drugs, he could amass the sort of money that could only be dreamt of.

His continual demands for larger supplies eventually attracted the attention of a young Colombian drug baron, Juan Carlos, who had immediately flown one of his lieutenants, Luis Fernando, to England. Jack had struck a deal with these people to become the sole importer of their drugs. The supplies would be shipped from Colombia, on a regular basis, into Northern Ireland from where Jack would smuggle the merchandise across the Irish Sea to the British mainland, using large, powerful speedboats.

However, there was another important detail that needed his immediate attention. He knew that it would be unrealistic to rely on local criminals to assist him with the Irish stage of the operation; they had nothing to lose and could not be trusted. There was also the possibility of their coercion with corrupt officers of the Royal Ulster Constabulary, which would inevitably lead to the pilfering of his drug shipments.

Jack's attention had been drawn to the Irish Republican Army who had become increasingly more active over the past few years, bombing police stations and utility installations in their struggle to overthrow British rule in Northern Ireland. The IRA was always in need of money, and if Jack could harness their assistance they might prove to be valuable allies.

When the iron gates clanged shut behind the departing vehicle, Jack dismissed his minders and stepped back into the entrance hall to see Levin appear from the study.

'Henry Jameson's on the phone. He needs a favour.'

'So what's new,' Jack said, following Levin. 'By the way, when's Lucy coming round?'

'Soon, I think. She and Sandra have been acting like a couple of kids.'

A car had been organised to take the young women to the Pink Pelican that evening where the Blues Knights were making a last appearance before their tour. It offered Jack a chance to keep the promise he had made to Sandra. Needless to say all the stops were being pulled out; nothing would be too much trouble for the boss's wife.

'I'd like to know what Andy Rivers has got that I haven't,' Levin remarked, pointing to the waiting phone.

Jack picked it up, shielding the mouthpiece. 'A guitar and a big dick,' he said, deadpan. Levin returned a two-fingered response.

Jack settled back into his comfortable leather chair. He swivelled round to gaze out the window, taking a moment to enjoy his extensive property. It boosted his ego: made him feel good. Levin sat quietly in front of the desk. The infrequent moment of frivolity had passed. Jack raised the phone to his ear. It was business as usual.

'Hello, Henry, what can I do for you?'

'Jack, I have a major problem that I fear only you can deal with.' The voice had an insistent edge to it.

'What kind of problem?'

'It appears that this Petrov individual, that Andy Rivers has brought in from Poland to be his personal manager, is not what he seems.'

'Who the hell's Petrov? Hold on a moment,' Jack said, looking across at Levin. 'Do you know anything about Andy Rivers taking on a personal manager?'

Levin frowned and shook his head.

Jack returned to Jameson. 'This is news to me. Sounds like we need a word with Sharmer?'

The irrelevant chatter exasperated the minister. 'Never mind Sharmer, dammit. Petrov's a Russian spy!'

Jack took a moment to reply. 'What are you talking about, Henry? Have you been at the booze or something?'

'I'm deadly serious. Andy Rivers took him on as a favour to his sister who was under the impression that Petrov wanted to marry her. Apparently, Rivers offered him a job as his personal manager to help him earn better money. It was a bloody scam. Petrov immediately started to involve himself with a hostess at Redwing House with the intention of gaining information from her. The woman has been sleeping around with some senior ministers. Doesn't take a genius to work out where it's all leading. When Rivers confronted Petrov, the smug bastard threatened to expose Rivers' affair with *me*, denouncing us both as homosexuals. He also threatened to accuse Rivers of complicity in espionage, and considering it was Rivers that brought him into the country, that would be an extremely plausible accusation. Imagine the implications of all this?

The secret service agencies would immediately be alerted, and we don't need those bastards sniffing around, eh, Jack?'

Levin watched his friend closely. He could hear an excited babble coming through the phone, but the words were lost to him.

Jack had been concerned after Levin had told him of the conversation with Sharmer, revealing Andy Rivers' homosexuality. But the pop star's huge earning potential had forced him to accept the fact. Now all his fears had been realised. You simply couldn't trust queers, and what with Rivers' involvement with Jameson, it just kept getting worse. The gangster's huge fist crunched around the handset.

'What a fuck up!' he cursed, lowering the phone to his chest. He threw a black look at Levin. 'Apparently this Petrov is a bloody spy. Can you believe that?'

Levin's eyes widened in disbelief.

Jack went back to Jameson. 'So the scumbag's expecting a free ride right into the heart of the government at our expense. What do you suggest we do about him?'

'How you deal with the matter is up to you, Jack. Surely you must realise that I can't be involved in such a discussion,' Jameson said softly.

'Of course you can't, Henry,' Jack replied, with blatant cynicism. 'Meanwhile, there's something *you* can do for me.'

'Sure, what is it?'

'I need names of some senior guys involved with Sinn Fein, or the IRA.'

'What's this, another business deal?' Jameson probed.

'Something like that,' said Jack.

'That shouldn't be a problem. I know a few members of the Stormont Parliament in Belfast. Most of them are Unionists, and keep a wary eye on their Sinn Fein counterparts,' said Jameson. 'I'll get back to you in a couple of days.'

'Thanks, Henry. And as for that creep, Petrov, play it cool. He mustn't suspect anything.'

There was a threatening chill to Jack's voice as he hung up.

*

A table had been positioned to give the closest, uninterrupted view possible for Sandra Bronson and Lucy who were eagerly fingering their champagne flutes in anticipation of the evening's performance. A soulless looking man was sitting alone at a discreet distance to ensure their privacy from the rest of the club's patrons, fuelling intrigue as to the attractive women's identities. Mutterings began to circulate, much to the girls' amusement.

The house lights were darkened. A single spotlight drew the audience's attention towards a brightly lit set of red velvet curtains surrounding a half-moon stage. The friends exchanged excited glances as they listened to the uncomplicated introduction.

'Ladies and Gentlemen...Andy Rivers and the Blues Knights!'

As the heavy drapes swung back, the impact of the bass guitar in the opening chord hit Sandra squarely in the stomach, taking her breath away.

She was captivated by the husky voice of Andy Rivers rising above the solid, rhythmic backing of his group. There followed an hour of thrilling music: ranging from hard rock to soulful blues.

*

Jerry Wilson hammered his sticks across every drum in the sparkling silver kit, finishing with a smash of cymbals that seemed to engulf the dying moments of Andy Rivers' howling Fender Stratocaster, bringing the set to an abrupt finish. There followed a brief, mesmerised stillness, before an eruption of applause and cries of appreciation filled the darkened space.

When the lights went up, the relief band introduced a smoother sound to the club's smoky atmosphere, returning the place to a murmur of relaxed conversation.

'That was brilliant,' Sandra said, clinking glasses with her friend.

'What a group...*what a man*,' Lucy breathed lustfully.

Sandra laughed. 'Steady, girl. Would you like to meet him?'

Lucy hunched her shoulders like a thrilled little girl. 'Are you kidding? Do you think we could?'

'My husband *owns* the Diamond Agency. A wife's perks wouldn't you say,' Sandra winked, beckoning the manager, Steven Bradley, with a discreet finger.

*

Steven Bradley knocked on the dressing room door and entered to find Andrei alone, placing his guitar back in its case.

'Sorry to bother you, Andy, but a couple of

young ladies have requested that you join them for a drink.'

'Give me a break, Steve, I'm tired, and I'm really not in the mood. Some other time maybe,' Andrei said, clipping the case shut.

He had managed to dismiss Stefan Petrov from his mind during the band's performance. But now the problem had come flooding back, and he wanted to be alone with his thoughts.

'*Please*, Andy,' the manager begged. 'One of the women is Sandra Bronson. Her husband owns the place. It would be a huge favour to me if you could spare them a few minutes?'

Steven Bradley came across as a decent guy; it was difficult to refuse him. Andrei breathed a resigned sigh. 'Okay, Steve, what the hell, I could use a drink.'

*

Sandra had requested that they be moved to an area curtained off from prying eyes. Their initial thrill of expectation gave way to quiet fascination when the charismatic man joined them. Andy Rivers was everything a superstar should be: tall, slim, and extremely handsome, wearing a red silk shirt and black leather trousers, his stature enhanced by a pair of high-heeled Cuban boots.

He accepted a glass of champagne and flashed them a stunning smile. 'I understand your husband owns this club. It's a great place isn't it,' he said, looking directly into Sandra's eyes.

His attempt at polite conversation suddenly caused Sandra acute embarrassment, like she had summoned some underling into her presence. She hadn't meant it to be like that.

'Yes... I suppose it is...I have to say, it's very kind of you to spare us the time...' she waffled self-consciously. *Silly Cow! Jack's a powerful businessman. Act like it, you idiot,* she screamed silently to herself.

Lucy gazed doe-eyed at the man, blissfully unaware of her friend's dilemma.

'Not at all, it's my pleasure to meet you,' Andrei soldiered on, baffled by Sandra's apparent discomfort.

'Oh to hell with it, I'm sorry about this. I'm acting like a complete idiot. Let's start again shall we. My name's Sandra Bronson and this is my friend, Lucy.'

She smiled and reached over the table.

'And I'm *still* Andy Rivers, at your service,' he joked, taking her hand with a flamboyant bow of his head. All three of them dissolved into laughter, instantly transforming the mood.

Lucy discovered her voice and proceeded to commandeer the proceedings, asking all the usual questions that Andrei had heard countless times before. It wasn't until she left for the *Ladies Room* that Sandra managed to get a word in.

She enquired about his past. The similarity between the pop star's lowly upbringing, and subsequent rise to fame, seemed uncannily similar to her husband's remarkable success in the business world. She thought it best to say nothing about Jack also owning the Diamond Agency, not wishing to undermine Doug Levin's authority.

'I'm sure my husband would love to meet you at some time. You'd probably have a lot in common. Do you have a private number?' she asked, rummaging in her evening bag to produce a silver-barrelled pen.

'Sure,' Andrei said, leaning forward to write his number on a coaster, causing the talisman to hang out of his open necked shirt. Sandra wondered why a wealthy pop star would wear such a cheap wooden charm.

'What *is* that, Andy? I noticed it when you were on stage. Does it hold any special significance?'

Her seemingly innocent request caused a sudden change in his demeanour; she had touched a nerve. The confident professional had suddenly become vulnerable. He took hold of the talisman to show her. She leaned forward to examine it more closely. It was a simple, almost primitive carving in the shape of a guitar.

'That was made by a childhood friend of mine many years ago,' he said quietly. 'The poor kid had a tragic life.'

There was deep sorrow in his voice, making her wish she hadn't asked the question. 'I'm sorry. I didn't mean to -'

'That's okay No need to apologise,' Andrei was quick to reassure. 'As I said, he was a close friend. Sadly he went away before I had a chance to say goodbye.' He let the talisman drop back against his chest.

Sandra caught a sudden hint of his fragrant cologne. She unwittingly voiced Andrei's thoughts. 'I wonder what became of him.'

'Probably scraping a living as an odd job man, he was always good with his hands,' he said with a sad smile

Chapter 23

Sharmer had been in the middle of a phone conversation when his office door flew open to reveal the burly figure of Jack Bronson striding into the room, followed by Doug Levin. He cut the call short, planted a grin across his face, and got to his feet.

'What a pleasure to see you guys.'

'Shut up and sit down,' Jack ordered.

Levin closed the door and stood in front of it to prevent anyone else from entering. Sharmer's grin faded. He dropped back onto his seat, experiencing a cold sense of fear as he watched Jack walk around the desk to confront him.

'What's this all about?' Sharmer asked, turning his chair around to look up into a menacing face.

'It's about Stefan Petrov,' Jack snarled, narrowing his eyes.

'I was going to tell you about him, honest. He's no big deal,' Sharmer babbled. 'I didn't want to bother you with unimportant stuff. I know you're a busy man.'

Without another word the young gangster lifted Sharmer up by his lapel and slapped him hard across the face, sending him crashing to the floor.

'*Unimportant stuff,*' Jack raged, glaring down at the cowering man. 'Petrov's a Russian spy you stupid bastard!'

Sharmer looked stunned. 'I had no idea, believe me,' he cried, shaking his head. 'What could I do? I had no choice. Andy Rivers insisted that Petrov was to be his personal manager.'

The agent scrabbled back to his feet, soothing an angry red patch spreading across his cheek.

'Do you think Rivers knew about Petrov? Are they in this together?' Jack demanded

'All I know is that Petrov was supposed to be marrying Rivers' sister, and Rivers wanted to help him earn some decent money. That's it, I swear, there's nothing more to tell.'

Jack swung his eyes towards his friend. 'What do you think, Doug?'

'I've only met Rivers once,' Levin answered. 'A flash little sod, but then these pop stars usually are. To be honest, he didn't strike me as anything other than a regular rock guitarist. But hey, what do I know?'

Jack quietened. He stared at Sharmer for a few moments, and then moved towards him. The agent flinched as Jack raised his hand again, but this time it was to gently pat down Sharmer's ruffled jacket.

'Sorry about the rough stuff, Ben, sometimes I get a little pissed off. You really should let me know about these things,' he said in a silky voice, throwing an arm across Sharmer's shoulders.

'Sure, Jack, I understand totally. From now on I'll tell you everything. It won't happen again, I promise,' the agent gabbled cringing at the man's touch. He was terrified, and felt lucky to be alive.

'I want you to act like everything is normal in front of Petrov,' said Jack. 'Now, where can I find him?'

Sharmer hurried to his desk for the address. 'What are you going to do about him?' he asked, handing over a piece of paper.

'Questions like that can get a man into trouble, Ben. Just keep your mouth shut.'

Sharmer had no intention of saying anything. He held his smile until the two men had left the office. *I knew that bloody Petrov was bad news*, he thought. *Fucking foreigners!*

*

It was late evening when Petrov left the bedsit. He walked purposefully towards the Bayswater Road, keeping his eyes peeled for a black cab to take him to the Soviet Embassy in South Kensington. He still cursed himself for his reckless behaviour with the girl at Redwing House. He should have known better than to risk so much so soon. A good agent would have taken time to study his options, and make contingency plans for unforeseen events that might jeopardise his cover. Of course he knew what he *should* have done only too well.

As a committed communist, he loathed the decadence and greed epitomised by western culture. Greedy Jews like Ben Sharmer, and rich, perverted pop stars cavorting with corrupt politicians like Henry Jameson, filled him with revulsion. These were the things he found increasingly more difficult to deal with, impairing his judgement and destroying his effectiveness: he had been in the job too long.

He knew his threats against Andrei Wolenski would only buy him a limited respite. Something would eventually be revealed, and that could prove to be a diplomatic embarrassment for the Kremlin. After the tedious groundwork he had put in with that empty-headed woman, Maria Wolenski, to get close to her brother, he had squandered a perfect opportunity. His position was now compromised and his usefulness was at an end. It was time to come clean with his superiors. Stefan Petrov was about to destroy his career. After failing his motherland, he saw it as the only honourable thing to do.

He paused at a pedestrian crossing, preoccupied with his thoughts. He hadn't noticed the car that had been kerb crawling behind him. It slowed to a halt, inviting him to cross. Petrov waved an acknowledgement and stepped off the kerb.

He flinched at the sudden squealing of tyres as the dark saloon pounced. There was no time to scream. Just excruciating pain as the impact shattered his spine, sending his horrified face rushing to meet the tarmac. The car dragged him beneath its metal belly, bouncing over his body, before spewing out his bloodied remains.

A pedestrian's solitary cry was Stefan Petrov's brief obituary.

Chapter 24

Dawn was breaking across the capital, sending thin shafts of light to probe the half closed slatted blinds of Mike Robson's office. The simply furnished room was situated in North London on the 6th Floor of MI5 headquarters, a plain, unimposing building that overlooked the busy junction of Euston Road and Gower Street. The Operations Controller had called a meeting with two of his senior officers after receiving a police report concerning the death of a suspected Russian agent.

Robson lived solely for the purpose of defending his country. After an exemplary career in the army, he had been invited to apply for a position within the Secret Service. Once out of uniform, he attached no importance to civilian clothes, taking on the unlikely appearance of a mildly eccentric academic. But at thirty-eight years of age, his harsh military training had developed a fiercely uncompromising attitude. His tough, hard-headed approach to the job had earned him a respected reputation, and swift promotion. He was sitting at his desk, thoughtfully tugging a knitted brown tie free of its collar, poring over a wad of papers. A tweed Dunhill sports jacket and creased cavalry-twill trousers hung from his gaunt frame.

An attractive brunette and a serious faced, clean-cut young man sat opposite him in obedient silence.

Jan Stevens typified that classic combination of brains and beauty. After leaving school she had worked hard to pass the necessary exams to gain a place at Hendon Police College. While serving as a young policewoman, her good looks had often proved to be a distinct disadvantage when trying to win the respect of her superiors. But her dogged perseverance and commendable record finally paid off, gaining her a coveted transition into the ranks of MI5.

By comparison, her fellow operative was a relative newcomer to the department. Peter McCann had benefited from a public school education, followed by a successful three years at Oxford University. A respectable degree, coupled with a rowing blue, had proved to be a definite advantage in his successful application the previous year. The single vent blazer and sharply pressed grey flannels disguised a trim but powerful physique, maintained by regular training in the use of martial arts. His courage and enthusiasm for the job proved to be a saving grace for his occasional lapses in discipline.

Robson finished reading and looked up, brushing an unkempt mass of dark hair from his eyes.

'Our Soviet friends must be hopping mad. This Petrov individual was a sloppy sod,' he began with a facetious smirk. 'He not only gets himself killed crossing the road, but has also left a most informative document for us in his Bayswater bedsit. It's been compiled by the KGB, and I reluctantly admit to being impressed by their sources of information. We need to step up our efforts in eradicating these bloody leaks. Put some feelers out, Stevens. See what you can dig up.'

The young woman nodded her compliance. 'What exactly have they found out, sir?' she asked.

'Well apparently, this Junior Cabinet Minister, Henry Jameson, is a homosexual and was involved in an affair with the pop star, Andy Rivers, who brought Stefan Petrov back from Poland to be his personal manager. The police have already spoken to Rivers and his agent, a man called Ben Sharmer, who have both denied any knowledge of Petrov's true motives for being in the country. Whether they're lying or not remains to be seen, but more intriguing is the revelation of Jameson's close ties to the gangster, Jack Bronson.'

'We all know about Bronson,' the younger man cut in, 'that thug is untouchable. But I find it hard to believe that a man like Jameson could be mixed up with him.'

He drew a cautionary glance from his female colleague. Their boss disliked being interrupted.

'I'm not interested in what you believe, McCann,' Robson barked. 'Take it from me that he bloody well is!' He reached for a mug of steaming black coffee, taking a minute to savour the hot drink. It seemed to pacify his fleeting displeasure.

'In fact it might be a good idea if we got to know Jameson a little better,' Robson went on. 'Why don't the pair of you pay him a visit? Feel him out about his involvement with this pop star, Rivers. See if there could be any connection between Rivers and the KGB? Then ask him about his dealings with Bronson. That should rattle his cage. Petrov's death could open up a whole raft of opportunities for us. Lean on Jameson, hard.'

'Is that wise, sir?' Jan Stevens cautioned. 'He's a Junior Cabinet Minister. He'll be on to our Director General in a flash. We wouldn't want to drop the department in it.'

Robson's two officers were fully aware of the professional animosity that existed between himself and the head of MI5, a shamelessly ambitious individual who gloried in the successes of the department, but was quick to distance himself from any operation that failed to achieve its directives.

'You let me worry about him,' said the Controller. 'We have stumbled across a threat to our country's security. If necessary I'll talk to the Home Secretary. That would give him something to think about.' He paused with a self-satisfied smile. 'That man hates anyone going over his head.'

Chapter 25

Knowing how much the little boy looked forward to seeing his grandmother, Sandra had sent a car to fetch her over for Sunday lunch. Ever since the death of Mr Hurwitz she had felt responsible for Jack's mother, encouraging her to spend as much time as possible at Greystone Manor. Despite the old lady's fierce independence, a strong bond had been forged between them.

After the family meal, Jack retired to his study, leaving the two women to relax in the opulent living room. Mrs Hurwitz sat in an armchair, playfully bouncing Marek on her knee. Sandra had curled up on the sofa, turning the pages of the morning newspaper, baffled by reports of a Russian spy being involved with Jack's agency. She never dwelt on her husband's business affairs, but her feminine intuition told her that he genuinely seemed to have had no knowledge of the matter.

She jumped up with a start. 'Damn, I nearly forgot. Jack wanted to see the news.'

She hurried across the room and opened the doors of a teak cabinet to turn on the television. It took a few moments for the black and white picture to emerge, revealing a familiar face.

'Jack!' Sandra shouted into the hallway, 'it's the

BBC News. Ben Sharmer's on the telly.'

Jack was quick to enter the room and join his wife on the sofa. Mrs Hurwitz settled Marek quietly on her lap.

Sharmer could be seen leaving the Diamond Agency's office, accompanied by a minder, with a pack of scrambling reporters jostling for position around him. He had been provided with a statement prepared by Jack who watched with uncertainty, unsure how the man would react in front of the cameras.

'Please, if you could just be quiet for a moment.' The television speakers amplified Sharmer's voice above the noisy barrage of questions. When the commotion died away, he produced a folded sheet of paper from his pocket and cleared his throat loudly.

'On behalf of the Diamond Agency, I would like to express how deeply shocked we are to discover that one of our colleagues, Stefan Petrov, was a Russian spy. We understand that his death is currently under investigation. We would also like to emphasise that this agency, and the pop star, Andy Rivers, who we represent, had no knowledge of this man's activities. Rest assured that we will co-operate fully with the authorities regarding this dreadful disclosure. Now, if you'll excuse me…'

The throng of reporters closed in tighter, blocking the men's path towards the waiting car.

A tousled haired woman thrust a microphone into Sharmer's face. 'Will Andy Rivers be making a statement?'

'He has no reason to. I've already done that for

him,' he replied, shoving his way forward.

'Can you confirm that Petrov accompanied Andy Rivers when he performed at Lord Fanthorpe's parties?' she asked, fighting to keep her place in the scuffle.

'Lots of celebrities play at society functions, and of course Petrov was with him, he was his agent. But we had absolutely no idea that -'

'Wasn't it Andy Rivers who introduced Petrov to your agency,' another hard-nosed journalist called out, elbowing the woman aside, 'and didn't they both come from Eastern Europe?'

Sharmer was getting flustered. 'Yes, but -'

'Is it true they slept with prostitutes at these functions?' he threw in, hunting for a scandal.

Before Sharmer could answer, another reporter yelled, 'Couldn't that have been a security risk, considering the politicians that were present?'

'No comment!' Sharmer shot back, looking anxious.

Jack was becoming concerned. *It's getting too hot, you idiot. Get out of there.*

The female reporter re-appeared with a mean glint in her eye. 'Mr Sharmer, is there any truth in the rumour that Andy Rivers is a homosexual? Could he be involved with anyone? Will the police be talking to him?'

'This is all rubbish. I have no more to say.' Sharmer shouted, glaring at his minder who began to manhandle the relentless news hounds from their path. The two men disappeared through the car's open door chased by a clatter of camera shutters.

Jack sprang to his feet. 'That bloody Rivers guy

is becoming a liability,' he barked, striding across the room to hit the *off* button.

Marek stared wide-eyed at his father, disturbed by the raised voice and sudden change of mood. Sandra met the old lady's eyes; Mrs Hurwitz knew it was best to go. She got up and led the small boy through the french windows into the garden. As Jack started to leave the room, Sandra reached out and caught his hand.

'Jack, darling, please wait a minute.'

He sat down beside her with a muffled groan, knowing what to expect.

'I've met Andy Rivers, remember, he's a nice person. There's no way he could be mixed up in any of this spy stuff. It's a joke,' she said with a tiny laugh, hoping to win him round.

'Look, sweetheart, you've just heard the press,' he reasoned, trying to remain patient. 'Rivers has been sleeping around with prostitutes and politicians. He then meets up with Stefan Petrov in Poland, who just *happens* to be a KGB officer, and brings him back to England, demanding the guy be made his personal manager. Come on, you have to admit, it doesn't look good does it?'

'Well no, put like that of course it doesn't,' she admitted. 'But you do own the agency. It wouldn't hurt to meet with him. I'm sure you'd feel differently if you did? And after all, he *is* a Polish guy like you.'

'What difference does that make, and anyway I'm not Polish, I'm Russian. That damn country did me no favours,' Jack said, getting up to leave.

'Jack, please call him?' Sandra begged, 'I have his number.'

He cradled her chin in his strong hand and kissed her mouth. 'Okay, I'll think about it. Leave his number in my study.'

*

Crowds had been gathering in Victoria Square since early afternoon. The city was in the throes of witnessing its share of mass hysteria caused by every Blues Knights appearance. When the doors were eventually opened a large body of police had been forced to link arms, channelling countless clamouring fans towards the impressive columned entrance of Birmingham Town Hall. The Victorian building had been designed along the lines of a Roman temple. It seemed a fitting venue for the adoring worshippers, flocking to pay homage to their gods.

Inside the impressive building the mood in the dressing room was subdued. Sharmer's pavement interview had been screened over all the afternoon news bulletins, and very soon Andy Rivers would be leading the Blues Knights on stage for their next scheduled gig. How would the fans react? Had they even heard the news? The allegations of the singer's homosexuality, and his association with a dead KGB spy, could prove disastrous for the group's popularity.

The members of his band had been stunned by the disclosure of Andrei's involvement with Stefan Petrov. But Mark Jacobs knew his place would always be at his friend's side whatever the outcome. He silently drew Andrei's attention towards the other two group members who were half-heartedly sifting through a few dog-eared magazines. Andrei acknowledged his concern. He forced a small cough to get their attention.

'Look, guys, we need to talk about this. I have to know you're with me, right? I'm as shocked as anybody about Petrov. Hell, it was me that brought the man into the country. This whole damn business is getting seriously out of hand.'

Mick Brightman came back immediately. 'We know you got conned by Petrov, and of course we're with you, but your judgement's crap.'

Mark Jacobs was quick to defend his friend. 'That's not fair, Mick. There's no way Andrei would have wanted this. He's got as much to lose as the rest of us.'

'Okay, I'm sorry, Andrei. But that's not the point. What the hell must *they* be thinking out there?' Mick Brightman said, jabbing his thumb towards a distant roar that could be heard from the growing multitude of fans.

'I know. That's why I've got to do something,' Andrei replied. 'You've all got to trust me. When we get out there I'm going to meet this thing head on.'

'Whoa, that sounds serious, man,' Jerry Wilson said, starting to lay out his stage clothes. 'Are you sure that's a good idea?

'I've had enough of this shit, Jerry,' Andrei argued. 'I can't just sit back and let the press rubbish me. I'm going to throw myself on the mercy of the fans. They scream their bloody heads off at me every night, so let them really prove they love me.'

'Great, and if they don't, then what?' said Mick Brightman, irritated.

'Then I guess that will be the *end* of the Blues Knights,' Andrei retorted, angered by Brightman's negative attitude.

Mark Jacobs stepped in. 'Come on guys let's cool down. Arguing amongst ourselves won't help. We've got a gig to do.'

The room fell silent. Andrei had never felt so alone.

*

Jack needed some space. He had returned to his study to wait for Levin who had been asked to report back to him on the recent developments in London. By late afternoon he was still at his desk, gazing through the window, watching long shadows follow Marek and the old lady as they enjoyed the last moments of sunshine. He was suddenly aware of footsteps approaching his office

Jack swung his chair round to see Levin enter the room.

'Hi, Jack.'

'This whole thing's a balls-up!' Jack shouted angrily. 'This bloody Petrov business could be disastrous. Those reporters made a laughing stock out of Sharmer. He's useless.'

'Be fair, it's not easy taking flak from those sods,' Levin answered.

Jack heaved a calming sigh. Levin was the only one who could get away with such criticism.

'Look, we had no choice,' Levin went on. 'We had to take Petrov out. Can you imagine the risk of allowing him to function inside the agency, let alone Redwing House?'

'Maybe,' Jack conceded, 'but you can bet your

life there'll be some government agency sniffing around out there. We should have taken more care and searched Petrov's place for anything that might have identified him?'

'Come on, Jack, we're all bloody brilliant in hindsight,' Levin said, anxious to move the discussion on. 'More importantly, you wanted the guy dead, and he is. Anyway, the truth about Petrov would have come out eventually.'

'I suppose. But these security agencies could be bad news,' Jack argued, knowing they played rough, like him; it was something he could do without.

'I'm sure the whole thing will go away,' said Levin. 'Petrov was only in the country for a short time. What damage could he have done?'

'You could be right', Jack replied, unconvinced. 'But I don't like what I'm hearing about Rivers with his Eastern European connection, and all this homosexual stuff with Jameson. Is there any reason to be worried?'

Levin looked unsure. 'It's too early to say. We'll have to see how it develops.'

'Yeah, well, if it develops we don't sod around. We deal with it, understand?'

*

Andy Rivers walked determinedly to the front of the stage, leaving the rest of his group to take up their positions behind him. Ordinarily they would have blasted straight into the opening song while the crowds were still cheering, but not this time.

They all stood perfectly still, leaving their instruments untouched. Andy Rivers' blonde ponytail shone beneath a bank of powerful spotlights. The chrome fittings on his guitar flashed intermittently. He waited until the huge audience had settled into an uneasy calm, before pulling the microphone towards him.

'I need to talk to you,' he began, as if addressing a roomful of friends.

The amplification bounced his voice around the auditorium, inviting the sporadic response of a few whistles and squeals that quickly died away.

'You people are not stupid. You've seen the news, and you've read the papers.'

This time there was no reaction. The musicians swapped anxious glances.

'The newspapers are saying I was involved with a Russian spy called Stefan Petrov, but I knew nothing about that. I hired him to be my manager, and he used me to get into this country. They're making accusations about my sexuality. Well damn them. That's none of their business. You can believe what you want,' he cried defiantly. 'But more importantly, I've seen too much ugliness in this world and I don't wish to become a part of it, I've done nothing wrong. All I've ever wanted is to play my music...*for you!*'

A long, lingering silence was eventually broken by a solitary handclap. Very soon the entire building had erupted into thundering applause. Mark Jacobs had immediately counted the band in over the long-lasting ovation. As the Blues Knights sustained a pounding rhythm, Andrei walked back and forth behind the footlights waving his thanks to the multitude of fans. He eventually stopped, centre stage, and lifted his guitar as a salute to them. Above a roar of excitement, he swung his hand down across the strings to smash the chord that would lead his musicians into their first song of the evening. Andy Rivers had won his approval.

*

London's Royal Albert Hall was the last venue for the Blues Knights' four-month tour. Due to Andrei's much publicised speech in Birmingham they received a hero's welcome, finally assured of their continued popularity and no longer threatened by the headlines that continued to swamp the front pages.

The hardest thing for Andrei had been trying to console his sister. Not only did she feel responsible for the bad publicity surrounding her brother, but to have been so cruelly deceived by a heartless man had been the ultimate humiliation.

Chapter 26

Henry Jameson experienced a sickening fear as he opened the door of his Holland Park town house to see a tall, serious faced young man standing in front of him, accompanied by a neatly dressed female colleague. He had received a call the previous day advising him of their visit.

'Good morning, Mr Jameson, we're from MI5. My name is Peter McCann, and this is my fellow agent, Jan Stevens,' the young man announced.

Jameson peered at their identity cards before inviting them in. He faked a welcoming smile, and led them towards the living room. Once they had taken their seats the minister sat back in his armchair, trying to appear relaxed.

'This must be an important matter to justify a visit from MI5?' he began.

'I'm sure you're aware of the recent news concerning the dead Russian agent, Stefan Petrov?' said Peter McCann.

'Indeed, but with respect, what would that have to do with me?' Jameson replied, assuming a look of mild astonishment.

'Well, sir, it appears that you have been intimately involved with the pop star, Andy Rivers, who was responsible for bringing Petrov to Great Britain.'

Jameson glared with indignation. 'How dare you! My private life is none of your damn business.'

'I'm afraid it is when it involves a security threat to our country, Mr Jameson,' McCann answered in a steady voice. 'I'm simply asking if you think this Rivers character is as innocent as he claims to be?'

'I don't think for one moment that Andy Rivers had any idea what Petrov was about,' Jameson replied adamantly. 'He was as shocked as anyone when he discovered the truth. He brought the Russian into the country as a favour to help the man earn a decent wage. Petrov was supposed to be marrying Rivers' sister for God's sake. Apart from anything else, I can vouch for Rivers personally. Being a Cabinet Minister, I am fully aware of my position, and I choose my liaisons very carefully.'

'Actually, you're a *Junior* Cabinet Minister, sir,' McCann corrected, 'there is a difference. But what you say does confirm what Rivers has already told the police.'

Jameson scowled back at the MI5 agent. His initial fear was turning to outrage at being subjected to such ridicule. *Who the hell does this little bastard think he is? I don't have to put up with this. I'm a senior member of parliament.* 'Good, that's settled then,' he exclaimed, rising from his chair. 'And just for the record, young man, I do have *considerable* influence. You might want to remember that. Now, maybe you'll be good enough to leave me in peace? I have ministerial duties to attend to.'

'We haven't finished yet, sir,' said Jan Stevens, entering the conversation. 'There's also the matter of your association with the gangster, Jack Bronson?'

Jameson's stomach flipped. The whole business was getting seriously out of hand. It was time to pull rank and fight back.

'The only association I ever had with Bronson was when he helped fund my election campaign back in 1958, along with many other benefactors I might add. Of course, I have since discovered that he is an unsavoury character, and I no longer have anything to do with him. How dare you suggest otherwise.'

'Unfortunately that is not what we understand,' Jan Stevens said in a softly, threatening tone. 'We have irrefutable evidence tying you to various property transactions with Bronson, as well as favours you've afforded him using your *considerable* influence.'

Henry Jameson's world had begun to implode. He stared at the young woman who looked directly back at him, unblinking, expressionless, waiting for the answer she knew he could not give. He lowered himself slowly into his chair with as much dignity as he could muster.

'I have nothing more to say without legal representation. I think it's time I spoke with your Director General,' he muttered, grasping at the last sanction left open to him.

Jan Stevens raised a confirmatory eyebrow at her companion. His nod was barely perceptible. They had done their job and it was time to leave.

Jameson heard the front door click shut; the brief visit was over. He was left alone in the stillness of his living room, contemplating the end of his career to the persistent tinkling of a French carriage clock.

*

It was the evening rush hour. Robson looked down upon a mass of tiny figures hurrying towards Euston Square Tube Station. In his eyes they represented a microcosm of the British people enjoying the privileges and freedoms of going about their business in a hard won democracy that he had sworn to protect.

As a soldier, he had fought against the communists in Korea, being part of a British task force sent by the United Nations. It had almost been a forgotten war. The British people knew, or cared little about its outcome. But Robson cared. The faces of many good friends who had died in that inhospitable land would often return to haunt him. It was their sacrifice that kept him focused on doing what was right for his country.

Peter McCann stood in front of the desk, looking sheepishly at his boss. A problem had arisen: they had lost Henry Jameson. It appeared that the minister had panicked and gone into hiding after his visit from MI5.

'I'm sorry, sir, I have no excuse. We were simply not expecting this. But you did order us to lean on him, so we did.'

The Controller continued to gaze through the window, half listening.

'Sir?' McCann was thrown by the lack of response.

Robson emerged from his thoughts and turned to face his officer. 'He'll turn up eventually, and anyway he's only running from himself. He knows he's ruined. Once the facts become public, that will be the end of him.'

'But surely, we could still get useful information from him about Jack Bronson?'

'That's true. He probably knows things that would be of interest to us, but I do have other sources.'

Peter McCann wondered what they might be. 'Do you believe his story about this pop star, Andy Rivers, being ignorant of Petrov's true identity?'

'Strange though it may seem, I do. Jameson seemed adamant that Rivers was innocent of any collusion with Petrov, and I believe him. He's the sort of person who would have been quick to expose Rivers if it had meant saving his own skin. You caught him unaware. He didn't have time to invent any elaborate stories. The background I've managed to dig up on Rivers suggests to me that the young man is innocent of any wrongdoing. It seems pretty conclusive. His real name is Andrei Wolenski. He comes from an impoverished Polish family. His sister was a simple enough girl, infatuated with this Petrov character who picked her up in some bar. Wolenski is the proverbial poor kid made good. He doesn't appear to have any political affiliations, so why would he risk losing his newfound wealth and celebrity status by involving himself in the grubby world of espionage?'

'Then it appears we have nothing more to chase?' said McCann. 'Petrov's dead, so he's no threat to us anymore. The Soviet Embassy has predictably distanced itself from him. And that corrupt minister, Jameson, is ruined. I would think that puts this spy saga to bed. Job done wouldn't you say, sir?

'Our job is *never* done, McCann.'

Robson's curt reply signalled the end of their conversation. His eyes wandered back to the busy scene in the street below.

Peter McCann recognised his cue to leave.

Chapter 27

The two friends were working on a new song. Mark Jacobs was insisting that the chorus was not strong enough. It simply didn't generate the instant appeal that most of their material possessed. Andrei was trying out a new chord sequence in the hope that an inspirational melody would jump into his head. A shrill ringing echoed through the apartment, interrupting his creative process.

'Shit, I nearly had it then,' he complained, putting down his guitar to answer the phone. 'Hi, who's this?'

'Hello Andy, it's me, Henry,' said a quiet voice.

'I've told you before. I really have nothing more to say to you. Now please-'

'Maybe not, but *I* have something to say to you,' Jameson interrupted. 'Please listen carefully.'

Andrei beckoned Mark Jacobs towards the earpiece to hear the venomous voice of Henry Jameson proceed to threaten him with his intentions of going to the press about their sexual encounter. He would denounce the famous singer, claiming him to be a communist sympathiser who had used their relationship to pass state secrets to his bogus manager, and co-conspirator, Stefan Petrov. The media would have a field day, especially after Andrei's widely reported declarations of innocence in front of his fans. The pop star, Andy Rivers, would be ruined. Put simply, Jameson wanted money: a great deal of money.

There was no choice but to agree to his demands and a meeting was arranged at the apartment for the coming Sunday afternoon. Mark Jacobs derived no satisfaction in knowing how right he had been about his friend's disastrous involvement with the man.

A rising panic gripped Andrei as he lowered the phone. 'I can't believe it,' he groaned, grabbing a fistful of hair at the back of his head. 'One stupid mistake is all I made. What the hell have I got myself in to?'

'That's irrelevant now. You're involved with him whether you like it or not. With what's been going down lately, something like this was bound to happen sooner or later,' Mark Jacobs said, making a cold assessment of the situation. 'We must start getting the money together straight away. In fact, I think we should pay the bastard off and get out the country while we still can. We're big stars, Andrei. Hell, there are agencies out there that would leap at the chance to sign us.'

Andrei was surprised by the bold suggestion. 'Do you seriously think we could? What about Jerry and Mick? Would they go along with us?'

Mark Jacobs looked thoughtful. 'Well they weren't too happy about you addressing the crowd in Birmingham, and that turned out okay. I think they'll go along with us. In some ways they don't have a choice. You and I *are* the Blues Knights. We write the songs, remember?'

Andrei shrugged uncertainly.

Mark Jacobs threw an arm around Andrei's shoulder. 'Hey, stop worrying. Leave it with me, I'll speak to them.'

Andrei made no comment. Everything Mark Jacobs said made sense.

*

Jameson had insisted on an evening meeting inside the Pink Pelican, reasoning there would be enough customers in the club to minimise the possibility of any threat to his safety. With the promise of big money at his disposal, the ministerial fugitive felt remarkably confident as he approached the two men waiting at a table close to the bar.

Jack and Doug Levin sat in silence while Jameson told them about his financial arrangement with Andy Rivers. He explained how necessary it had become for him to leave England after his visit from MI5. The subdued manner in which the two men listened gave the impression that even they were now more afraid of what *he* might do to them.

'You're a businessman, Jack,' Jameson concluded boldly, 'and as you well know certain things can be worth a fortune if the timing is right. My silence is golden at the moment, so it doesn't come cheap. Andy Rivers was only too pleased to accommodate me. Of course, I wouldn't dream of demanding money from you, after all the favours you've done for me. But there is something you could help me with. It goes without saying that my lips would remain sealed about your dealings, and our various *arrangements* over the years.'

Jack stared at Jameson, saying nothing. Levin spoke for him.

'What do you want, Henry?'

Jameson held Jack's gaze. 'I need the use of your light aircraft to leave the country. It would be in our best interests if I could disappear.'

'So what's your plan?' Levin persisted.

Jameson finally turned to Levin. 'I shall be collecting the money from Rivers at his apartment this Sunday. If you meet me there we can drive straight to the airfield, and then your pilot can fly me across the Channel to a destination of my choice in France.'

Levin looked at Jack who gave a poker-faced nod.

'Very good,' Levin agreed, 'Sunday it is. We collect you from Rivers' apartment, fly you to France, and in return we can rely on your continued discretion?'

'Most definitely,' Jameson promised, holding out his hand.

Levin shook it. Jack smiled thinly without uttering a word.

'Thank you, gentlemen, I knew you would oblige me,' Jameson said, getting up from the table. He knew better than to outstay his welcome. 'I'll see you on Sunday, Doug.'

'I'll be there,' said Levin. 'And make sure you're alone with Rivers, or the deals off. I don't want any other sods involved in this.'

'I will, don't worry. This is strictly between us,'

the minister replied. He left with a feeling of extreme satisfaction. His plan was coming together perfectly.

Jack battled to restrain himself until the man had gone.

'That bastard has signed his own death warrant. Does he honestly think he can blackmail *me,* and walk away? *Unbelievable!*' he bellowed.

A few of the club's patrons glanced briefly in their direction. Levin smiled back an apology, before turning to his friend.

'Don't worry, Jack, I'll get it sorted. And we'll be getting rid of *both* problems together... right?'

The suggestion pacified Jack. 'Yeah, and make sure Jameson dies badly. It's a shame about the singer. God knows who he's been sleeping around with, and his involvement with that Russian was bloody dangerous no matter how innocent he claimed to be. We have a multi-million pound organisation at stake and he's a problem we can do without. These loose ends have to be tied off.'

'We'll soon find another politician, but a pop star? Not so easy,' Levin said with a cynical grin.

'It's too bad,' Jack sighed. 'He was a good earner, and my Sandra liked him. She won't be happy,'

'You'll have to take up the guitar, Jack.'

There was the hint of a smile on the rugged face. 'I'll leave the arrangements to you, Doug, but from now on no more poofs. You can't trust the buggers.'

*

The following day Jack made the effort of

returning home for lunch. It was Marek's third birthday and the opportunities of dining together as a family were all too rare. The red-faced little boy's spirited attempt to blow out his candles provided an amusing highlight to their meal.

'Just like his father, he won't let anything beat him,' Sandra giggled.

'Quite right, too,' Jack agreed, ruffling Marek's black curls.

Sandra dropped her serviette and rose from the table. 'Do you fancy a coffee in the garden?'

'Good idea, it's a nice day,' Jack said, lifting Marek from the chair.

The housemaid moved forward to clear the dishes. 'I'll bring them out in a few minutes, Mrs Bronson.'

'Thanks, Ellie,' Sandra said, hugging her husband's free arm as they walked from the room. 'Well, have you spoken with him?'

Jack's heart sank.

'Who?'

'Andy Rivers, of course,' she said with an impatient tug.

'To be honest ...'

Sandra coloured up. 'Jack, you're impossible!' she cried, pulling her arm away. 'Andy's a nice guy. Why don't you *ever* consider anything I say?'

'Sandra...darling,' he called after her as she stormed off.

Bloody Andy Rivers, what is it with that man? I'll be glad to see the back of him. Jack raged silently to himself. He continued on his way to the garden with Marek. What had promised to be a pleasant afternoon was now ruined.

*

Sounds of a busy dockyard filtered through the metal-framed windows of Levin's office. He spoke in a clinical manner, outlining his plan, explaining exactly what he expected of the four men sitting in front of him. Their job was to kill two people. They were hardened professionals, and few comments were made as they listened to their instructions.

'After dealing with Jameson, empty that into Andy Rivers,' Levin continued, pushing a sealed packet across the desk towards one of the men who slipped it into his pocket. 'It's a lethal mix of drugs, shouldn't take him long to die. Once he's unconscious, take off his clothes and smear Jameson's blood over him. Maybe leaving the syringe in his hand would be a nice touch.' The suggestion was coldly matter of fact. 'So there we are, gentlemen, a classic lover's quarrel. They have a row. Rivers kills Jameson, who was threatening to expose their relationship, then being overcome with grief he takes his own life with an overdose.'

The man who had taken the package grinned at his accomplices. 'A regular poof's punch-up, eh fellas.'

The coarse laughter was cut dead by Levin. 'More importantly, don't forget the blackmail money. Any questions?'

There were no replies.

'Good. Jameson should be arriving early on Sunday afternoon. You'll have no trouble getting into the apartment. Just ring the door bell, he'll be expecting to see me…and *don't* screw it up.'

Chapter 28

The leather holdall stood on the dining table crammed with money: a stark reminder of one reckless act. Earlier in the week, Andrei and Mark Jacobs had received another call from Jameson to say that Levin would also be joining them at the Bayswater flat, suggesting that he might be another victim of the minister's blackmail. But they knew little about the man, and were past caring; they had their own agenda.

'You shouldn't be alone with Jameson,' Mark Jacobs protested by the open door. 'He's a conniving sod, and I don't trust him.'

'Mark, I'll be fine, really,' Andrei said, guiding his friend from the apartment. 'He specifically stated that it should just be him, Levin and me. Why mess up the arrangements now? All he wants is the money. You wait outside in the car. When you see him leave with Levin come back here and we'll start getting our stuff together. We'll have plenty of time to make the airport. Now stop worrying.'

*

Peering through the tinted windows of the parked Mercedes, Mark Jacobs instinctively slid down into his seat as the portly figure of Henry

Jameson paid off the taxi and entered the building.

Events were now in motion and very soon he, Andrei, and the rest of the band would be leaving this nightmare behind to embark upon a new future together. He had managed to convince Jerry Wilson and Mick Brightman to join them on a flight to the United States later that evening. Being hot property on both sides of the Atlantic, their intention was to approach one of the big American agencies and fight whatever court case might be necessary to start afresh.

His daydream evaporated at the sound of slamming doors. A large saloon had swung onto the forecourt, coming to a halt in front of the apartment block. Four men were hurrying up the steps towards the building's entrance.

Mark Jacobs had expected to see Levin, but not these people. It was possible that they had nothing to do with the meeting. However, the urgency of their arrival was unsettling. Almost unconsciously he clicked open the car door.

*

The corrupt politician was greedily fingering the bank notes. 'Don't need to count it to know there's a lot of money here,' he gloated, drawing the zipper closed.

Andrei watched with contempt. 'Just take it and get out. Blood money never brought happiness to anyone.'

'Spare me the lecture, Andy. You can afford it, and it's cheap at the price,' Jameson said, dragging the heavy bag off the table. 'Don't be a sore loser. I'll be out of your life very soon.'

The doorbell sounded.

Jameson checked his watch. 'Perfect timing, that will be our friend, Mr Levin,' he said, looking pleased with himself.

He walked across to open the front door. Violence and horror struck in one terrifying moment, as four men barged into the apartment. Jameson's head was snapped back by a powerful hand gripping his throat, distorting his set smile into a grotesque grin. His jacket was pulled from his back and his trousers dragged to his ankles, causing him to stumble backwards in a humiliating scramble towards the bedroom. A rock hard forearm was clamped across his mouth, silencing his cries, while the rest of his clothes were torn away. He felt helplessly vulnerable, aware of his nakedness, as the two attackers held him down on the bed. *What the hell's happening? Are they going to rape me?*

A third man entered the room brandishing a carving knife. Jameson's eyes bulged in terror as his assailant walked swiftly towards him, and without hesitation, plunged the blade several times into his quivering stomach. A pillow was crushed over his face to dampen the screams of agony. He was eventually released to roll onto his side, whimpering pitifully, clutching at the bloodied mess that began to seep between his fingers.

It took Henry Jameson several minutes to die.

*

When the intruders burst in, Andrei had leapt to his feet only to be pushed backwards by one of the men who knelt on his chest, pinning him to the couch. He twisted his head round to witness Jameson being hauled away. Another man crashed around in the kitchen and emerged with a knife, making straight for the bedroom. Jameson's muffled screams were suddenly followed by unexpected chiming from the doorbell, accompanied by a forceful hammering.

Andrei seized the moment to punch his fazed attacker hard between the legs. Breaking free from the moaning thug, he ran for the kitchen. If there were more of them at the door it would be his only means of escape.

The man appeared from the bedroom clutching a blood stained knife. It was all the incentive Andrei needed to take a reckless gamble. He threw a stool through the kitchen window, and followed it, knowing that the fire escape ran directly below. His gamble paid off. He dropped several feet onto the steel walkway, landing heavily with a resounding clang, to clamber down the narrow stairs. When he reached the ground at the rear of the building, he stumbled away, cut and bruised, creating as much distance as he could between himself and the killers. His mind was reeling from the sudden savagery. *Who were those maniacs? Who sent them?*

*

Against his better judgement, Mark Jacobs had crept cautiously down the softly lit corridor to pause outside the apartment. Distant screaming prompted him to lean on the bell, and begin thumping the door, until the sound of smashing glass and aggressive voices panicked him. His courage failed. Moments later he was careering down the utility stair well, vaulting several steps at a time, to reach the downstairs lobby. He rammed open the large doors, startling an older woman who was entering the building. Jabbering his apologies, he ran past the Mercedes towards the main road, cursing his inability to drive, waving his arms wildly to hail a passing cab.

*

Jack nodded approvingly as he watched Levin leave the study. He opened his desk pad, took up a pen, and drew a line through the name of Henry Jameson. Directly underneath he made a new entry: the name and telephone number of a man called James Doyle, bracketing the letters IRA beside it. He closed the pad with a callous smile. The junior cabinet minister had met his final obligation.

Henry Jameson was dead. And despite Andy Rivers' escape, Levin had managed to convince Jack that the unplanned outcome would still be resolved to their advantage. The hired killers had been quick to improvise damning evidence to incriminate the musician, before sending an anonymous tip-off to the police. It would only be a question of time before he was arrested, and with trumped-up testimonies from bribed witnesses his conviction would be guaranteed. If for any reason his actions were deemed to be a crime of passion, thereby avoiding the death penalty, he would be killed in prison by well-rewarded fellow inmates.

With Jameson dead and Andy Rivers framed for his murder, together with a generous haul of cash, Jack was content with the outcome.

*

When the police arrived at the apartment and discovered the minister's body, MI5 had been alerted immediately.

Jan Stevens never ceased to be amused at the predictable coolness shown towards her by the CID who seemed to harbour an inherent dislike of the secret service agencies. She arrived soon after the plain-clothes officers, receiving little assistance from them as she made her own, independent examination of the crime scene. While inspecting the bedroom, she stopped to look over the pathologist's shoulder as he examined the bloodied corpse that lay in a foetal position across the bed.

'How long has he been dead?' she asked, with professional detachment.

The man paused from his work. 'Not that long actually, the body's still stiffening, maybe two or three hours at the most. Must have been a terrible death, multiple stab wounds to the lower abdomen, intense pain, and a lot of blood to lose before you die…nasty.'

'That's queers for you,' a brash voice interrupted.

The woman looked round to see a sullen-faced detective standing at the entrance to the bedroom, lighting a cigarette.

'Homosexuals can be vicious bastards,' he said, with smoke wafting from his nostrils. 'I've seen a fair bit of these jealousy killings around the London clubs. No more than they deserve if you ask me.'

'I see, so with your *extensive* experience, the

obvious suspect would be this celebrity, Andy Rivers, the owner of the apartment,' Jan Stevens said, riled by the man's bigotry.

'You don't have to be a genius, or even an MI5 officer, to work that out,' he taunted, taking another pull on his cigarette, 'and surprise, surprise, our men have even found drugs, a carving knife, kitchen rubber gloves, and one of those expensive silk shirts, saturated in blood, dumped in the communal dustbins behind the building. No prizes for guessing who the shirt belongs to.'

She shook her head in despair. 'The rubber gloves suggest there will be no fingerprints, and unless you found Rivers inside his shirt what does that prove? It's all too convenient, almost insults the intelligence, and why would he throw a stool through the kitchen window when all he had to do was open the front door?'

'The murder weapon was a knife,' the policeman argued, 'there must have been one hell of a fight going on. The stool was probably thrown by Jameson in self-defence.'

'Any prints on the stool?'

'Not as far as I know, but the forensic guys haven't completed their work yet. I'm telling you, Rivers is definitely our man. We've put out an APB on him. It won't be long before he's picked up.'

'As I say, all *very* convenient,' Jan Stevens repeated, growing weary of the conversation. She pushed past the detective and left the room.

'It's an open and shut case,' he shouted after her. 'You people love to make a big deal out of everything, don't you?'

The woman stopped in her tracks, spun round, and shot him a withering look. 'I would think that a Cabinet Minister found naked and savagely knifed to death in a top celebrity's apartment is a big enough deal without any help from *my people,* wouldn't you? I expect a full report from your senior officer on my Controller's desk first thing in the morning. And that's not a request, that's an *order!*'

The pathologist struggled to hide a smile from the red-faced policeman who was quietly choking on his cigarette, glaring after the MI5 agent as she swept out of the apartment.

*

Mick Brightman was shocked by the appearance of Mark Jacobs standing at his front door in such a distressed state. Jerry Wilson had driven over to join them immediately after being told the news. The two group members' first reaction was to call the police, but they soon realised that Jameson's blackmail demands could raise dangerous implications for Andrei. Without knowing exactly what had happened in the apartment, it wasn't difficult to imagine that something awful had gone down. There was nothing any of them could do except wait.

Their proposed flight to America had become a remote prospect, as the most important priority now was to establish Andrei's safety. No matter how disheartened they had become about their future, they had no intention of leaving without him. It was almost midnight when the phone rang. Mick Brightman answered it.

'Hello...reverse the charge...no problem, put him through.' He handed the receiver to Mark Jacobs whose face brightened at the sound of his friend's voice.

'Andrei, thank God you're all right. What the hell happened in there?'

'I think Jameson's dead...it was bloody terrible...I'm sure they were out to kill me too...'

'Okay, calm down, who's *they? Who* tried to kill you?'

'I have no idea, but Levin must have had something to do with it. He was supposed to have been there this afternoon. But he never showed...just those killers. I can't call the police...what would I say? They'd never believe me. What the hell am I going to do? Who would want *me* dead, Mark?'

'I have no idea, but that can wait. Where are you now?'

'I'm in the Oceanic Terminal at Heathrow Airport, as we arranged. I didn't know where else to go. I managed to hitch a ride from some old guy...not a pop fan thank God.'

Andrei's brave attempt at humour was lost on Mark Jacobs who sensed imminent danger. 'Damn it, you shouldn't have gone there. Try and stay out of sight. You need to lay low.'

'I'll do my best, but I've got no money. Can you meet me here? I must get away and figure out what to do.'

'Of course, I'll be as quick as I can, and Andrei...*Andrei?*'

*

The police reasoned it would only be a question

of time before Andy Rivers showed up at one of the country's docks or airports. Before he could finish his conversation, a couple of alert plainclothes officers had pulled Andrei from the phone booth and were dragging him forcefully across the busy concourse. People stared, flashlights popped, and scuffles broke out among the ever-present prowling paparazzi. Their pictures would command large fees from the daily tabloids.

Chapter 29

Sandra was speechless, appalled by the dramatic photographs of Andy Rivers' arrest. She pushed the morning paper across the table towards her husband, silently inviting him to look at the headline. He drank his coffee, reluctant to comment, knowing how fond she had become of the man, until he glanced down at the front page. His eyes became transfixed. Crashing the cup on its saucer, he lifted up the newspaper to examine it more intently.

Sandra look startled. 'Jack, are you okay? What's the matter?'

He sat motionless, unable to speak. Suddenly he slammed the paper down in front of her with a haunted look. 'In the picture…tell me, what do you see?'

She checked the photo again. It showed a close-up of the dishevelled pop star being restrained between two policemen. Apart from feeling saddened by his public humiliation, she wondered what she was supposed to be looking at.

'It's dreadful,' she sighed, 'I can't believe that -'

'Never mind all that,' he said impatiently, 'what do you see…*there*…hanging around his neck?' He leaned across the table, stabbing his finger at the photograph.

'Oh *that*,' she said, studying it more closely. 'It's just a cheap wooden talisman. He showed it to me on the night I met him. Apparently some friend carved it for him back in Poland when they were children. He wears it all the time, quite sweet really,' she said, handing the paper back.

There followed a brief, uncomfortable silence.

'*Christ!* I've been so stupid. How the hell could I have missed it?' Jack groaned, collapsing back in his chair, staring at the grainy black and white picture. 'He was always playing the guitar as a kid. But he's so different. I mean...his face, that pony tail...I would never have known...but now, looking at him...'

Sandra's eyes narrowed. 'What are you saying? Do you *know* this guy?'

He swallowed hard to clear his throat, staring at the paper. 'Yes, I know him. His name is Andrei Wolenski. He was my best friend...the *only* friend I ever had back in Poland. He probably saved my life, but that's another story. The last time I saw him I was eleven years old...*I* carved that talisman for him.'

The colour drained from his face. Sandra got up from the table and moved round to stand beside him.

'I knew there was something special about that man. How did it all come to this, Jack?' she said, kissing him gently on the top of his head. 'Is there anything you can do for him? Surely you don't believe he could be responsible for such a terrible murder?'

Jack felt a surge of remorse sweep through him. It was an alien experience. He had forgotten how to feel pity for anyone except his own family. But then Andrei Wolenski *had* been his family: Andrei, his mother and sister, Grandma Anna.

Childhood memories streamed back into his consciousness: he was back at school in Kielce, forced up against a wall, hugging his head in his arms as a group of young ruffians rained blows on him. Suddenly, a tall, fair-haired boy appeared out of nowhere and confronted the bullies, saving him from a serious beating. Then he was reliving the stabbing horror: the sickening squelch as the knife entered Gustav Wolenski's neck, the warm, sweet smell of blood, distant screams. Once again, Andrei was with him. The tall, fair-haired boy, holding him…comforting him…

Jack looked up at his wife. She was shocked by the semblance of a tear in his eye. Sandra had never seen him like this, even after the death of Samuel Hurwitz.

He reached up to hold her hand. 'You have my word that Andrei will walk away from this,' he said, with a small tremor in his voice. 'Andy Rivers, the superstar, will be restored to his rightful status.'

*

There was a lot to be done. Jack spent the rest of the morning in his study with strict instructions to Sandra that he was not to be disturbed, insisting that she keep their conversation to herself.

Levin was astounded by Jack's call, but he knew better than to query direct orders from his boss: and the orders were explicit. The man they had set out to kill, and subsequently frame for murder, was now to be exonerated from all charges brought against him. Levin was told to contact Jack's solicitor with instructions to hire the best defence barrister available. If necessary, bribed witnesses would be provided to supply whatever testimonies were required to assist in securing Andy Rivers' release.

He was then given instructions to approach a contact in the Foreign Office to organise entry visas for the pop star's mother and sister who would be given the opportunity of attending the trial. Lastly, Jack was adamant that his name should not be divulged to anyone until his permission was given. If pressed, Levin was to say that an anonymous, wealthy admirer had insisted on financing Rivers' defence.

*

Robson sat in his office, studying the assorted newspapers lying in front of him. They all bore the same headlines about Henry Jameson's murder, and photos of Andy Rivers being dragged off by the police.

Jameson's death had come as no surprise, considering his close ties to the gangster, Jack Bronson. But Robson had his doubts about the famous celebrity's alleged guilt. Jan Steven's report on the crime scene suggested a most unimaginative attempt at implicating Andy Rivers in the murder. Then there was the hit and run incident resulting in Petrov's death. A witness testified that the car had appeared to accelerate deliberately towards the man, before accelerating away at great speed.

The common denominator with these three people was Jack Bronson. Jameson might well have made too many demands of the gangster? The spy, Stefan Petrov, would have certainly been a dangerous liability to Bronson's organisation, as would Andy Rivers, who had unwittingly brought the man into the country.

Logic demanded that the gangster was a prime suspect for the recent killings: he had been doing a spot of house cleaning. Truth be known, Robson couldn't give a damn. A criminal organisation carrying out executions to their mutual advantage was the ultimate paradox.

Chapter 30

A pungent odour of stale tobacco and disinfected floors hung in the air. The green painted room contained three chairs, grouped around a wooden table where a metal ashtray, crammed with twisted cigarette buts, stood as evidence of a previous occupant's interview. Andrei sat on one of the chairs, dressed in his blue prison fatigues, waiting for his lawyer to arrive. A stern faced prison officer stood beside the door, straight backed, feet apart, with hands clasped firmly behind his back, eyeing his longhaired ward like some rare curiosity.

During his first few days spent on remand the other inmates had constantly clamoured for the pop star's attention, disrupting the smooth running of the jail, forcing the prison authorities to put him into solitary confinement. Ironically, at that moment, it seemed the only welcome privilege his fame had ever brought him.

Andrei had adamantly denied any involvement in Jameson's murder, exercising his right to silence by refusing to answer the questions put to him under police interrogation. Mark Jacobs had taken immediate steps to appoint legal representation, only to be told by Levin that it had already been organised by a rich admirer who had chosen to remain anonymous. It seemed a strange gesture, as the pop celebrity was certainly wealthy enough to afford his own counsel. But Levin was adamant, and when it was revealed that the person in question was Stuart Desmond QC any doubts were immediately dispelled. In spite of a dubious reputation for his cavalier approach to the law, he was arguably one of the most successful criminal defence barristers in the British legal profession.

Andrei also drew comfort from the knowledge that his mother and sister had been flown over from Poland, and were staying in an expensive London hotel, courtesy of the same mysterious benefactor. As much as he longed to see them, he adamantly refused to let them visit him languishing in jail.

The echoes of banging doors and jangling keys grew closer, heralding the arrival of the barrister, a tall, cadaverous looking individual with steel grey hair and dark, piercing eyes. He was accompanied by a smaller, conservatively dressed man. They pulled out the empty chairs opposite Andrei and sat down, prompting the prison officer to wait outside in the corridor. The tall man dropped his worn valise onto the table.

'Good afternoon, Mr Wolenski. My name is Stuart Desmond, and this is Mr Browning, the solicitor who instructed me,' he began, motioning to his associate who gave a silent nod. 'Subject to your approval I shall be representing you at your forthcoming trial.' He offered his hand with a customary smile.

Andrei shook it despondently. 'That's fine by me, but who's paying your fee?'

'The same person who has offered to post bail, for a great deal of money I might add, allowing me to secure your release pending the trial.'

'That's great news. So who do I have to thank for this?' asked Andrei.

Browning gave a cautionary shake of his head at the barrister.

'I'm afraid I'm not at liberty to answer that,' Stuart Desmond said, unbuttoning the jacket of his blue pinstriped suit. He produced a fountain pen from his inside pocket and flicked open the valise to draw out a writing pad. 'All I can say is that he's an extremely wealthy person who feels a strong compulsion to offer you assistance in your time of need. An ardent fan of yours I would imagine.' Stuart Desmond selected a fresh page, and slipped on a rimless pair of spectacles. 'Now, there is much to be done. Would you be good enough to tell me, in your own words, exactly what transpired in your apartment on that Sunday afternoon?'

The lawyer sat expressionless, listening carefully, occasionally jotting down a few details. As Andrei spoke, the more painful the memories became. He finished by expressing his suspicions about Levin having had some involvement in the attempt on his life, and Jameson's subsequent murder.

Stuart Desmond answered with a condescending chuckle. 'I don't think so, Mr Wolenski. He's a rich businessman, with many interests. What possible reason would he have to kill you, or Jameson, for that matter?'

'I have no idea,' Andrei admitted. 'But why did those murderers arrive instead of him? He *knew* Jameson and I would be there at that precise time. And I'm pretty sure Jameson must have had something on Levin, otherwise why would he have agreed to join us?'

'I really couldn't say,' said the barrister. 'But Mr Levin has assured me that he was delayed in a meeting with your agent, Ben Sharmer, at the offices in Denmark Street. He tried to telephone your apartment, but got no answer. Of course, now we know why. He saw no point in keeping to the arrangement if nobody was there. It sounds like a logical decision to me.'

Andrei could not recall any phone call. He reasoned that it might have been made after his escape. 'Then if it wasn't Levin, who else would have wanted us dead?' he argued, refusing to be appeased.

Stuart Desmond plucked off his glasses and beckoned Andrei to lean in closer. 'Mr Wolenski, let's be realistic about the situation. The fact that Jameson was trying to blackmail you suggests that he desperately needed money, probably to leave the country. He was a known homosexual who had held a fairly senior post in government. I would suggest that he had got himself involved with some bad people, and was under some kind of threat. If they found out he was planning to visit you, they probably thought it would be the perfect opportunity of killing him, while framing you for his murder. I'm sorry to say that after your, what shall we call it, *indiscretion* with

Jameson, you would have made the perfect scapegoat. Of course, it's all pure conjecture on my part.' He waved a dismissive hand and sat back from the table. 'More importantly, you escaped with your life, and my job now is to get you cleared of this murder charge.'

'Easier said than done,' Andrei sighed. 'With the evidence they have stacked against me, what chance do I stand?'

The barrister rose above the defeatist remark. 'If we can prove that you were somewhere else at the time of the murder the prosecution's case would be indefensible, their so-called evidence would be worthless, and -'

'But I wasn't anywhere else,' Andrei cut in, confused.

Stuart Desmond appeared irritated by the interruption. 'Please, let me finish. If you want to walk away from this you *must* do as I say.' The insistence in his voice commanded attention. 'Mr Levin and Mr Sharmer are willing to testify that you were with them at the Diamond Agency offices on that Sunday afternoon.'

Andrei threw a surprised glance at the solicitor who returned a faint smile, before re-examining a sheet of paper he was holding.

'I don't believe it. Then if Levin really *is* blameless, what about the real killers, they would know it was a lie?' Andrei protested, turning back to the barrister.

Stuart Desmond laughed. 'Mr Wolenski, those people are hardly likely to come forward.'

Andrei cringed, embarrassed by his thoughtless remark. 'Okay, sorry, that was stupid. But supposing I went along with your suggestion, how on earth would it explain Jameson's presence in my apartment?'

'Fair question, and the answer to that is simple. You were closely involved with the man, so it's not unreasonable to expect that he might have had access to your home. We will merely suggest that he had arrived unexpectedly and was awaiting your arrival, during which time a person, or persons unknown, entered the apartment and killed him.'

'But that close involvement, as you call it, meant nothing. It was ages ago. I never saw him again socially.'

'A jury won't know that, and besides, his being there might even prove useful to us.' Stuart Desmond's last comment was almost lost as he began to twist the top back on his pen. 'I really must be going now, Mr Wolenski. I have all the information I need for the moment.'

'Hold on, I don't understand,' said Andrei, 'in what way could Jameson's presence in my apartment be useful?'

'Never mind that for now,' the barrister answered, securing his valise. 'Apart from yourself, and Mr Sharmer, the only other person who knew Mr Levin was supposed to be at the apartment was Jameson, and he's dead, so you see there's really no one to disprove their testimony.' Stuart Desmond paused to breathe a confession. 'Alright, I suppose we are stretching things a little. But let's face it, you know you're innocent. There are three possibilities here. You could go to the gallows, spend the rest of your days in prison, or continue with your life as a successful pop celebrity. Not exactly a hard choice is it.'

Both men stood up and made for the door. As the solicitor opened it, Andrei called after them.

'Actually, there is someone else who knew Levin was supposed to be there.'

The barrister looked back with a questioning frown. 'And who might that be?'

'My friend, Mark Jacobs.'

'Ah yes, Mr Jacobs, I'd almost forgotten.'

'But I know Mark, I can guarantee he won't be a problem,' Andrei confirmed immediately.

'I'm sure you're right,' said Stuart Desmond who smiled and followed the solicitor out the room.

Chapter 31

Andrei and Mark Jacobs sat at the kitchen table, silently sipping their coffees. The cereal bowls remained empty and the toast had gone cold. It was the morning of the trial. In a short while Andrei would be called upon by representatives of his defence counsel who would accompany him on his drive to court, where he would meet for a preliminary discussion with his barrister, Stuart Desmond QC. Andrei had been instructed not to discuss anything about his case with anyone before the trial, which included his partner, Mark Jacobs.

That had been the most difficult thing to deal with, as Mark Jacobs had proved to be Andrei's rock. Without him, Andrei genuinely wondered if he could have maintained his sanity. The recurring nightmare, waking up drenched in sweat with a noose tightening around his neck, continually haunted him. Mark Jacobs' brave humour, and his positive belief in a successful outcome, had sustained Andrei in the weeks leading up to the trial. The prospect of being found guilty was a scenario that neither of them wished to contemplate.

Mark Jacobs lifted the percolator, offering to

replenish Andrei's cup.

'No thanks, one more drop and I think I'll throw up,' Andrei said, with a forced smile. 'You've been such a good friend, Mark.'

The young man reached across the table to clasp Andrei's hand. 'We're much more than friends, Andrei. We're inseparable.'

*

The murder trial had stirred up a media frenzy. After only two days of legal deliberation Stuart Desmond QC played his trump card. Doug Levin and Ben Sharmer were called as witnesses to provide a solid alibi for the pop star at the time of the killing. As anticipated, the prosecution's case was thrown into disarray.

The following morning Mark Jacobs had arrived early to avoid the army of fans who turned up every day to keep vigil outside the Old Bailey. He was seated in the courtroom, still mystified by the previous day's developments. Levin and Sharmer's evidence had come as a shock, but if the lie meant securing Andrei's freedom he was willing to go along with it, in the same way he'd agreed to appear as a character witness to further assist in his friend's defence. Apart from a natural apprehension of being called to the witness box, he saw no harm in agreeing to the barrister's request.

He turned round to look up at the crowded public gallery where Mick Brightman and Jerry Wilson were quick to smile back their support. Beside them he saw the anxious faces of Marta and Maria Wolenski. The buzz of noisy speculation was suddenly silenced by a formal announcement.

'Be upstanding.'

The red-robed judge swept importantly into the room, clutching a bundle of papers that were neatly bound by a slender black ribbon. He settled into his chair, poured a glass of water, and invited the proceedings to begin.

The prosecution started by expressing their displeasure at the late introduction of the defence team's testimony, with veiled insinuations as to its reliability. They endeavoured to put forward theoretical possibilities that might still prove Andrei's guilt, suggesting that he could have simply paid a third party to carry out the murder, while using his meeting at the Diamond Agency as an alibi. Andrei's defence counsel vigorously countered their arguments, raising objections and pouring ridicule on their theories, until the moment finally arrived when Mark Jacobs was called to be sworn in.

Andrei was thrown by the unexpected development. *What possible reason could there be for calling Mark to the witness box?* His concern was heightened by the behaviour of his Counsel who seemed to be avoiding eye contact with him.

Stuart Desmond started with the usual formalities, before embarking upon a series of amicable questions that confirmed just how close the friendship was between Mark Jacobs and the pop celebrity, Andy Rivers. After a while the prosecuting barrister rose to his feet, querying the relevance of it all, reasoning that two members of a successful band would predictably speak well of one another. The Judge upheld the objection and asked the defence counsel to justify his current line of questioning. It was then that matters took a sinister turn.

'If the Court will bear with me,' said the QC, 'I am about to unveil certain facts that will strengthen my client's defence indisputably.'

The Judge gestured with a slow flick of his wrist, allowing the barrister to continue. Stuart Desmond's face lost its congenial expression. He turned to look gravely towards his witness.

'Mr Jacobs, would you describe your relationship with Andrei Wolenski, better known as the pop star, Andy Rivers, as being normal...in the accepted sense?'

Mark Jacobs threw a questioning stare at Andrei, who looked back from the dock in astonishment.

'Please answer the question.' The voice had become aggressive.

'Er...what exactly do you mean?' Mark Jacobs stammered.

'Am I right in saying that you are a homosexual, and that you are, in fact, utterly smitten by Andrei Wolenski? Remember that you are under oath.'

'Well...yes, but...' his reply seemed to resonate loudly around the murmuring courtroom. Tears of frustration welled in his eyes. *What is this man trying to do? He's supposed to be on our side...*

'You were besotted with Andrei Wolenski, weren't you?' The accusing voice grew louder. 'You hated him after hearing rumours about his alleged intimacy with Henry Jameson, a known homosexual. I'm suggesting, Mr Jacobs, that *you* could have murdered Jameson yourself.' Stuart Desmond was poised like a predatory animal stalking its kill. 'It would have been so easy for you to lure him to the flat and then stab him in a jealous rage, framing Andrei Wolenski for his murder. How might I put it, two birds with one stone?'

The courtroom erupted at the allegation. Mark Jacobs was dumbstruck. He could say nothing about Levin and Sharmer's blatant lies as they would only incriminate Andrei further. And who would believe him? Knowing how prejudiced public opinion was against homosexuality, anything he might say would be treated with scorn. He shook his head, feeling helpless and cruelly betrayed.

The prosecution lawyer leapt to his feet, his protests drowned by the rowdiness from the public gallery, forcing the Judge to raise his hand and demand order to the proceedings. The courtroom fell silent: primed, ready to explode.

The Judge looked directly at the defence council. 'This is all theoretical, surely. Do you have any evidence to uphold these suppositions?'

'I do, your Honour,' Stuart Desmond replied, running his eyes across the jurors' faces, as an actor might survey his enthralled audience. 'Not only am I suggesting that Mark Jacobs had the motive, and the opportunity, but I *also* have a witness, an elderly resident who saw him running from the apartment block in a distressed state at the time of the murder.'

In that instant Mark Jacobs knew he had been set up, having completely forgotten about the woman he had almost knocked down in his rush to leave the building. He stared piteously towards Andrei who looked dazed and heartbroken by the disastrous turn of events.

The courtroom chatter began to rise as the Judge allowed the stunned witness to step down. He ordered an adjournment, dismissed the jury, and informed the clerk of the court to summon the two barristers to his chambers. There were important issues that needed to be resolved before the trial could continue.

In the aftermath of the defence counsel's damning disclosures the case against the accused had become so tenuous that the judge had no option other than direct the jury to bring in a verdict of *not guilty*. The papers were awash with stories about the trial's sensational outcome. And regardless of wild speculation, the identity of Andy Rivers' mysterious benefactor still remained shrouded in secrecy.

*

Andy Rivers appeared outside the Old Bailey under a bright winter sun to be feted by an adoring crowd. He smiled bravely for the cameras, surrounded by his triumphant legal team, his only thought being to rejoin his soul mate, Mark Jacobs, as soon as possible.

Later that day he managed to escape the media attention and return to the sanctuary of his apartment. The moment he opened the front door a sense of uneasiness came over him. He called out Mark's name, but there was no reply. He pulled open the hall closet to find his friend's coat missing, and immediately hurried to the bedroom to discover a few articles of clothing scattered across the bed. Mark's guitar case was still leaning against the wall, but his large clutch bag, the one he always favoured when they were touring, was gone. Andrei wandered into the living room where he was devastated to discover a note sitting on the coffee table. It simply read:

'I will always love you...Mark.'

*

The police decided to act upon the new developments that had come to light at the trial and bring Mark Jacobs in for questioning, only to discover that he had left the country and disappeared without trace. It appeared that the man's actions had proved his guilt beyond question. His file was left open, and any further investigations into the murder of Henry Jameson were brought to a close.

*

Early in the New Year, Andrei sold the Bayswater apartment and bought a house in Cheyne Walk, Chelsea, insisting he be left alone with his family for a few months to recuperate after the trial. Levin had no choice but to respect his wishes, especially in light of Jack's newly found interest in their famous celebrity. He was desperate to discover exactly what the connection was between his boss and the fair-haired musician.

Ben Sharmer had been instructed to give the Blues Knights top priority by the Diamond Agency's promotional team. Their continued success was to be its sole undertaking. The band still had enough material to release a couple of new records, as well as unseen film footage to play through the media, which would be more than enough to keep them in the public eye, while Andrei spent time away from the glare of publicity.

The recording company had started to put pressure on the agency for the group to release a new album to coincide with a possible European tour planned for the following year. Meanwhile, auditions were underway to find a new bass player. Andrei found it painful to accept the reality of replacing Mark Jacobs, leaving it in the hands of his fellow musicians. Apart from losing his partner, he had also lost an inspirational driving force behind their song writing.

Chapter 32

Torrential rain spoiled a fine summer's evening, creating an oppressive humidity across Belfast's city centre. Jack and Doug Levin hurried across the wet pavement to their waiting car. Two of their men were already waiting in the front seats. The driver pulled away from the hotel's entrance and continued along Divis Street, before joining the Falls Road.

'It seems that Jameson came up with the goods again. He was a useful bugger,' Jack said, with scant regard for the man's demise. He sat back in his seat, rolled down the window, and loosened his collar. 'The three guys we're meeting are top ranking Republicans. Apparently James Doyle wields the power behind Sinn Fein, while Dennis Flynn and Patrick O'Neil are two high-ranking commanders in the IRA paramilitary. With those people handling this side of the operation, I can't see any of the local Irish yobs interfering with the shipments.'

'They'd be dead men if they did,' Levin remarked. 'So where is this Kellys Bar?'

'Some place called Andersonstown in west Belfast. It's a Republican stronghold, so we should be safe there. The directions were phoned through just before we left. These people are paranoid about security. Apparently there are British undercover agents everywhere.'

'The sooner we get this over with the better. I don't trust Irishmen, they're all lunatics,' Levin complained.

Jack laughed. 'Just the sort of people I like doing business with.'

Levin shook his head with a despairing smile.

*

The driver parked the car a short distance from Kellys Bar. As the four men approached, the sound of an Irish ceilidh band could be heard above the noisy commotion coming from inside. One of the minders pulled open the door to allow Jack and Levin to enter. The room suddenly fell silent. Jack's men stepped forward with their gun hands resting lightly inside their jackets. An assortment of inquisitive faces stared blankly at the intruders.

'Friendly bastards,' Levin whispered.

Jack remained unfazed. 'We're here to see James Doyle,' he announced loudly.

'Then you've come to the right place,' a voice cried from the depths of the smoky room.

The band struck up immediately, as if on cue, prompting the rumble of conversation to continue. A burly individual, wearing jeans and a loose denim shirt, walked towards them offering his hand.

'Welcome to Ireland, my friends. My name's Patrick O'Neil. Come and join us?'

O'Neil led them to a table at the back of the bar where James Doyle and Dennis Flynn were seated, watched over protectively by two surly looking men standing behind them.

James *Jimmy* Doyle's lined face, silver hair, and soft Irish brogue personified that of a kindly grandfather. But hardened Republicans like Doyle, who had taken up arms against the British forty years ago, were a breed apart. While serving as a young conscript in the Republican Army, he had been personally involved in murdering senior officers of the Royal Irish Constabulary. His duties also included punishment beatings of those loyal to the British government. Shattering a man's kneecaps with a pickaxe handle, oblivious to the screams and pleas for mercy, required a particularly cold mindset.

Dennis Flynn looked to be in his mid-forties. His father had been a contemporary of Doyle's back in the early days. They had been involved in many gunfights with the despised Black and Tans, a British paramilitary group that had been set up to help restore order to Northern Ireland. The Tans, as they were known, comprised mainly of ex-British soldiers, demobilised after the First World War, who were infamous for their drunkenness and ill-discipline.

In 1920, as a reprisal for IRA attacks, they sacked and burned many small towns, one of them being Balbriggan, home to the Flynn family. Dennis Flynn's father had been dragged from his house and made to kneel in front of his young family who were forced to witness his execution: a bullet to the back of his head. As a five-year-old child, Dennis Flynn's memory of that day was vague, but his hate for the British knew no bounds. Even as a boy, he attended every anti-British demonstration he could. In those days he threw stones: now he threw grenades.

The third member of the group, Patrick O'Neil, was a younger man who had been born in Londonderry to an English father, and a Catholic Irish mother. His parents' marriage had been despised by the local people, resulting in him being subjected to constant hostility as a child. His father had been killed after a drunken brawl, following an argument about his English roots. The tragedy only served to strengthen Patrick O'Neil's resolve to be accepted by the Catholic community. His perseverance finally paid off after meeting James Doyle at a Republican gathering. Doyle had taken pity on the younger man's predicament and used his considerable influence to endorse O'Neil's successful enlistment into the IRA. His drive and enthusiasm for the cause gained him huge respect and saw him quickly elevated up the chain of command to become a senior paramilitary commander.

After the introductions had been made, Jack settled into his chair and addressed his hosts. 'Before we talk, allow me to buy a round? What will it be, pints of the Black Stuff?' he grinned.

'Guinness? I bloody hate it,' said James Doyle. 'Make it whiskies all round.'

Jack laughed and turned to his men. 'Get them in and wait by the bar. I'll call if I need you.'

Once the drinks had been brought to the table, they immediately got down to business. The boisterous crowd had begun to join the ceilidh band in a rousing folk song that conveniently prevented any chance of them being overheard as Doyle explained the plan.

He started by instructing Jack to contact his Colombian suppliers and arrange for the ship carrying the drugs to weigh anchor at specific co-ordinates off the Antrim Coast, where it would transfer the illicit cargo to a smaller boat, before continuing its passage to the port of Larne. The shipment would then be brought to a cove near Portrush. From there the drugs would be driven overland, changing vehicles at Armagh to confuse any inquisitive members of the Royal Ulster Constabulary who might consider following them. They would eventually arrive on the east coast at Dundrum Bay. The final leg of the journey would be undertaken by powerful speedboats that would transport the drugs across the Irish Sea. They would skirt the northern coast of the Isle of Man, to avoid the busy ferry lanes, and arrive at a beach near Whitehaven on the Cumbrian coastline where Jack's men would be waiting to collect the merchandise.

'Sounds like you've done your homework, Jimmy,' Jack said to Doyle. 'But you mentioned changing vehicles. Do you expect trouble from the RUC?'

'We mustn't underestimate the sods,' Doyle replied. 'But we'll have a few surprises lined up for them. Some of our people will be bombing specific targets when we make the drugs run. They'll make useful diversions, and the attacks will be a bonus for our cause.'

'The British government pour scorn on our

efforts,' said Dennis Flynn who had remained silent up until now. 'I'll admit that our 'Operation Harvest' campaign hasn't succeeded in throwing the bastards out of our country. But the drugs money will give a big boost to our struggle.'

'I'll drink to that,' said Patrick O'Neil.

The five men joined their glasses together with a resounding ring.

'It looks like we have a deal?' Levin smiled.

'Excellent,' Jack said, keen to move on. 'Right, let's cut to the action. The first shipment is due in two months, so we have plenty of time to prepare. As you know, I am financing this one myself. We have agreed the percentage you will receive for your part in the venture and subject to its success another, much bigger deal will be arranged for the following year. I'm proposing that you share a third of the costs for setting that one up. The initial outlay will be high, but the returns will be huge.'

O'Neil laughed. 'Is this a touch of the English blarney?'

'No, Patrick, I'm talking *millions*'.

A stunned silence followed.

James Doyle frowned. 'A third of the costs means a third of the profits. So does that mean you'll be taking two thirds?'

Jack shook his head. 'No, Jimmy. I'll need the assistance of another guy who runs things in south London. We'll need all the help we can get. He can provide more manpower for our UK distribution, and he'll be useful in helping to share the expense.'

Doyle considered Jack's proposal. He had

doubts about working with people he didn't know, but the promise of such rich rewards was too tempting to let go. He glanced towards his two companions who silently confirmed their agreement.

'You won't regret it, gentlemen,' said Jack. 'A large proportion of the drugs will be flown over to Europe by my people, where the distribution network is even bigger than the UK. If you consider the street value of the cocaine, it doesn't take a genius to work out the rest.'

'We'll win this bloody war. You'll see if we don't,' Dennis Flynn said, with a rush of enthusiasm. 'That'll wipe the smile off those Protestant bastards in Stormont.'

'Whatever,' Jack interrupted, growing tired of the politics, 'but it'll put a big one on mine. I'll be in touch.'

He and Levin shook hands with the Irishmen and left the bar, escorted by their bodyguards.

*

The caller's quiet voice and broad Irish accent forced the Controller to listen intently as the important information was being divulged.

'This is good stuff,' said Robson. 'And remember, I want surveillance only. No intervention. Let the bastards get on with it. We'll land the big fish later. Well done, and watch your back.'

The caller hung up without another word. Robson replaced the scrambler phone back on its cradle and leaned forward to speak into the intercom. 'Get McCann and Stevens into my office straight away.'

He released the button and took a moment to focus on this latest development. His Irish informant had just given him the news he had been hoping for. Jack Bronson had made his move by enlisting the assistance of the IRA in his drug smuggling operation. This could be the opportunity of striking a crippling blow against the terrorists, as well as bringing down a powerful criminal organisation.

Robson knew his boss slavishly ran the department by the book, and MI5 was supposed to function within strict government guidelines. Unfortunately, criminals and enemies of the State acted under no such restraints. If the Director General had the slightest idea of what was going through Robson's mind he would be incensed.

The Controller's lined face stretched into a scheming smile. It might be a dangerous game, but a lot could be gained by riding on the back of a tiger.

Chapter 33

The Colombian vessel had managed to transfer four large crates of cocaine onto the small boat. It had been a dangerous manoeuvre, allowing for the huge swell of the Atlantic. But the ships masters were experienced seamen, and the substantial financial rewards made for a greater incentive for their crews to succeed.

The moment the small boat had weighed anchor near Portrush, a series of organised attacks by the IRA commenced across Northern Ireland, drawing attention from the route being used for the drugs run. Dennis Flynn had insisted on taking charge of the operation. As a senior IRA commander, he should not have been involved. But his passion for Irish independence drove him to personally undertake the most hazardous missions, regardless of any risk to himself. He was in command of six men, five of whom were sitting in the back of the covered lorry, as it barrelled through the darkness heading out of Armargh towards the east coast.

Flynn sat beside the driver, continually checking the wing mirror, keeping a wary eye on a set of headlights that had been following them for some time. They had stopped in the town, as planned, to transfer the crates into another vehicle, but despite efforts to deter any unwanted attention the headlights were still there. After a few more miles, he ordered the driver to pull over. As the pursuing car drew closer, Flynn jumped from the cab. His suspicions were confirmed as the vehicle ignored his gesture to slow down and accelerated past him, disappearing into the night.

Flynn walked to the rear of the lorry and pulled back the canvas sheet. A rattle of five bolt-action rifles rang out of the darkness.

'Whoa, steady, lads!' Flynn cried. 'Save that for a more deserving bastard.'

'You frightened the shit out of us. What's the problem, Dennis?' asked one of the men, lowering his weapon.

'We've had a car tailing us for some time, probably the RUC making a bloody nuisance of themselves. Nothing better to do I guess. I'm just warning you to stay alert for the rest of the run.'

'Do you think they're on to us?' asked another gunman.

'Not a chance,' Flynn answered with confidence. 'Only James, Patrick and I knew exactly what time we were making our move this evening.'

*

Two speedboats cut their engines and drifted silently up to the beach a few miles south of Whitehaven on the English coast. Their occupants, dressed in heavy waterproofs, dropped over the side and pulled the boats clear of the water. Flickering torch beams appeared out of the night as Bronson's men moved towards them across the sand. It didn't take long for the crates to be manhandled away to a waiting trailer that stood harnessed to a dark green Land Rover.

'Sweet as a nut. Well done guys. Who said the Irish were useless?' said a gruff-voiced gang member, throwing a tarpaulin across the crates that were already strapped down in the trailer.

Dennis Flynn was not amused. 'Very funny, and so bloody original. You can tell your boss we had a good run. There was only one incident.'

'You're bullshitting me?'

'I never bullshit, my friend. A car was tailing us for a few miles. As soon as I tried to flag it down it buggered off. I thought it might have been the RUC?'

'Could be dodgy? I'd better tell Bronson.'

'If it makes you feel better, but I doubt it's anything to worry about. If they'd had anything on us I wouldn't be standing here talking to you, now would I?' said Flynn. 'Anyway, I've been here long enough. I hate this fucking country. We're gone,' said the Irishman, beckoning his men back to the boats.

*

Doug Levin phoned Jack with the news. The drugs had arrived safely and were already being distributed to their various destinations. He mentioned Dennis Flynn's experience about the car that had been tailing them. Jack took the same view as Flynn. If the authorities had been on to them they would have been arrested without hesitation. The RUC were renowned for their brutal commitment to strike at the IRA at any given opportunity.

Chapter 34

'Our guests have arrived, Jack.'

Levin stood up and closed his jacket against the cold November morning as he prepared to greet the occupants of a two-tone brown and cream Rover 95 that was nosing its way up the frost-covered drive.

Jack looked over his shoulder to follow Levin's gaze. His initial reaction had been one of deep concern when MI5 had called on his private line to demand a meeting. It seemed that Dennis Flynn's report about them being tailed that night had been more significant than they originally thought. But after reflecting on the situation, Jack felt encouraged by the fact that the RUC had mysteriously failed to intervene during the drugs run, and that MI5 had also taken the time and trouble to contact him personally. Whatever they had in mind would have to be to their mutual advantage otherwise they would have come down on him much sooner, and much harder.

Levin returned, guiding two men and a woman into the study.

'Mr Robson, I presume?' Jack said, getting to his feet.

'You presume correctly,' the Controller replied, giving a short handshake. 'And these are my colleagues, Peter McCann and Jan Stevens.'

The three MI5 officers took seats opposite Jack. Levin moved across the room to stand behind his boss. Robson wasted no time in opening the meeting.

'Mr Bronson, I'll be as brief as possible,' he said, unfastening his duffle coat. 'We've spent the last few months compiling a comprehensive report on your organisation and its activities. We are convinced that you were responsible for the deaths of Stefan Petrov and Henry Jameson. In fact, whether you realise it or not, you have actually been useful to us. That said, you can't go around killing anyone you please.' He paused with a reproachful look in his eye.

Jack broke into a sardonic smile. 'Of course not, unless it suits your purpose.'

'Quite so,' said Robson, whose two officers remained aloof from the small talk.

'Your accusations are one thing,' Jack said, 'but proving them is another matter, so enough with the bullshit and tell me what you're doing here.' He aimed a belittling glance at the brunette, signifying his displeasure at having to negotiate with a woman.

You rude bastard, she thought, returning a steely glare.

'Excellent, straight to the point, that's what I like,' the Controller said, slipping the catches on his attaché case. He pulled out a folder and placed it on the desk. 'It's all there in the report. We know about your trip to Northern Ireland in July, and your meeting in Andersonstown with the Republicans. It seems that you and your friend, Mr Levin, are planning another extremely ambitious drugs run?'

Levin looked astounded.

Jack looked curious. 'I'm impressed. You know almost as much as I do. Perhaps you'd like a piece of the action? I mean, how much can a job like yours pay?' he asked with an impudent smirk.

'Sufficient for my needs, thank you,' Robson replied, unmoved by the insolence.

'Bribery is a serious offence, Bronson,' Jan Stevens cut in sharply.

'You should keep her on a leash,' Jack taunted.

She scowled back at him. The man was definitely getting to her.

'You watch your mouth,' McCann threatened, knotting his fist angrily.

'Let's all calm down shall we,' Robson cut in. 'This sort of nonsense achieves nothing.'

Jack was losing patience. 'So what do you want from me?'

The Controller fixed the gangster with a commanding stare. 'I *want* James Doyle, Dennis Flynn and Patrick O'Neil. And I want *you* to give them to me.'

'Oh I see, just like that,' Jack said, struggling to keep his cool.

'Yes, just like that,' Robson echoed. A smile twitched across his lips. *That's slowed you down, you cocky bastard.*

Alarm bells were ringing inside Jack's head. *Where's this going? Where will it leave me? I need to strike a deal with this sod, fast.*

'You don't have enough to tie me into anything,

Robson,' Jack said, figuring a little token resistance would seem appropriate. 'A decent lawyer could tear your case against me into shreds. Sure, you could cause me some inconvenience. But my little deal would soon be back on track.'

Levin broke into a smug smile at his friend's reply.

'If you call millions of pounds a *little* deal, Mr Bronson, then I am impressed,' Robson answered immediately. 'I understand your next transaction will amount to something in that region, am I right?'

Levin's smile died.

Jack was desperately trying to figure out who the informant might be, already savouring the thought of what he would do to the bastard when he laid hands on him. He had wasted enough time. It was time to negotiate.

'Okay, I'm listening,' he said coldly.

'Cheer up, Mr Bronson. It's not as bad as you might imagine. What I'm proposing is a joint venture between my department at MI5, and you and your trusted colleague.' He paused to acknowledge Levin who did his utmost to look important. 'We will allow you to complete your drugs run and reap the financial benefits from your ill-gotten venture. In return, you will set up your IRA partners for us to deal with. These Irishmen are dangerous bastards who have been responsible for many atrocities in Northern Ireland, and on the English mainland. They are a bit like you, Mr Bronson, untouchable through normal channels.'

Jack ignored the gibe. 'Let me get this straight,' he said in the most composed voice he could manage. 'You will simply allow me to go free, unharmed, with all the money?'

'Well there's no fun in nothing,' Robson replied. 'By the time we've finished with the Irishmen they won't need their share. And you will be generously compensated for helping to eliminate your country's enemies. There is one other thing though?'

'There always is,' said Jack.

'In return for us allowing you to amass such a fortune, we would expect you to wind down your operation, and cease your criminal activities.'

Jack stole a glance at Levin who looked thrown by the demand.

'Are you asking me to go straight?' Jack said, turning back to the Controller.

'That is exactly what I'm asking. You're not a stupid man, and you know how difficult MI5 could make life for you if you were to refuse this request. Quite frankly, your criminal organisation is proving to be a major liability to the police, quite apart from the valuable resources they are forced to waste in your pursuit. And you have also become an embarrassment to the government no less. We want you out of the picture. I'm offering you an amnesty, Mr Bronson, and you'd be wise to take it.'

Jack sat back in his chair, drumming his fingers on the desk, considering his position. His worst fears had been realised. MI5 were on his case, and they could prove to be a formidable enemy. He might be forced to accept their demands: but he wouldn't trust them.

'It appears that we have a deal,' said Jack. 'I accept your amnesty. So in return for setting up three senior IRA commanders, and winding up my organisation, you will allow me to keep the money and walk away, free from prosecution?'

'That's correct,' Robson replied. 'We'll meet again later to discuss the details.'

The Controller glanced at his two officers, reached for his case, and stood up. They had spent enough time in the presence of these villains. The plan was activated and it was time to leave.

*

Mrs Hurwitz was sitting on the sofa, pouring their tea. Drops of rain had begun to tap against the French windows as Sandra let the net curtains float back into place after watching the Rover leave.

'Apparently they were important people from the government,' she said, walking back to sit beside the old lady. 'Jack has really come up in the world hasn't he?' She sank a spoonful of sugar into the hot drink, stirring it slowly. 'You can't help feeling proud of him, and especially for helping Andy Rivers get off that outrageous murder charge. What a miscarriage of justice that would have been.'

Mrs Hurwitz went back to her newspaper, hoping the conversation might change.

Sandra pursued the subject. 'Did you know that Jack knew the man?'

'What man?'

'Andy Rivers, of course, his real name is Andrei Wolenski,' she said, without thinking. 'He and Jack knew one another back in Poland when they were kids. Isn't that incredible?'

Sandra lifted the cup to her mouth. It took a moment to register before Mrs Hurwitz dropped the paper onto her lap.

'*Andrei Wolenski?* Are you sure?'

'Oh yes,' Sandra said, swallowing quickly. 'Jack only realised who he was after seeing that newspaper photograph of Andy Rivers' arrest. He noticed a wooden charm hanging around the man's neck. Apparently he'd carved the thing for Andy…I mean Andrei, as a parting gift. I don't mind telling you, I've never seen him look so upset, poor love.'

Mrs Hurwitz's efforts to remain calm were finally exhausted. 'And well he might,' she said in wounded disbelief. 'He should be ashamed of what he's become. That explains why we were all sworn to secrecy over the matter. To think he let his best friend go to prison. *He* should have been locked up, not Andrei.'

Sandra looked visibly shocked. 'Rachel, that's a horrible thing to say! Jack had no idea who Andrei was at the time.'

'That's as maybe,' Mrs Hurwitz argued. 'I read about Jameson's murder in the papers. Jack knew that man well. There's a lot more to this than meets the eye. And if he had nothing to hide, why didn't he reveal himself to Andrei? Why did he pay his legal fees? Andrei's a successful pop star. He's a very wealthy man. It smacks of conscience. You mark my words, Sandra, that son of mine is up to no good.'

'That's not true. Jack's a wonderful man. I admit he seems a little distant sometimes, but he has a lot on his mind, he runs a huge business.' Sandra jumped from the sofa and began to pace the room, anger smarting her eyes. 'I know you've always blamed him for Samuel's death, but you're wrong, Rachel. Jack loved his father. It's the last thing he would have wanted.'

'And my Samuel loved his son, *Yakov*,' Mrs Hurwitz sobbed, pulling a handkerchief from her sleeve. 'It was Jack Bronson that broke his heart. There's no doubt his young life was plagued by tragedy. That's why we brought him here to England. He was always such a quiet, passive child, but something changed him. I'm sorry, there's only so much you can forgive. He's not the same person I used to know.' She got up and hurried from the room.

The retort upset Sandra deeply. She never argued with Rachel. They had always been so close. Sandra often wished she could maintain the same dogged acceptance as her friend, Lucy, who simply banished Doug Levin's criminal involvement from her mind. Unfortunately, Sandra's state of denial would be shattered every so often, allowing reality to come crashing back into her life.

She gazed across the rain-drenched gardens of Greystone Manor. Her tears merged with the rivulets of water that were now trickling down the windowpanes.

Chapter 35

The Christmas lights in London's West End were legendary, and this year did not disappoint. Andrei had specifically asked his driver to take them along Oxford Street for the benefit of his mother and sister who looked in wonder at the twinkling spectacle.

He had been phoned by Levin requesting his presence at a Christmas Eve party to be held in his honour at the Pink Pelican. When pressed further about the evening, Levin seemed genuinely unsure of the arrangements. But soon all would be revealed as Andrei's new, dark blue Bentley swung into Regent Street, heading towards Soho.

They drew up alongside the pavement where a light flurry of snow sparkled in the neon lights above the club's entrance. For a passing moment it reminded Andrei of two small boys, wrapped up against the cold, waiting for a village bus. The doormen were quickly positioning themselves to create a clear exit from the car.

'Oh my gosh, look at the photographers, this is *so* embarrassing,' Maria giggled.

Her brother grinned. 'It's a taste of what I have to put up with.'

Andrei allowed his mother and sister to enter

the club, before stepping out into an explosion of flashlights. Shrieks of delight greeted him from a group of young women who had been waiting patiently for his arrival. *So much for a private party*, he thought, stopping briefly to acknowledge them.

Once their coats had been taken, Andrei insisted on being photographed with his family. Mrs Wolenski disliked the attention, but her daughter remained awestruck by the whole experience. Levin appeared in the foyer wearing a perfectly tailored dinner suit, and a broad smile.

'Welcome, Andy,' he proclaimed, 'and especially to your beautiful ladies.' He bent forward to kiss their hands, triggering another rush of crackling flashlights. Marta Wolenski looked mortified.

'Right, let's get you out of here,' Levin said, inviting Andrei and the two women into the relative calmness of the club.

The guests consisted of familiar faces from the music business and acquaintances that Andrei had made during his successful career. He saw Ben Sharmer, clouded in smoke, lighting a cigar at the bar. Mick Brightman, Jerry Wilson and the new bass player stood close by. They raised their glasses as he entered.

After mingling for a while, Andrei and his family were eventually seated at their own table. He was intrigued by the five remaining empty chairs.

'I think champagne might be in order,' Levin said, reaching into the air with a click of his fingers.

The small band stopped what they were playing and immediately struck up again with a lively *Mazurca*, a Polish folk song that Andrei had not heard since his youth. He looked baffled. 'What the hell's going on, Doug?'

'Hey, I just do what I'm told. You'd better ask the wine waiter.'

Andrei twisted round in his chair to see a heavily built man, with close-cropped hair and a mischievous grin, walking towards him, bearing champagne in a silver ice bucket.

'The service in this place is awful,' shouted the gruff voice. 'Do you realise we've been waiting sixteen years for this.'

It took a moment for the speechless pop star to grasp what was happening. Then it struck him: the inflection in the voice, that grin, those eyes.

'*Yakov?* Yakov Bronovitch…is that you?'

Jack laid the ice bucket on the table and looked down at his friend. His face became serious. 'Yes, Andrei, it's me, just another bloody immigrant who changed his name to Jack Bronson.' He looked around at the assembled crowd. 'The last Christmas Eve I spent with this man was as a child in Poland when I was lucky enough to discover the all-important star that night. Well, it looks like I've done it again. Ladies and gentlemen, I give you…*Andy Rivers!*'

Andrei rose to his feet. Jack looked him up and down and slowly spread his arms. They joined together in a warm embrace, to spirited applause.

*

It proved to be an emotional evening. Andrei

needed no introductions to Sandra and Lucy who were thrilled to witness the heart-warming reunion of the two men. He was particularly pleased to meet up again with his grandmother's friend, Mrs Hurwitz, whose kindness and generosity had given Yakov his new life.

When talking with the Wolenskis, Mrs Hurwitz had not been surprised to learn about Grandma Anna's passing, but was still saddened by the news. Likewise, they were sorry to hear about the loss of her husband. She was quick to steer their conversation away from the circumstances of his death.

By the early hours of the morning, Doug Levin had taken to the dance floor with Lucy. He finally appreciated the true reason for all the secretive arrangements insisted upon by his boss, and wondered how things might change now that the two men had been brought together again after so many years. Sandra had chosen to remain with the other women, enthralled by their stories of survival in war-torn Poland.

Andrei had become accustomed to leading a double life as himself and the superstar, Andy Rivers, but he found it strange hearing people address his friend as Jack Bronson. No one knew him as Yakov Bronovitch anymore. The two friends were sitting at the bar, their reminiscing finally exhausted.

'Doug tells me you have a busy time ahead of you next year. Another album, and a European tour,' Jack said, swirling the remnants of a cognac around his brandy balloon.

'That's right. We release our second album at

the end of March followed by a three month stint in Europe, finishing up at the Mojo Club in Hamburg.'

'Ah yes, Hamburg. Wasn't that where it all began with Ben Sharmer?'

'It was. But it seems a long time ago now,' Andrei mused. He turned to look at his friend. 'You know, Yakov, I can't believe that it's taken this long for us to meet. Don't you take *any* interest in the agency?'

Jack took pleasure in the sound of his old name. 'Andrei, you sound like my wife,' he laughed. 'Of course I'm interested in the agency, but only as a business, and a business has to show a profit. I saw you and your band as a lucrative cash cow. Be fair, this tall, handsome guitarist with the trendy ponytail is a far cry from the little blond kid I knew back in Poland. It wasn't until I saw the talisman around your neck in that newspaper photograph that I realised who you were. That came as one hell of a shock I can tell you. But I just knew you were innocent, and had to help,' he lied, wrestling with his conscience, trying to suppress the guilt of having almost murdered his childhood friend. 'Okay, so you got yourself involved with the wrong people, it happens. It must be difficult in your position, being surrounded by all those fawning idiots.'

'But why pay my legal fees, with all that cloak and dagger stuff? The sight of your face would have meant more to me than the money.'

'I just felt I owed you. And I'm a private person, Andrei. Can you imagine the media attention I would have received had I revealed my identity?'

Jack said, knowing he could never disclose the truth to his friend: a gangster posing as a respectable businessman. 'Am I so different from you? You are forced to maintain your public image as the famous Andy Rivers, but privately you must yearn for those moments when you can simply be Andrei Wolenski. No, it was better for me that way. And the final outcome was a great success. I always get what I want, and I wanted you out of harm's way. It was the very least I could do after what you did for me back in Kielce.'

'That was a long time ago, Yakov. Anyone would have done the same for a friend,' Andrei said, with deep sincerity, laying his hand on the man's arm.

Andrei's touch sent a quiver of emotion through Jack. He laughed to lighten the moment. 'Hey, you'll have me getting all sentimental. This is meant to be a happy occasion. We're together again. What could be better?'

Andrei remained serious. 'Yakov, without sounding ungrateful, was it really necessary for that damn barrister to denounce Mark the way he did? That was unforgivable.'

Jack was suddenly defensive, unsure how to answer. 'I have to agree, it was most unfortunate, Andrei. What can I say? We were in that lawyer's hands. And anyway, I had no idea that you and Jacobs were...well, you know...'

'Lovers? No, not many people did,' Andrei said, quick to ease his friend's discomfort. 'I'm sorry if it caused any problems for the agency.'

Jack put his arm around Andrei's shoulder.

'No, *I'm* sorry for the loss of your friend. You have nothing to apologise for, Andrei.'

The two men sat in silence for a while, reflecting on their conversation.

'It's strange isn't it, who would have thought that we'd be sat here together again as such wealthy men,' Jack said, handing his empty glass to the barman. 'We've come a long way since Kielce.'

'We certainly have,' Andrei agreed. He cocked his head with an inquisitive smile. 'Tell me, Yakov, what else are you involved in apart from the agency and the club? Your wife tells me you have many other business interests.'

'That's right. In fact too many to mention right now. But soon all of that will be over. I have one major deal to finalise in the New Year, before I leave it all behind. And then, my friend, we can spend more time together. But for now we'll keep that between ourselves.'

He reached for his freshly filled glass and toasted Andrei with a confidential wink.

Chapter 36

Levin sat in the back seat of the Rolls-Royce, gazing directly between the broad shoulders of two bodyguards. The object of his attention was a brown and cream Rover parked directly in front of them on the Vauxhall Embankment. Regardless of assurances that his boss would be unharmed, he was taking no chances. The meeting had been called by Robson who insisted they be alone, reasoning that the fewer people involved in the initial planning of the operation the less likelihood there would be of any leaks. Appreciating the risks involved to himself, Jack was more than agreeable to the arrangement.

After twenty minutes had passed, Levin was relieved to see his friend emerge from the steamed-up vehicle, draw up the collar of his sheepskin, and hurry back to the car.

'It's bloody cold out there,' Jack complained, pulling the door shut. 'Let's get out of here. I need a drink.'

Levin endorsed the command with a brief glance towards the driver who had been watching attentively through the rear-view mirror. The powerful V8 engine hummed into life, and soon the white Rolls-Royce was cutting swiftly through the freezing January mist.

*

Soho was still sleeping. A solitary street cleaner pushed his broom along the littered pavement. His breath billowed white into the chill, early morning air as he quietly cursed the idle rich after their Saturday night's revelry. He barely noticed two cars glide passed him to draw up outside the Pink Pelican. Their doors opened simultaneously, allowing four black men to step out from each vehicle into the watery sunshine. Two of them walked straight into the nightclub, while the others routinely scanned the deserted street through their tinted glasses before following.

The house lights were up, giving the club's interior the appearance of a spacious boardroom. A row of tables had been pushed together surrounded by enough chairs to accommodate those who were about to attend the meeting. The daunting figure of Jack Bronson was already seated at the head of the table with three men to his right, while their respective bodyguards stood positioned around the perimeter walls. Levin paced slowly behind Jack.

Clive Remus paused at the edge of the dance floor. He foppishly peeled off his leather gloves and slipped out of his coat, handing them to the man beside him. Smoothing down his blue mohair jacket, he eyed Jack with a defiant smirk. The disfigurement across his left cheek stretched into an ugly red weal.

'Good morning, Clive,' Jack said. 'You see how civilised it can be with a proper invitation. I'm pleased you've decided to come.'

The mobster fingered his deep facial scar. 'Perhaps I was a little hasty before.'

Jack ignored the remark and gestured to the three Irishmen. 'These are the people who'll be working with us, James Doyle, Dennis Flynn and Patrick O'Neil. Guys, meet Clive Remus,' he said, looking towards the black mobster.

'Must get a lot of sunshine in south London,' Dennis Flynn slipped out, straight faced.

Clive Remus glowered at Flynn, holding out an arm to prevent his minders from stepping forward. 'Easy, fellas, he's just a dumb fucking Irishman.'

'Not so much of the dumb,' Flynn replied, enjoying the wind-up.

'Leave it alone, Dennis,' Doyle ordered. 'You must forgive my friend, Mr Remus. He's never been fond of the coloureds.'

'Okay, you've had your fun,' Jack cut in firmly. 'My patience is limited, and so is my time. This is how it works. Clive, you and one of your associates will join us at the table. The rest of your men can remain standing alongside ours and watch one another. That way we'll all feel comfortable.'

Levin pulled out a chair next to his boss, signalling Remus and his gang member to follow suit.

'One of the reasons for this meeting was to introduce you all to one another,' Jack began. 'It's good to know who you'll be working with. Well, maybe not for Dennis and Clive,' he dropped in with a thin smile. 'But the main reason is to collect your stake money. The Colombians have advised me that the shipment will be arriving at the beginning of April, and they want their money. I'm meeting with them in two weeks time. I trust that is convenient for everyone?'

'Of course, although a couple of years ago things were a bit tight, no thanks to you, you bastard,' Remus replied. His lips parted into a crooked grin, revealing a glimmer of gold tooth.

'Glad you haven't lost your sense of humour, Clive. But that's how it goes. You hit me, so I hit you back. No big thing.'

'You're right. No big thing,' Remus repeated. 'How do I know I can trust you, Jack?'

'Trust is bullshit, Clive. Now stop sodding around. Are you in, or out?'

Remus sighed. 'Never a straight answer, eh? What the hell, I'm in. But I'll be watching my back.' He turned in his chair and beckoned one of his men to lay a suitcase on the table.

'And now yours, James,' said Jack.

Doyle lifted his hand: a signal for another suitcase to be brought forward.

Levin got up, reached for the cases, and carried them away.

'Doug needs to count the stuff. I'm sure you understand,' said Jack. 'We don't want to come up short. These Colombians are not the sort of people you upset. They're unforgiving bastards, but at least you know where you stand with them.'

'So apart from the drugs, how's the rest of the money going to be spent?' asked Patrick O'Neil.

'Fair question,' Jack replied. 'There are the

crews of two ships to sweeten, not to mention a bunch of corrupt security officers and border guards. We'll also need a couple of trucks and four powerboats, all of which will be burnt out after we've finished with them. The same goes for the Land Rovers, or whatever else we need, to get the crates off the beaches. We're leaving nothing behind that might incriminate us.'

'How long before we get paid?' said Remus.

'Not easy to answer that, Clive. It shouldn't take long to distribute the gear in the UK, in fact that will be down to you, but it might take a little longer in Europe. I've got an efficient German outfit handling things over there, and I have every faith in them. As soon as I get all the payments in, we can meet at my warehouse to collect our share of the money. Is everyone in agreement with that?'

Doyle looked apprehensive. 'Do you expect *all* of us to be there? Couldn't that be dangerous? I mean you're somewhat of a celebrity with the police. They could be watching the damn place.'

'You have a point, Jimmy,' Jack conceded. 'But that won't be a problem. There are plenty of other places in the area we could choose if it makes you feel more comfortable. And if you'd rather not be there to collect your money, send someone else. But bear in mind there are too many bloody thieves in my organisation to guarantee you wouldn't get robbed. Christ, I wouldn't want that responsibility.'

'Don't worry guys. I'll be happy to look after your share,' Remus sniggered, looking directly at Dennis Flynn who glowered back at him.

Doyle shrugged his acceptance. 'You've made your point, Jack. Just phone us with the time and place.'

Jack breathed an inward sigh of relief. For a moment he thought the Irishmen were going to be difficult about the meet. His cautionary bluff had worked.

'I knew common sense would prevail,' he said. 'Okay, that's enough business for now. Why don't you all join me at the bar for a small celebration? We're going to be extremely rich men.'

*

Leafless trees allowed broken bursts of sunlight to glint across the car's gleaming bonnet as it cruised through the Surrey lanes. The conversation had been sparse during their journey back from London. Jack's mind was elsewhere, his eyes allowing the bleak landscape to slip by without recognition.

Their meeting at the club had gone well enough, and the carefully structured plan was falling into place. The thought of getting out of the filthy business he was in, with a small fortune at his disposal, was appealing to Jack. But he was not happy; he knew Robson was lying. The man was not the Operations Controller of MI5 for nothing. It required a ruthless streak to run a secret service agency. Honesty and fair play were pointless considerations.

'We're going to need insurance, Doug,' he said suddenly.

There was a short, confused silence.

'Sorry?'

'Are you happy to be getting out the business?'

'I guess so,' said Levin.

'And do you want to enjoy your retirement with Lucy?'

'Of course I do. Sorry, Jack, what are you getting at?'

'There's no point in making all that money if we don't live to enjoy it, right?'

'Of course not.'

'Then we need a *get out of jail* card. Do you honestly think Robson is going to let us live? When we set up the Irish, he'll kill the bloody lot of us.'

'Christ, do you think so? What about the amnesty?'

'You're being naïve, Doug. You've got fat and lazy,' Jack laughed, digging his friend in the ribs.

Levin countered with a good-natured jab to Jack's shoulder. 'Seriously though, what are you suggesting?'

'We'll discuss it tomorrow,' Jack replied, as the Rolls-Royce pulled up outside Greystone Manor.

'Does Sandra know about our plans?' Levin asked, watching the electrically powered gates swing open.

'No, not yet, I'll tell her today. I've invited Andrei and his family over for lunch. It'll be the last chance we'll get to see one another before his European tour. I thought it would be a good opportunity to wish him luck, and announce our retirement at the same time. And there's something you can do for me. I want to take us all out for dinner at the best restaurant in Hamburg after his final gig. Can you organise that?'

'Leave it to me, Jack. I think it's a great idea.'

Andrei's Bentley was already parked alongside the stone steps that climbed to the entrance of the house, where Sandra's petite figure stood waiting to welcome them.

Later that evening, Jack's news was greeted with mixed reactions. Sandra was ecstatic. The end of her husband's criminal involvement meant no longer having to live in constant fear for his safety. She looked forward to a life full of holidays and family activities. Andrei, who had been expecting the announcement, welcomed the opportunity of spending time with his boyhood friend, and discovering the secrets of his success.

Mrs Hurwitz smiled a lot, but said little.

*

Two rapid taps on the door announced Peter McCann's arrival.

'Come in and sit down,' Robson said, signing off a few official papers. 'I've just heard from my Irishman. It's all set up for the last Saturday in April.'

'Who *is* this informant? Is he reliable?'

'You know better than to ask those sort of questions, McCann. And yes, he is *very* reliable,' Robson snapped back.

McCann shrugged off the reprimand. 'Fair enough, then we need to get organised. Any idea where the meeting will take place?'

Robson finished writing and looked up. 'No, not yet, it looks like being a last minute decision. Apparently our IRA friends were jumpy about being there, but it seems Bronson has managed to persuade them. Let's hope it all works out? How many men will you need?'

'I was planning on six officers and myself. They're all top marksmen, and well disciplined. None of us will be carrying identification, so if anyone doesn't make it nothing will be traced back to the department. We'll be ready to move by road, or boat. Bronson not only has his warehouse at the East India Dock, but also various clubs and venues around London. We'll need as much notice as possible from your informant.'

'He's fully aware of that. As soon as he finds out we'll be the first to know.

'I assume we're taking *all* of them out?' McCann asked.

'You assume correctly,' the Controller replied bluntly. 'I don't honour deals with gangsters.'

'Do we know how many will be there?'

'About twelve at the moment, but that could change,' said Robson. 'I doubt it will be a walk in the park, McCann. They're all dangerous buggers, and they'll be armed.'

'I'm ready for that, sir. It's in my job description,' he replied with an impertinent grin.

Chapter 37

Leaving his men in the car, Jack paused briefly to look up at the fading facia that read *'Sam's Café'*. Apart from needing a coat of paint, everything was exactly as he remembered it. The *'CLOSED'* sign was displayed, but Mrs Hurwitz had left the door unlocked in readiness for her son's visit. He found his mother sitting at one of the tables, toying with an empty cup.

'Sorry I'm late,' he said, bending forward to kiss her cheek, noticing her stiffen slightly. 'It's good to see the old place again, but you shouldn't still be working. I wish you'd consider selling up.'

'And do what, Jack? Where would I go? This is my home. It's where my Samuel is.'

Jack had always regretted his father's death. His mother would simply not accept that it was a cruel world out there. He was only trying to make things right, redress the balance, but there was no point in pursuing the subject.

'Mum, I have a favour to ask.'

'So, ask.'

'I need somewhere quiet to meet in this area with Doug, and a couple of other guys, on Saturday evening at about nine o'clock. This place would be perfect.'

Mrs Hurwitz reached across the table, clutching

her son's hand in one final plea. 'Jack...*Yakov, please*, no more. Whatever you're planning, I *beg* of you not to do it.'

Jack hated seeing her this way. It would be his last job, and soon it would all be over. He desperately wanted to explain the situation, but one look at her face told him it would be a waste of time.

'Please, try not to worry, everything will be fine,' he said, gently folding his other hand over hers.

The warmth faded from her eyes. Her voice was harsh. 'Very well, do what you must. I'll expect you Saturday night.' She snatched her hand back and got to her feet.

Jack ached watching her walk away. He tried to call after her, but the words froze on his lips. The flat door banged shut, leaving him alone in the empty café.

The cold rejection had been a painful reminder of how much he still missed his mother's affection. He slumped back into the chair and closed his eyes, imagining the sounds of clattering dishes and chattering customers. He recalled the satisfying experience of relaxing with his parents after a hard day's work just to earn a modest income. It all seemed a long time ago. His life had changed out of all recognition. Had he been happier then?

A group of youngsters passing by outside suddenly burst into raucous laughter. His eyes sprung open, banishing his thoughts. He took a slow look around, before getting up to walk to the flat door.

'I'm off now, Mum. See you on Saturday. Don't forget to lock up.'

There was no answer.

Chapter 38

It was Saturday morning. McCann and his team would be hitting Bronson and his IRA collaborators that evening. Jan Stevens had just seen him and Robson leave the building. They had caused a rush of activity in the department, discussing final preparations for the mission, and now the place had lapsed into a quiet murmur of operational routine.

She sat at her desk, doodling an intricate pattern of squares on her blotting pad, bored and irritated by the way Robson had excluded her from the assault team. She had completed her firearms training successfully and was in good physical shape. She and McCann made a good team.

Robson was a decent boss: shrewd, protective, loyal to his officers, and fearless in his undertakings. Stevens often wondered if he stretched his protectiveness a little too far where she was concerned. But she valued her job too much to dare challenge him about it. He could be extremely volatile when upset: one of his few emotions that occasionally surfaced.

Although there was no personal attraction between her and McCann, she still held a soft spot for the man and feared for his safety. The young officer could be rebellious at times, and not known for his diplomacy, but she secretly admired his attitude. She saw him as a young Robson in the making.

One of her colleagues shouted across the open plan office.

'There's a call for you, Jan. Line three.'

She lifted the phone and pressed the button.

'Jan Stevens.'

A man's hushed voice answered. 'I know Robson's your boss, and I have important information for him.'

'I'm afraid you've just missed him,' she said, checking to see if there was anyone more senior to take the call.

'I'm aware of that. That's why I'm talking to *you*,' said the man, sounding irritated. 'It's to do with this evening's assignment, and it's urgent.'

An alert registered in her brain. She knew Robson's informant was Irish, and this person had no such accent. He would also have used the scrambler.

'Okay, so what's the message?' she asked suspiciously.

'I can't give it to you on an open line, you idiot. Meet me outside on the corner of Gower Street.'

Stevens mind was racing in different directions. *The guy just answered my question about the phone, so he obviously knows the procedure. He has to be genuine. Should I take another officer with me? To hell with it, I'm a big girl, and it's only just outside the building. This would keep me involved, and give me a genuine reason to contact Robson with important intelligence. It's got to be done.* 'Okay, but how will

I recognise you?' she asked.

'It doesn't matter. I know what you look like. Be there in five minutes.'

The man hung up.

Jan Stevens retrieved her bag and got to her feet. The prospect of a clandestine meeting with an unknown caller caused a sudden surge of adrenalin.

'I won't be long,' she shouted to the colleague who had patched the call through to her.

He waved a response and went back to his paperwork.

*

Robson was back in his office. He and McCann had returned to MI5 HQ with their Director General earlier that afternoon after a meeting with the Home Secretary. Assurances that their covert operation would eradicate the three main ringleaders of the IRA's 'Operation Harvest', that had plagued the British Government for the last few years, had been met with enthusiastic approval. And disposing of Jack Bronson, London's most notorious gangster, was seen as a most welcome bonus. Robson's plan had originally been dismissed out of hand by the Director General, but the man's sudden change of heart in front of the Home Secretary, wallowing in the glory of its initiative, had tested Robson's patience to the limit, leaving him in a cantankerous mood.

Unfortunately, his temper had not been improved by the latest incident. Robson had been disturbed by Stevens' disappearance after she had left the office that morning without explanation. His concern had been justified. He crashed down the phone, livid at Bronson's audacity. He had been expecting a call from his informant, confirming the location of the evening's meeting, but not from Jack Bronson telling him that one of his officers, Jan Stevens, would be held as *insurance* until the operation was completed.

'Do we call off the mission, sir?' McCann asked, fearful for his fellow officer's safety.

'Absolutely not,' was Robson's curt reply. 'As soon as we know where the meeting will be, we proceed as planned. Stevens was bloody careless in allowing herself to be taken. But I'm confident that she'll suffer no harm, except possibly to her pride. It means that you and your team will have to be particularly careful not to harm Bronson and his men. You said they were marksmen. Well now is their time to prove it.'

'Did he say where they're going to meet?'

'No. He knows we have a mole in his camp, and we'll find out anyway. He's playing everything close to his chest now.'

'I'm sorry, I don't like it' McCann argued. 'Anything can happen in those situations. It's too dangerous. One mistake and Bronson's men would kill her. He's a bastard, sir. And he'd do it.'

'I'm not interested in your opinion, McCann,' Robson said darkly. 'After what we've just committed our department to in front of the Home Secretary, there's no turning back. It'll be bad enough having to spare Bronson, let alone call the whole thing off. Sorry, it's not negotiable.

Either you carry this through, or I'll assign another officer to the task. It's your decision.'

'Very well, but it'll be on *your* head,' McCann answered rudely.

'I'll pretend I didn't hear that,' said the Controller. 'Now bugger off and simmer down. I'll see you later at the briefing.'

*

Mrs Hurwitz had left the four men in the café and returned upstairs to her flat. She sat on the landing, feeling miserably alone, listening tearfully to every word of her son's conversation drifting up the stairwell, all uttered with no hint of conscience or remorse.

Jack was explaining to Doug Levin, and two gang members, how they would be attacked by government agents during the coming meeting. He gave them his assurance that they would not be harmed because of the hostage he had taken. The prospect of receiving their partner's share of the money was reward enough to risk the hazardous undertaking.

The harsh reality of his criminal involvement cut deep into his mother's soul. The resentment she now harboured towards him was beyond forgiveness. She had lost her son; he had become a stranger to her.

*

A full moon shone across the East India Dock. The distant masts and funnels of rusting cargo ships created jagged shapes silhouetted against the night sky, forming a bleak backdrop to the isolated pier looming from the dark, lapping water of the River Thames.

Jack Bronson, Levin, Remus and four gang members were standing alongside the Rolls-Royce and a white van that were parked facing the river at the end of the jetty. Clive Remus and his two bodyguards were blithely unaware of why their four associates had distanced themselves from them. The men watched as two sets of headlights approached the pier. One car stopped at the entrance, while the other continued cautiously down the wooden landing stage to draw up a short distance in front of them.

'Okay, this is it. When I give the word move fast. You won't get a second chance,' Jack whispered sharply, barely moving his lips.

His three companions mumbled a nervous response. They watched Jack step forward to greet the four men who were exiting the cars. Two of the Irishmen drew revolvers, levelled towards Jack and his associates. Remus's face hardened. Jack cast a warning glance at his party; he didn't need any reckless moves. The elderly figure of James Doyle walked towards them, accompanied by Dennis Flynn.

Jack shook their hands. 'Good evening, Jimmy. Why the guns, don't you trust us?'

'Nothing personal, Jack, just business,' said Doyle.

'Where's Patrick?' asked Jack.

'What's it to you? Do you have a thing about Irish boys?' Flynn taunted, predictably offensive.

Jack bit his lip. Levin wondered how much more abuse his friend would tolerate from the man.

Doyle shrugged. 'Dennis's idea of a joke, Jack,

but to answer your question, O'Neil's waiting in the other car. We thought it would be sensible for one of us to keep an eye out for any intruders. It *is* the only way in and out of this jetty.'

'If it makes you happy,' Jack grumbled. *MI5 can worry about that one,* he thought briefly.

'So are we getting our money, or what?' Flynn demanded. 'We've got a load of guns to buy if we're going to throw you bastards out of our country.'

'Dennis, I can put up with most of your crap,' Jack answered, surprisingly calm, 'but don't *ever* accuse me of being British. I'm just a hard working immigrant, and proud of it.' He looked over his shoulder. 'You heard them. They want to see their money.'

The Irishmen could hardly believe their eyes as Clive Remus signalled his men to pull open the double doors of the van to reveal countless bales of bank notes tightly stacked up to the roof of the vehicle.

At that precise moment, shadowy figures, wearing black combats and balaclavas, materialised silently out of the darkness above the sides of the jetty. The sound of clattering canisters was swiftly followed by an intense hissing as billowing, acrid smoke engulfed the pier. The IRA gunmen swung round, loosing off a couple of rounds into the haze.

'Down! Get down! Now!' Jack yelled.

His warning was almost lost in thunderous gunfire flaming out of the darkness as Sterling sub-machine guns delivered their deadly payload into the gathering of screaming men, cutting them to pieces where they stood. Jack and his companions flattened themselves to the ground, clamping their hands over their ears, their bodies flinching wildly under the violent onslaught.

It ended abruptly. A few moments passed before their ravaged senses adjusted to the distant drone of outboard engines powering a clutch of inflatable dinghies back up river.

The four shaken survivors climbed to their feet with handkerchiefs pressed over their mouths against the spent tear gas drifting away into the night. They peered cautiously into the surrounding darkness, guns drawn. Jack turned at the sound of squealing tyres to see Patrick O'Neil's car hurtling away into the night. He wondered how the man would explain this away to his IRA henchmen.

'You won't need the guns,' Jack said, surveying the aftermath with cruel satisfaction.

He wandered between the seven contorted bodies that lay, covered in blood, ripped apart by the savage torrent of split-nosed shells. James *Jimmy* Doyle was staring sightlessly into the moonlight, a look of horrified astonishment set across his pallid face.

Jack formed a grim smile. 'As you said, Jimmy boy, nothing personal, just business. And as for you, you insolent bastard,' he said, studying the remains of Dennis Flynn. 'The only Irish boys I like are dead ones.'

He promptly kicked the bloodied corpse in the head.

'That's *enough*, Jack,' Levin shouted forcefully. 'Don't you think we should be leaving? It's going be full of coppers, very soon.'

The distant sound of sirens could be heard, clearing a path for the squad cars that were already racing towards the river.

'You're right,' Jack called back. 'Let's get the hell out of here.'

One of his men secured the doors of the van and climbed into the cab to start the engine. Jack looked across at the body of Clive Remus.

'So much for watching his back, they hit him in the chest,' he laughed, stepping into the back of the Rolls-Royce.

*

Dark figures stood hidden in the shadows, guarding the warehouse entrance. Inside, the place was alive with activity. Jack and Doug Levin watched closely as gang members packed the vast amounts of cash into canvas bags ready to be flown to Switzerland in the early hours of the morning.

Once they were satisfied with the progress, they made their way to the end of the building and entered the office. Two men got up from a card game to greet their boss. Sitting beside the desk, a bitter-faced Jan Stevens angrily crushed out her cigarette.

'About bloody time,' she fumed, 'how dare you, Bronson. Get me out of here immediately.'

'I thought we might have a drink before you go, to celebrate our success,' he suggested.

'Screw you! I could lose my job over this.'

One of the men produced a bottle of Scotch and poured out three drinks. Levin took one, and Jack picked up the other two, offering a glass to the woman.

'Come on, no harm done. You're far too pretty to sack. Here, have a drink.'

'What the hell,' she relented, and gulped down the neat whisky, letting out a small gasp. The drink kicked her professionalism back in. 'I presume everything went to plan?'

'Let's just say your people were extremely efficient, and I'm glad to say their aim was good.'

'Robson's a professional. He would never deviate from a plan, unlike present company.' Her accusation was teamed with a look of disgust.

Jack refused to be goaded. 'That's because I didn't *allow* him to deviate from the plan. In fact I'm surprised that he underestimated me. You see I never trust anyone. That way I avoid disappointment, *and* stay alive.' His ruggedly handsome face held a stubborn smile.

'I've heard enough of your crap, Bronson. I just need to get out of this place, *if* that's alright?' Her tight-lipped response drew the conversation to a close.

'Of course, there's a car at your disposal,' Jack said casually. 'And give my regards to your boss. He should be reasonably pleased with the night's outcome. At least he got two of the Irishmen.'

One of the men moved forward to open the door.

Jan Stevens snatched up her bag and stopped to look straight into Jack's eyes. 'Would you really have been prepared to kill me?'

He dropped his smile. 'What do you think?'

She left without another word.

*

In the aftermath of the multiple shootings, high-ranking police officers were immediately summoned to MI5 HQ to attend a meeting with Mike Robson and his team in order to produce a credible press statement.

Expediency with the truth was finally decided upon by describing the incident as a failed drugs deal, culminating in a gunfight between South London gangsters and members of the IRA who had been looking to fund their subversive activities. It was expected that after the usual bout of media speculation, the whole affair would eventually be forgotten.

Chapter 39

Doug Levin met Patrick O'Neil at the entrance to the warehouse and led him through a gauntlet of heavily armed men towards the office at the end of the building. Jack had insisted upon maximum security; he was still alive, and that's how he intended to stay. MI5 would not be happy at having their plans disrupted. Their Controller was a determined individual who would stop at nothing to achieve his goal, and the young gangster had no intentions of allowing him to do so.

It had been just over a week since the attack on the jetty and Jack had wondered how long it would take for the IRA to contact him. O'Neil must have considered it necessary to allow the dust to settle, before phoning to arrange a meeting.

'Someone to see you, Jack,' Levin said, opening the door to usher in the Irishman.

'Good evening, Patrick. I see you're still in one piece. Can I offer you a drink?'

Patrick O'Neil glared across the desk. 'What the fuck happened out there? Who were those bastards? And how come you managed to survive?' he shouted.

'When your IRA guys started shooting, we just

hit the deck,' Jack replied quietly.

'And what about the money?'

'It wasn't touched, I salvaged the lot.'

'You mean those people, whoever they were, never took it?

'No, Patrick. They were government agents,' Jack said in an even tone.

O'Neil's temper began to settle. He looked guarded. 'You've got to be joking? How can you be sure?'

'Because they weren't interested in the money,' Jack answered, as if stating the obvious. 'They were there for one reason only, to *kill* all of us.'

There was a moment's silence.

'So Flynn was right,' O'Neil muttered. 'We have a rat in the camp.'

'Yes we do,' Jack said, becoming irritated by a conversation that was leading nowhere. It was time to reveal some stark facts. 'Sit down, Patrick. I have something to explain to you.'

The Irishman pulled up a chair.

'That rat in the camp, as you call him, shopped *me* to MI5 who then blackmailed me into setting up that meeting on the jetty. Their intention was to kill the three major players in the IRA, namely you and your friends, Doyle and Flynn. It didn't take a bloody genius to figure out that I would also be on their list. I run a huge crime syndicate. The bastards have been after me for years. Imagine how convenient that would have been for them. Gangsters and the IRA taken out in one hit, bloody perfect.'

O'Neil took a moment to reply. 'So it was *you* who betrayed us?'

'*No*, Patrick, it was the MI5 informer in *your* camp who betrayed us. What was I supposed to do? Lose out on a multi-million pound deal to save a madman like Dennis Flynn and his suicidal war against the British. I had no choice. It's called survival, my friend.'

The Irishman looked accusingly at Jack. 'Then how come they didn't kill you and your men? I think you're a lot cosier with MI5 than you'd have me believe.'

'You stupid sod, do you think they spared me for being a good boy,' Jack countered. 'I'm alive because I took one of their officers as insurance. A simple trade: our lives for their agent.'

'And what about Remus?'

'He was a bonus. The bastard's been a pain in my backside for a long time. I allowed them to do a small favour for me. So where do we go from here?' Jack asked, leaning back in his chair.

O'Neil looked hesitant; he was on dangerous ground.

'Well there'd be nothing gained by killing me would there,' he said warily. 'Look, I can't condone what you did, but I understand why you did it,' he said, letting out a long sigh. 'We've lost two of our most senior men. But our share of the money will go some way in appeasing my compatriots. I'll simply tell them it was this damn rat that shopped us to MI5. That way we can both walk away from this. I'm no Dennis Flynn, Jack, I'm a realist. It's far better to live and fight another day. Meanwhile, we'll have to flush out this bloody traitor.'

'That's good with me,' Jack said, feeling the

tension begin to ease. 'But I must be honest. After you disappeared, I couldn't risk the cash lying around. Most of it has already left the country. It might take a few days to get your money organised.'

'No problem. It'll give me time to prepare a story for the guys in Belfast. They're seriously angry men, baying for blood, but I'm sure the money will sweeten things. By the way, that was a ballsy move, kidnapping an MI5 agent. She must have been pissed off at being taken like that. It wouldn't have gone down well with her superiors.'

'Probably not,' Jack mumbled.

O'Neil got up to leave. 'Well if it's all the same to you, I'll be off. I could murder a pint. Call me when you've got the money.'

'As I said, it might take a couple of days,' Jack repeated. 'Why don't you show Patrick out, Doug?'

Jack watched the two men leave the office. A dark shadow fell across his face. *I never told him our hostage was a female?*

Chapter 40

A black Riley and a dark green Wolseley were parked opposite the entrance to a dilapidated block of flats. The car's occupants were armed. Robson had been advised by his informant that Bronson would be arriving at the rented flat in Paddington at six o'clock that evening to hand over the IRA's share of the money. It would be the perfect set-up. They would catch him red-handed, and he would be summarily killed while *resisting arrest*. McCann was behind the wheel of the Riley with another officer sat beside him. Robson was in the back seat, next to Jan Stevens, having decided to involve himself personally with the operation.

The Director General had managed to defer his meeting with the Home Secretary, reluctant to admit that one of his officers had been taken hostage by Jack Bronson, allowing the gangster to survive the shooting. MI5 would be made to look a laughing stock, and that would reflect directly upon him. His furious voice, demanding a successful outcome to the present assignment, still rang in Robson's ears. That's why the Controller had taken no chances by arriving an hour before Bronson's scheduled meeting. But that time had long passed and there was still no sign of activity.

'How long have we been here?' Robson asked, peering at the drab building.

McCann checked the time. 'Nearly three hours, sir. Do you think he's got wise to something and called it off?'

'But how would he know?' said Jan Stevens. 'Surely Bronson hasn't got someone inside MI5?'

'Impossible', said Robson. 'Only you, McCann and I knew about it. The other officers were pulled in literally just before we left HQ. I'm beginning to have a bad feeling about this.'

'Should we move in?' asked McCann.

'Have we got the back of the building covered?'

'Yes, sir.'

Robson didn't take long to decide. 'Right, let's do it.'

McCann left the car and gestured silently to the men in the other vehicle. Within seconds, eight armed officers were moving swiftly across the road towards the building's entrance.

*

Doug Levin extinguished the lights and turned off the engine. He left the Rolls-Royce and hurried up towards the front door of Greystone Manor to report on his successful assignment. Jack welcomed him in. The two men were soon settled down with a drink in the study.

'So you hit him early this morning?' Jack asked.

Levin grinned. 'That's right. We got the bastard out of bed.'

'I assume you had no trouble finding the place?'

'No, and what a shit hole it was too.'

'Very appropriate for a rat,' said Jack. 'Did he

have anything to say?'

'Not really, mind you, our boys were quite inventive. It would have been difficult to say anything after they'd dealt with him.'

'I suppose so,' Jack answered, with a cruel smile. 'And what about MI5, when did they turn up?'

'We left someone watching the building. They arrived in two cars about an hour before you were supposed to be there. They'll have sore arses by the time they make their move, which could be about now I guess,' he said, glancing at his watch. 'I can't see them hanging round much longer.'

'Good work, Doug. By the way, I just spoke with Andrei before you arrived,' Jack said, totally dismissing the previous topic. 'The tour has been a sell-out. He's looking forward to our night out in Hamburg next month. Hell, it'll be great to see the guy again.'

*

When they arrived on the second floor landing, Robson knocked loudly on the flat door. There was no answer. He stepped aside and signalled one of his men to break it down.

The burly officer tumbled through the doorway, followed by another who rapidly checked the place out, arms outstretched, with a double handgrip on his gun. Patrick O'Neil was tied to a chair facing the door.

Robson strode into the room, flanked by McCann and Stevens. He stopped in front of O'Neil's body. The Irishman had been garrotted by a length of wire, and his tongue had been cut out. The blood had congealed around his chin, suggesting he had been dead for some time before their arrival. A bloodstained scrap of paper was pinned to his pyjama jacket. Robson used a handkerchief to tug it free. He read the message.

'Punished for treachery, find yourself a new rat.'

'Short and to the point,' the Controller growled, showing the note to his officers. 'Bronson is proving to be an elusive bastard. But how the hell did he find out? O'Neil was one of our most experienced informants.'

'Probably through some stupid mistake,' said Jan Stevens. 'That's usually the way these things happen. And I'm the last one to point a finger,' she added, looking sadly at the mutilated body.

'Was he an MI5 officer?' McCann asked.

'Not exactly,' said Robson, 'but an extremely brave man, nonetheless.'

The young woman dragged her eyes from the gruesome sight to look at the Controller. 'How on earth did we manage to recruit a senior member of the IRA?'

Robson shrugged. 'Now he's dead I suppose there's no harm in telling you. Patrick O'Neil's father was an Englishman who married a local girl while working in Northern Ireland for a British manufacturing company. Being English, and living in the predominantly Catholic area of Londonderry, inevitably caused a great deal of resentment with some of the locals. Sadly, it resulted in the man being killed after a drunken brawl outside a local pub. It was no secret that young Patrick O'Neil had witnessed his father being beaten to death.'

'Poor kid,' McCann murmured.

'But why join the IRA after such a terrible experience? You'd have thought he'd hate the Irish after what they did to his father?' Stevens said, looking puzzled.

Robson lapsed into a grim smile. 'Oh, he hated them alright. So much so, that he channelled all that hate into becoming one of them in order to bring about as much chaos and discord into their ranks as he could. Once he had secured an important position within the Republican movement, he offered his services to us. The rest, as they say, is history.'

'Just like him, poor sod,' McCann remarked. 'What a horrible death.'

Robson ignored the comment and shifted into positive mode. 'Right, let's call in the incident team and get this lot cleared up. We'll meet in my office next Monday at ten o'clock sharp. I want a de-brief of the whole operation to date.'

*

Jack Bronson had been quick to inform the Republicans of Patrick O'Neil's death, and reveal his true identity. Their initial astonishment and disbelief at the news eventually turned to fury, instigating rigorous security checks into their members' backgrounds. It created the perfect scenario for Jack to explain their betrayal to MI5, resulting in the assassination of the IRA commanders. He lied about the cash being confiscated by the secret service and made much of the fact that his own partner, Clive Remus, had died in the attack, and how lucky he had been to survive himself. Finally, he made a point of informing the IRA that he would be winding up his drug smuggling operation now that MI5 had made his position untenable.

After the huge disruption in their ranks, their influential leaders disposed of, and the loss of desperately needed funding, the Irish Republican movement fell into disarray, seriously compromising their effectiveness. Any hope of resurrecting their border campaign had been finally dashed, bringing a fragile period of calm back to Northern Ireland.

Chapter 41

The de-briefing had done little to lessen Jan Stevens' acute embarrassment at being held as an unwilling guest of Jack Bronson. She was still riled by her stupidity in falling for such a ridiculously simple ploy: a phone call asking her to meet outside the building, leading her straight into the clutches of Bronson's thugs.

'I think we can safely congratulate ourselves on a successful conclusion where the Irish Republicans are concerned,' said Robson, 'but as for Bronson, that's another matter.' He levelled an anxious frown towards Jan Stevens. 'Shame about your visit to the warehouse. Had us all worried there for a while.'

Peter McCann felt some sympathy for his colleague. Their boss had a way of calling you an idiot, without actually saying it. The young woman knew it was best not to answer.

'Well, I mean, if McCann *had* been ordered to dispose of Bronson you'd have never drawn your pension would you? Let that be a lesson, Stevens. Don't ever drop your guard.'

She threw her eyes to the ceiling, missing the Controller's sly wink at McCann.

'Point taken, sir,' she breathed through gritted

teeth, feeling like a chastened schoolgirl. 'So what *is* to be done about Bronson?'

'I'm still considering the problem. We need to regain a few brownie points for the department. The Home Secretary wasn't best pleased at our failure to deliver Bronson's head on a plate. Mind you, it was worth it just to see the Director General squirm,' he chuckled.

'Why can't we simply eliminate him?' she grumbled.

Robson got up from his chair with a disapproving frown. 'There's nothing *simple* about eliminating someone, Stevens. We've already tried that twice, dammit. Bronson will have formed a ring of steel around himself now. If we stand any chance at all of nailing him, we need to catch him off guard. And there might just be an opportunity.'

His last comment was mumbled quietly to himself. He shoved his hands in his trouser pockets and began to pace the room with furrowed brows. After a long moment he stopped dead and turned to face his officers.

'Something rather strange has turned up out of the blue.'

They remained silent, looking intently towards their boss.

'Scotland Yard has contacted me with information they've received from the West German police. An Englishman has been arrested in Hamburg on charges of drug dealing. The man has given his name as Mark Jacobs, the one who did a runner after that Andy Rivers murder trial. They thought it might be of interest to us, considering Bronson's involvement with the agency that represents Rivers.'

'What are you suggesting, sir?' asked McCann.

'All in good time,' Robson replied. He folded his arms and leaned against the desk. 'I've been doing a little homework of my own. I picked up a copy of the *Melody Maker* newspaper, and it seems that this pop star, Andy Rivers, is appearing with his band in Hamburg next month. It will be the final performance of his European tour, and our friend, Mr Bronson, has every intention of being there.'

Jan Stevens looked intrigued. 'How can you be sure of that?'

'Because I asked Ben Sharmer, the man who runs his agency.'

'But surely he would have alerted Bronson straight away?'

'Why would he? He had no idea who I was.'

'How on earth did you get away with that?' she said.

'Not too difficult,' Robson replied airily. 'I had to adopt the coolest voice I could manage. I believe that's the correct terminology isn't it?'

McCann raised his eyebrows; Stevens suppressed a smile.

'Well anyway,' Robson went on, ' I told him I was promoting a pop festival on the Isle of Wight, and wanted to arrange a meeting with him and Bronson next month to discuss the possibility of booking the Blues Knights. Mr Sharmer told me, rather pompously, that matters like that were left to him, adding that Bronson would not have been available anyway, as he would be in Hamburg for the Blues Knights' final performance.'

Jan Stevens smiled. 'Very devious, sir, but what's your angle?'

Robson paused with a familiar gleam in his eyes. 'You are.'

Her mouth fell open.

'There are many ways to skin a cat, Stevens,' Robson replied. 'Go pack a bag and get your passport. You're going to spend a little time with the Hamburg Police. I'll explain everything on the way to the airport.'

*

'*There* you are. I've been looking all over for you,' Sandra said, entering the study, carrying her small son.

Mrs Hurwitz had arrived at Greystone Manor earlier that morning on one of her regular visits. She was sitting behind Jack's desk and looked startled by the interruption.

'I could have sworn Marek left his toy train in here. I've been searching everywhere for it,' she announced, getting up to fuss around the desk top.

The little boy fidgeted to get down at the sight of his grandmother. He was released to run into her arms for a hug.

'Don't worry. I'm sure it'll turn up. He's not exactly short on toys,' said his mother. 'Rachel, there's something I've been meaning to ask you.'

'Of course, what is it?' Mrs Hurwitz said, gathering up her grandson.

'Jack tells me you won't be coming to Hamburg with us next month.'

'It was kind of him to invite me. But to be honest, I really couldn't tolerate a long journey. And as much as I love Andrei, his music is a little too loud for my liking.'

'I can understand that, so I was wondering, why don't you stay here at the house and look after Marek for us? Obviously the staff will be around to help out. My parents did offer, but I would prefer him to be in his own home. What do you think? I've spoken to Jack and he thinks it's a great idea.'

'I should like that very much.' Mrs Hurwitz's reply seemed far away. There was a hint of dampness around her eyes.

'Are you alright, Rachel?'

'Yes I'm fine, my love, just tired. I haven't been sleeping too well lately,' she said, giving the child a kiss, before lowering him to his feet.

Sandra looked concerned. She gently took the old lady's hand. 'We were going outside for a walk. Why don't you join us?'

'What a good idea, I could do with a breath of air,' said Mrs Hurwitz, allowing herself to be led from the room.

*

Jan Stevens had disembarked from her Lufthansa flight to be greeted by two smartly dressed German police officers. She was amused by their stiff click of heels and firm handshakes. They escorted her out of the airport to a waiting BMW, and were soon speeding towards the city centre.

West Germany was still reeling from the huge import of drugs that had swamped Europe, some of which had crossed its own borders. Cocaine was fast becoming an escalating scourge, and the German authorities had been more than willing to join forces in a plan to stem the source of the evil trade.

As her journey came to an end she glanced up at a blue sign that read *'Polizei Hamburg'*, before the vehicle dropped down into an underground car park. Within minutes, the MI5 officer was being led along a series of brightly lit corridors to an office that bore the black painted inscription *'Polizeihauptkommissar'* across its glass door. She was offered a cup of strong coffee and left alone for few moments. Eventually, a tall, fair-haired police officer entered the room, removed his peaked cap, and stepped forward to shake her hand.

'You are the MI5 officer, Jan Stevens, I presume?' he said in guttural English. 'Please allow me to introduce myself. I am Police Captain Ernst Schuster.' His manner was polite, but formal.

'I suppose you are aware of the reason for my visit?' she said, placing her unfinished coffee on the desk.

'I have been briefed by my superiors and been instructed to afford you all the co-operation you require,' he answered. 'We have Mr Jacobs waiting in a cell downstairs. He is aware of your visit, but we have told him nothing about the reasons for it. You will appreciate that I am merely acting as a go-between. The people that hold the real authority are your opposite numbers in the BND, the West German National Security Agency. One of their officers will be on hand to finalise the details with you, assuming that you succeed in your efforts to coerce Mr Jacobs into this venture.'

'That sounds good to me, Captain Schuster,' said Stevens. 'And now I would like to meet with Jacobs. Time is of the essence you understand.'

'Of course, please follow me,' he replied, stepping back to open the office door.

When Jan Stevens entered the cell she was confronted by an unwashed, longhaired young man dressed in soiled jeans and a grubby black shirt. He was sitting on a firm, steel framed bed with his knees curled under him. She drew up a chair, having asked Captain Schuster to wait outside, and sat quietly looking at Mark Jacobs who stared back at her, saying nothing. The harsh neon light cast stark shadows around his eyes that were sunk deep into their sockets. His cheeks were drawn, with a yellow pallor to his skin. After a while he started to shiver and scratch at his arms: the first signs of withdrawal.

'Hi, Mark, my name is Jan,' she said suddenly.

His vacant stare didn't waver.

'I've come to offer you help. God knows, you look as if you could use some.'

'What could you possibly do for me?' he snivelled, drawing a sleeve across his nose.

The shadow of a smile crossed her face. *At least I've got him talking.* 'I know how badly you were treated, Mark, with all those terrible accusations that were made against you. And you were innocent weren't you. How would you like to see Andy Rivers again? I could easily arrange it. Did you know he'll be coming to Hamburg soon?'

'Of course I do, you stupid cow. This is where it all began, just him and me. What the hell is it to you, anyway? You know nothing,' he rambled. 'I loved Andrei...he was my life...you couldn't begin to understand...'

Stevens made a mental note. *So it's Andrei is it? This is good. I've got him on a roll.* 'You're right, Mark,' she replied. 'I could never understand how you feel about Andrei. There are many things I don't know. But I *do* know how much you'd like to take revenge on the bastard that did this to you.'

Another long pause followed, before the young addict rolled on to his back, trembling and hugging his sides. 'Christ, I need a fix,' he groaned.

Stevens retrieved a small paper packet from her bag and reached across to place it beside him. Mark Jacobs tore it open and immediately rubbed the white powdered contents into his gums. After a while the trembling subsided. He leant up on his elbow, suddenly coherent, focussing on Stevens' face.

'What the hell do you want from me?' he pleaded, tears forming in his eyes.

'Nothing, Mark, I want to do something *for* you. Listen carefully to what I'm about to tell you,' she said, holding up another small packet. 'All you have to do is point a gun at the man who ruined your life and pull the trigger. He's a bad man, Mark, a gangster. This is the man who took Andrei away from you, and denounced you as a homosexual. In fact, if you do this for me I can get you off this drugs charge. I can promise you a new life with Andrei, anywhere you choose. And okay, if you need a supply of the white stuff it can be arranged.'

Mark Jacobs looked back at her through a haze of confusion. 'Would it really bring Andrei back to me?' he whispered.

'Of course it would. He knows all about this. He can't wait to see you again,' she lied, bare faced. 'We'll take you to a restaurant and point the man out to you. He's called Jack Bronson. Once you shoot him, get back outside as quick as you can. We'll have a car waiting to take you away to a safe place. We're the police, Mark. You'll be doing this with the law on *your* side. You can either stay here and rot in this cell, or go far away with Andrei. What do you say?'

His confused mind was desperately trying to grasp what was being asked of him. *Kill Jack Bronson…a safe place with Andrei…far away…*

'Well, Mark? Will you do it…for Andrei?'

There was a short silence.

'Yes, I'll do it. I'll kill the bastard,' he sobbed.

Jan Stevens rose slowly to her feet. 'Good boy. We'll come for you in a couple of weeks. If there's anything you want, just ask,' she said, lobbing the remaining packet onto his bunk.

*

The Blues Knights were back in Hamburg. The tour had proved to be their most successful to date, gaining them another legion of fans across Europe. After the previous gigs, the Mojo Club would be tiny by comparison with an audience consisting mainly of the media and a gathering of show business personalities, together with a few fortunate fans who were wealthy enough to afford the exclusive tickets.

The management had allowed the famous group access to the empty club in the early hours of the morning. The next evening's performance would be the last of their current tour, and having not been back for three years Andrei wanted to familiarise himself with the place once again.

Nothing had changed much. If anything it looked worse than he remembered. The carpets were badly soiled: scorched by cigarette burns and imbedded with discarded chewing gum. Even the dim lighting couldn't disguise patches of paint peeling off its walls. It was hard to imagine how this shabby establishment could still command such an unrivalled reputation.

The new bass player was enjoying the novelty of wandering around the club, studying framed photos of other top names that had appeared at the legendary Reeperbahn venue. His fellow group members were sitting at a table, quietly sipping at their drinks.

Andrei was first to break the silence.

'I have mixed feelings about this gig...too many memories.'

Jerry Wilson dropped his voice tactfully. 'You're not alone. The new guy's great, but without Mark it all seems...oh, I don't know...'

Mick Brightman nodded slowly in agreement. 'You're out with your friend, Jack Bronson, after the gig aren't you?' he asked Andrei, turning the conversation.

'Yeah, that's right. My mother and sister will be

there too. Should be good. How about you guys?'

'Bed,' Mick Brightman said, putting down his empty glass.

'Who with?' Jerry Wilson laughed.

No I mean it, I'm bloody knackered. It's been a long four months.'

Chapter 42

Jack had invited his guests for a drink, providing an opportunity for them to relax and enjoy a quiet conversation before travelling to the Mojo Club for the Blues Knights' evening performance. They were seated on comfortable couches in the bar of the Fairmont Hotel, overlooking the Alster Lake. Streetlights on the surrounding road cast their glow over the surface of the water, enhancing the unusual feature that lay close to Hamburg's city centre.

'This must be the only pleasant view in Hamburg,' Marta Wolenski remarked. 'The rest of the city is so depressing. I suppose that's the price you pay for starting a world war.'

Maria looked through the large window with a wistful gaze. 'It is, mother, just like our little town of Kielce. It was beautiful until the Germans invaded. And now the communists have succeeded in destroying what's left of it with their hideous apartment blocks and oppressive regime.'

Sandra broke into a sympathetic smile. 'It must be heartbreaking for you both. But at least you're out of there now. You have a new life to look forward to. In fact, we all do,' she added, cuddling her husband's arm.

Jack grinned broadly: it was a sight rarely seen. 'I have to admit it sounds like a welcome prospect,' he said. 'Don't you agree, Doug?'

Doug Levin turned to Lucy who looked lovingly into his eyes. She caressed his face between her hands and drew him into a passionate kiss.

'I think that's answered my question,' said Jack.

Marta Wolenski smiled. 'Yakov, the last time I saw you this happy you were helping Andrei sort out presents under the Christmas tree.'

'Marta, no, please don't bring that up,' Sandra cautioned. 'He hates talking about those days.'

'That's okay, Sandra,' Jack said. 'It doesn't seem to matter anymore now that we're all together again.' He slid back his sleeve to check the time. 'Okay, drink up everyone. It's time we left. We have an important gig to go to.'

*

The Reeperbahn had descended into chaos. Animated waving by white-gloved traffic police did little to ease the congestion caused by the endless flow of limousines drawing up outside the Mojo Club. Only a privileged few would gain entrance to the place, but it hadn't deterred crowds of young people from lining the street, hoping to catch a glimpse of their heroes.

The dance floor had been sacrificed to accommodate the long list of guests still pouring into the club, allowing Jack's party to take a table directly in front of the stage.

'This is the second time my wife's seen The Blues Knights. She's becoming a regular groupie,' Jack teased, resting his arm around Sandra's shoulders.

His friends grinned back at him, while a waiter moved around the table filling their glasses. Lucy and Doug Levin were seated beside Sandra. Opposite them were Marta and Maria Wolenski, excitedly awaiting Andrei's performance. It would be the first time they had seen him on stage as the world famous Andy Rivers.

'To old friends,' Jack said, raising his glass towards the Wolenskis.

As they drank, the cellar darkened and the first crashing chords of the group's latest release ripped into the smoky atmosphere. Sandra snuggled closer to her husband. Her eyes grew expectantly as the crowd roared and spotlights swung onto the stage. Marta Wolenski was overcome by emotion. She gripped her daughter's hand, her heart swollen with pride at the sight of her handsome son being feted by his audience.

Having been partly responsible for his friend's success, Jack felt a warm sense of fulfilment. It went someway in repaying Andrei's courage and kindness in befriending a vulnerable, small Jewish boy all those years ago.

*

The long wheelbase Mercedes was swamped by a crush of teenagers as it drew up outside the fashionable restaurant. The combined efforts of its own commissionaires and a small army of policemen managed to hurry the pop star and his entourage inside, before the limousine slid away to park behind the building in readiness for a discreet departure later that night.

Ignoring the frowning disapproval of the officious maître d', smartly dressed customers were constantly approaching Andrei's table, begging for his autograph. He graciously obliged, signing napkins, shirt cuffs, menus, and anything else that was produced, much to the amusement of the others.

'I understand that girls throw their knickers at you,' Jack said, with a mischievous grin, receiving a sharp nudge from his wife.

'Sadly wasted on me, wouldn't you say?' Andrei quipped, to polite laughter around the table.

His mother and sister smiled dutifully.

'Excellent choice of restaurant, Doug,' Sandra broke in, desperate to change the subject, embarrassed by the two friend's banter. 'The food's great.'

Doug Levin raised his glass in acknowledgement: too busy chewing to speak.

*

The maître d' had been summoned to the front desk to greet two smartly dressed men who smiled courteously as he approached.

'Good evening, we have a reservation for two,' said a small, dapper man, with a soft Irish accent.

'Of course, sir, and what name would that be under?' asked the maître d', hovering his finger over the list of bookings.

'Doyle, Brendan Doyle,' the man replied.

'Ah yes, here it is. Would you be kind enough to follow me?'

The maître d' led the two men into the restaurant, winding his way between the tables.

'You'll be sitting close to a celebrity this evening,' he said importantly. 'We have the pop star, Andy Rivers, dining with us.'

'Is that right?' said the taller, heavier built man. 'Maybe we could get his autograph?'

Brendan Doyle smiled.

'I would ask you to refrain from doing that, sir, if you don't mind. Although I'm sorry to say that some of the guests have ignored my request. Apart from interrupting our celebrity's meal, it causes such disruption in the restaurant.'

'Don't worry,' said Doyle, 'we wouldn't dream of disrupting your restaurant would we, Michael?'

Michael pulled a serious face and shook his head.

'I appreciate that. Thank you, sir,' the maître d' said, seating them at their table. 'Enjoy your meal.' He summoned a waiter who immediately offered both men a leather bound menu.

Two weeks prior to the Irishmen's arrival in Hamburg, an anonymous phone call to the IRA had revealed Jack Bronson's involvement in their betrayal to the British secret service. James Doyle's son, Brendan, had been incensed, vowing to avenge his father's death at any cost. His IRA masters had been against the operation, reasoning that the risk was too great. But Brendan Doyle was adamant, and this was the moment he'd been waiting for. He allowed the waiter to leave before speaking quietly to his companion.

'We couldn't get much closer if we tried,' he said, peering across the top of his menu at

Bronson and his guests. 'When shall we hit the bastard?'

'Why wait? I'm not here for the fucking food,' said the burly Irishman, reaching inside his jacket.

"Hold on, just a minute,' Doyle warned. 'What the hell's *this?*'

He drew his colleague's attention to a man making his way unsteadily across the restaurant towards Bronson's table.

At that moment, Levin also noticed the same person approaching. 'These bloody fans, shall I have him turned away? We *are* trying to eat,' he complained.

'That's okay,' Andrei said charitably, 'one more won't make a difference.' He turned to look at the man, while the others went back to their meal.

Something was wrong. This individual looked dishevelled, out of place in the stylish surroundings. He appeared to be drunk, lurching between the tables. There was something disturbingly familiar about him. Andrei's concern began to escalate. His heart pounded in his chest. *I know this person...it can't be... surely?* He stared in shock as Mark Jacobs collided heavily against the table between the two Wolenski women who shrunk back in alarm. Their fellow diners glared angrily at the intruder.

'Good to meet you at last, Mr Bronson,' drawled the bedraggled man.

Jack was furious. 'Who the *hell* are you?'

Andrei was dumbstruck. He could only stare in horror as Mark Jacobs lifted his right arm to point a gun directly at Jack who stared back in disbelief.

Sandra screamed. Levin leapt to his feet and grabbed the man's arm, trying to wrestle him away from the table. Three ear-splitting shots rang out across the crowded restaurant. Doug Levin's chest was torn open, splattering blood across the starched white tablecloth. He stumbled back from Mark Jacobs, hovering bizarrely for a few seconds, before crashing headlong onto the table. His life had been literally blasted away at point blank range. The vacuum of stillness that followed was cut short by a piercing cry as Lucy threw herself over his body.

Mark Jacobs' sunken eyes turned towards Andrei, then without another word he dropped the gun and pushed himself from the table to stumble away, leaving pandemonium in his wake. Women screamed, men shouted, chairs and tables were thrown aside, scattering cutlery and shattering glasses. Andrei battled through the chaos in pursuit of his friend's shambolic figure that was now staggering into the street. The doormen stood back against the walls of the foyer, anxious to let the gunman leave the building.

'Mark! *Wait!*' Andrei yelled, running out onto the pavement. His voice was followed by a sharp clap of thunder, triggering the start of a summer storm. A few loyal fans, waiting patiently behind metal barriers, could not believe their good fortune at the unexpected treat of their idol emerging from the restaurant.

Mark Jacobs turned to look at his friend, oblivious to the sudden cloudburst that drenched him where he stood. Flashes of lightning revealed a pitiful smile framed by long strands of wet hair flattening against his pale face. As he reached out towards Andrei, a succession of loud booms sent him reeling backwards, crashing to the ground.

The fans' squeals of delight turned to screams of terror. Andrei instinctively dropped to his knee. The sound of a car engine roared into the distance, leaving Mark Jacobs lying motionless on his back.

*

Marta Wolenski embraced her weeping daughter. They remained in their chairs, frightened to move. Violence had become a way of life to them.

Jack's survival instinct kicked in. There was no time to explain anything to the Wolenskis. He managed to prise Lucy from Levin's body, and with Sandra's help, drag the sobbing woman through the sweltering kitchens to the rear of the building. Once outside, he bundled them into the waiting car.

The driver was already holding the powerful Mercedes in gear, revving the engine. He swung round in his seat. 'I heard gunshots. What the fuck's going on?'

'Just get us to the airfield,' Jack ordered. 'Go...*go!*'

Oncoming vehicles swerved to avoid the accelerating limousine as it swerved out of the back alley to fishtail down the flooded street, heading for the outskirts of the city.

*

Grappling their way through the heaving mass of diners, the two Irishmen finally made it from the building and sprinted for their car. This had not been expected, and the matter was still to be resolved. Their driver had seen Bronson's Mercedes emerge from behind the restaurant, and within seconds they were in pursuit.

*

The rain fell harder, and the blare of police klaxons grew louder. Surrounded by a silent gathering of sombre faces, Mark Jacobs lay in Andrei's arms, bleeding profusely from gaping gunshot wounds to his stomach. He urgently searched his friend's eyes, frantic to tell him everything while there was still time. *The solace found in hard drugs while sleeping rough in the backstreets of Hamburg where they had first met…the understanding woman who had befriended him, and fed his habit… who had offered him a chance to avenge the evil that had ruined his life…the understanding woman who had promised to reunite him with his beloved Andrei…who had promised him so much…*

In the twilight of his surreal world he had explained everything; but not a word had passed his lips as he clung to the sight of Andrei's face. The coldness continued to spread through his body, deadening the pain…until he felt nothing.

Andrei gently stroked his palm across Mark Jacobs' eyelids, settling him into eternal sleep. He cradled his dead partner closer to shelter him from the storm, overwhelmed by a rising pain of unbearable sorrow. His brain could simply not accept what he had just witnessed.

*

The nightmare scenario that Sandra had lived with all her married life had suddenly returned.

She stared out the window through mascara-streaked eyes, hugging Lucy tightly. Her girlfriend was in a deep state of shock. Sandra could only imagine the misery she was going through; she would be inconsolable. Lucy's idyllic world had been torn apart. Doug Levin, the stylish, immaculately groomed figure had been her hero as well as her lover, providing her with an exciting and prosperous lifestyle: her saviour from a drab existence in the East End of London. Her sobbing had given way to a soft moaning, hardly audible above the screaming engine as the driver hammered the car away from the city.

Jack sat beside the women, haunted by a vision of Levin's body. Questions were flashing across his mind. *I always said you couldn't trust poofs, and how did a little ponce like that get his hands on a gun? That junkie had definitely been put up to it. But who could have organized such a hit? We're in Germany for Christ's sake...*

'What the hell!' the driver shouted, as a dark saloon came streaking alongside them, ramming their car into the side of the road.

He slammed on his brakes and frantically spun the steering wheel in a desperate attempt to ward off the attack: but it was too late. They careered off the slippery road over a steep embankment, and rolled down into a waterlogged field.

When the metallic groaning of the stricken Mercedes eventually ceased, the dazed driver clambered from behind the wheel to help Jack heave the two women from the car. The menacing snap of a loaded magazine forced both men to look upwards. Three dark figures stood in the rain, framed against the headlights of their stationary vehicle, with guns raised to their shoulders.

'*Shit!*' was all Jack could utter before they opened fire.

He grabbed Sandra and pushed her ahead of him into the darkness of the field. She ran, crying hysterically, before falling headlong into a muddy furrow. Jack dived to the ground and dragged himself towards her in a frantic crab-crawl. Bursts of water kicked up from the hail of bullets rocketing into the sodden ground around him, threatening to tear into his flesh at any moment.

When the shooting finally stopped he played dead, lungs fit to rupture. He fought to stifle his heavy breathing, until the distant sound of clumping doors and the ignition of a car engine finally told him it was safe to move. Gasping for air, he hauled himself up from the clinging mud and dragged his feet towards Sandra. She was lying, motionless, face down in the field. Jack dropped to his knees and gently turned her round. Her eyes stared blankly into his; there was no sign of life. A shiver of dread racked his body. He gently gathered her into his arms and struggled to his feet. Hugging her tightly, he staggered back to the wrecked Mercedes.

They were all dead. Sandra, Lucy and the driver, mown down like rats in a barrel. Jack fell back against the car. His knees buckled, sliding him to the ground, with Sandra's lifeless body lying across his lap. It should have been him, not

Sandra. The one good thing in his life was gone forever. His eyes wandered over her bloodstained silk dress, and his tailored suit that was now ripped and caked with dirt: the affluent, successful couple, torn apart, wallowing in a sea of mud. He started to laugh hysterically at the horrific absurdity of it all, until the manic laughter turned to convulsive sobbing.

*

Robson stretched out his arms and broke into a wide yawn. He looked
at the clock on the wall. It was two thirty in the morning: time for another coffee. Rolling the stiffness from his neck, he began to ease his chair back from the desk just as the phone sprang to life. He snatched it up.

'Robson.'

'It's not good, sir.' Jan Stevens' voice sharpened his wits.

'What do you mean?'

'Bronson got away.'

'For God's sake, I don't believe it. What the hell happened?'

'Mark Jacobs blew it. Levin fought with him and got himself killed trying to save Bronson. I never did like the idea of using a drug addict.'

'Did the Germans deal with Jacobs?'

'Affirmative, sir, although I have to say, I didn't appreciate they were going to kill the poor sod.'

'Don't be naïve, Stevens. The man was expendable. At least he can't shout his mouth off,' Robson said coldly. 'Do we have any idea where Bronson is?'

'Afraid not, but I'm receiving reports from the

BND of an attempt on his life. His car was shot to pieces a few miles outside Hamburg, but there was no sign of him. Incredibly, he must have survived. Unfortunately, Bronson's wife was among the dead.'

'Poor cow, what the hell was that all about?' Robson hated collateral damage. It simply wasn't professional.

'I have no idea, but it bore the hallmark of the IRA. Maybe they got wind of his double cross? Anyway, whoever it was, it had nothing to do with us.'

'I'm glad to hear it. I've had the bloody Director General on my case all afternoon, wanting to know what you've been up to in Europe. He'll go ballistic when he hears the news,' said the bleary-eyed Controller. 'I'll need your report first thing in the morning.'

'You're all heart, sir.'

'*Goodnight*, Stevens.'

*

Jack's phone call had left the household numbed with grief. The little boy was happily enjoying his morning play beneath the gnarled boughs of a solitary oak tree, oblivious to the tragedy that had befallen him. His nanny sat nearby, attempting to preserve an air of normality.

Mrs Hurwitz was still in the study. She was sat hunched over the desk, grief-stricken, clutching at a photograph of Sandra and Marek grinning back at her from happier times. It had been her painful duty to inform Mr and Mrs Woodman of their daughter's death. The howl of anguish from Sandra's mother still rang in her ears.

Chapter 43

The nightmare had returned. Andy Rivers and the Blues Knights were emblazoned across the front pages once again. The Diamond Agency was in turmoil following the events in Hamburg. The truth about Jack Bronson's position as head of a huge crime syndicate had finally been revealed. There could be no more pretence of him being a respectable businessman. The staff had not appreciated the extent of his involvement with the agency, and regardless of assurances from Ben Sharmer that their positions were secure, most had already left to get jobs elsewhere.

Andrei hired a private plane to fly his family and the members of his band back to England to avoid the media scramble that would have greeted them on a scheduled flight. His journey had been spent in heated discussions with his fellow musicians. Although genuine in their belief that Andrei had been ignorant of Jack Bronson's criminal activities, they were deeply concerned about the band's future. It was decided to withdraw The Blues Knights from their current schedules: decisions would have to be made as to their future. Andrei had no idea where his friend, Yakov, might be. He hoped the man would contact him: there were many things that needed to be said.

The first thing Andrei did after arriving home was to telephone Mrs Hurwitz. It struck him how strangely detached she had become. He put it down to an older person's weary acceptance of life's tragedies. She explained that her son had been in contact with her, but gave no indication as to his whereabouts. Her intention was to stay at Greystone Manor until his return. Marek would continue to be cared for by the nanny who had remained loyal to the family. The latest disclosures in the papers didn't bother her: she was a professional, and the child's welfare was her only priority.

After the deaths in Hamburg, the English press had been quick to run stories about Mark Jacobs, reminding their readers of his involvement in the Andy Rivers murder trial. The hapless young man's previous association with Andy Rivers was inevitably dragged back into the spotlight. But the group's latest spate of notoriety was conveniently overshadowed by scandalous headlines beginning to emerge concerning the beleaguered Conservative government.

Having clung to power for as long as possible, it finally lost an election to the Labour Party in the autumn of 1964. The lurid sex and spy scandals, involving dangerous breaches of security, had eventually destroyed the government's credibility with the electorate.

Chapter 44

Robson never enjoyed talking with the Director General at the best of times, and this latest conversation had been no different. Jan Stevens was sitting in front of his desk, maintaining a diplomatic silence.

'Well I'm sure you got the gist of that,' he said, replacing the receiver. 'What with a new government, and Home Secretary, our Director General has been grovelling more earnestly than ever. If he was ordered to burn the bloody building down he would. Where's the man's balls?'

Jan Stevens laughed. 'Only he can answer that, sir.'

Robson returned a wry smile. 'As you've probably gathered, we have been given a list of new agendas, one of them being to leave Bronson alone. I suppose we had it coming after three failed attempts at killing him. The bastard's got a charmed life. Personally, I think it's wrong. The man's like a wounded animal. He'll be more dangerous than ever after the events in Hamburg.'

'It's a damn shame. McCann's got tabs on him at last. He's back in the country. Do we really have to let it go?' Jan Stevens said, looking disappointed.

'I'm afraid so. Nobody would like to see Jack Bronson put away more than me, but orders are orders. It's just a job, Stevens.'

Chapter 45

After the shootings in Hamburg, Jack Bronson had immediately contacted his German accomplices who were more than willing to offer their assistance. He had made a great deal of money for them and was worth looking after.

He had stayed in Germany for over three months: long enough to allow things to quieten down, and regain his mental composure. Losing Sandra had almost broken him. He drew some comfort in knowing that young Marek was being cared for, but his sole purpose now was to avenge his wife's death. His wealth and power were still intact, and he would harness those resources to achieve his goal. Having recently returned to England, his first intention was to contact Andrei.

Jack stood on the pavement of Cheyne Walk, holding a large bouquet of flowers, taking stock of his friend's impressive house. There had been many things going through his mind on the journey over to Chelsea. He climbed the steps to the front door with a heavy heart.

*

Andrei had made it clear to Ben Sharmer that his band would be withdrawing from their forthcoming commitments. The agent had no problem with his demands. Knowing how vengeful and dangerous Bronson would be after the death of his wife, and long standing friend, Doug Levin, Sharmer knew it was time to disappear. His days at the agency were over. But that wasn't before he had revealed to Andrei the true extent of Bronson's criminality. Andrei had listened to Sharmer's disclosures in a state of shock. His friend's descent into such a world of evil was almost impossible to comprehend.

Despite learning the truth, Andrei had been relieved to receive a call from Jack. Regardless of the shocking discoveries, he still held a deep fondness for the man and was pleased that he had come to no harm. Marta Wolenski and her daughter had also found it difficult to accept the reality of Jack's criminal existence, even after the trauma of witnessing the violence in Hamburg. They could not believe how anyone would want to kill the young man whose kindness and generosity had brought their family together again after so long.

Andrei had been preoccupied all morning at the thought of seeing his friend. He paced the living room, unable to relax. What would he say? How would the conversation start?

A soft chime echoed throughout the house.

Maria was first to get the door. She opened it to see Jack Bronson standing in front of her.

'Hello, Yakov', she said with a small smile.

He handed her the flowers. 'Hello again, Maria, these are for you and your mother.'

'They're beautiful, thank you,' she said, inviting him to enter.

Andrei arrived in the hallway at the same time as his mother. There was an awkward silence while the four of them faced one another.

Marta Wolenski rescued the moment. 'I'll make some coffee. Why don't you men go into the living room? Maria -'

'I know, mother', she laughed, 'I can help you in the kitchen.'

The small token of humour eased the tension.

'Shall we?' said Andrei, leading the way.

Jack unbuttoned his coat and took a seat on a crimson, regency striped sofa.

'Let me take your coat. You are staying aren't you?' said Andrei.

'Sadly, no,' Jack replied.

Andrei hid his disappointment, and settled on the edge of an armchair. 'Yakov, there is so much to discuss. I don't know where to start?'

'Yakov is gone, Andrei. I don't know him anymore,' Jack replied, with no hint of humour.

'How can you say that? You're still the same person you always were, just bigger and uglier,' Andrei teased, with a tentative smile.

'Bigger and uglier I would agree with, but the same person? I'm afraid not,' Jack said, becoming serious. 'As you will have gathered, I'm the boss of a large crime organisation. It's a choice I made a few years ago, and I make no excuses for myself. The way I see it, we live in a shitty world. I think recent events in Germany have proved me right.' He paused to collect himself as the memory of Sandra crept back into his mind.

'I'm not judging you, Yakov. But surely you can turn things around? You said yourself that you were going to leave all that behind,' Andrei reasoned.

Jack scowled. 'That was before those bastards killed my Sandra. I've lost my parents, my stepfather, and now my darling wife. I've had enough, Andrei. People are going to pay.' His voice lightened. 'Anyway, the reason I came here was to apologise for putting you and your family through that terrifying experience in Germany. It was stupid of me to involve you in my affairs. We have both risen from hardship, and reaped the spoils of our success, but we tread very different paths. You're a successful pop star, and I'm a successful gangster. You entertain people, and I kill people,' he said, with a humourless laugh

Andrei ignored the flippancy. 'What are you trying to say, Yakov?'

'I'm trying to say that I love you, Andrei. You're like a brother to me. And as my brother, I don't want any harm to befall you, or your family. I have things to do, things that you mustn't concern yourself with. And now, my friend, I must go. I've taken up too much of your time already,' he said, getting to his feet.

'Yakov, you can't just walk out on me again after all these years?' Andrei pleaded, his voice thick with emotion.

'You're not listening are you?' Jack said, laying a hand on Andrei's shoulder. 'Yakov left you a long time ago. It's Jack Bronson that's leaving now, and he's not worth fretting about. I'm sorry, Andrei, I truly am, but it's the only way.'

He slid his hand down to gently squeeze Andrei's arm. There was a finality about the gesture that rendered any further conversation pointless. As he turned to leave, Marta Wolenski entered the room carrying a tray.

'Yakov, where are you going? What about your coffee?' she asked, looking surprised.

Jack's expression hardened. He glanced at his devastated friend. 'Andrei will explain, Marta, perhaps another time?'

Chapter 46

Greystone Manor had become a forbidding place. Its sparsely furnished rooms no longer enjoyed a woman's touch that had given it the warmth of a real home. The large property was now surrounded by an expanse of uncut grass and long strips of heavily overgrown flowerbeds. Its swimming pool lay drained and littered with debris. The ornamental lake, choked by a mass of unchecked waterweed, had taken on the appearance of a stagnant swamp with its small boathouse and landing stage rotting into disrepair.

When Jack had returned home, Mrs Hurwitz went back to her flat, refusing to be in the same house as her son, declining his offers of financial help. Sam's Café still continued to trade under the management of a younger couple, who leased the small business from her. Jack had managed to retain the services of Marek's devoted nanny who remained at Greystone Manor to care for the child, but the rest of the domestic staff had been replaced by a group of cheerless men whose sole job was to protect their boss.

After the tragic deaths in Germany, it was obvious to Jack that he and Doug Levin were to have been the real targets that night in revenge for double-crossing the IRA, and he had his suspicions about their betrayal. Clive Remus's South London gang were under no illusions as to how their boss had died, and were proving to be a constant menace to his operation. Then there had been the question of Mark Jacobs turning up at that Hamburg restaurant, where Levin had died saving Jack's life.

These threats had to be eliminated, hence the meeting that was about to take place. In the bleak winter's morning a long line of cars were parked, bumper to bumper, along the leaf covered driveway. Heavily coated figures roamed the boundaries of the sprawling acres ready to discourage any unwanted guests.

As the gang members arrived they were shown into the spacious sitting room where Jack was seated, surrounded by bodyguards. He had become a dangerously embittered individual who had aged noticeably since the summer. There was a chilling remoteness about his eyes that almost rendered him expressionless. He motioned to a bottle of whisky standing on the table beside him: a signal for one of the men to refill his glass.

'Your attention please, gentlemen.'

His voice was harsh and aggressive, silencing the room. He lifted the drink to his lips, relishing the only thing that brought him any real comfort, taking time to study the dour faces assembled in front of him. Levin had been Jack's right hand man, and after his death there was talk of Jack becoming vulnerable. A few members of the organisation had begun to display signs of disloyalty, one of whom was sitting directly in front of him, flaunting an insubordinate smirk.

'You all know why I've called you here,' Jack began. 'It's time to punish those who have chosen to cross us. My close friend, Doug Levin, died saving me from a bloody queer who blamed me for losing his lover. I've spent a great deal of time and money to find the person responsible for his death. It seems that MI5 collaborated with the German secret service in putting Mark Jacobs up to it. A man called Robson is the Operations Controller at MI5. That treacherous bastard blackmailed me into doing a deal with him, and then tried to kill me. He's going to die for that.' Jack raised a hand to quell the sudden rumble of unease. 'After he's been dealt with, we wage war on the black mob south of the river. It had to be those arseholes that betrayed me and Doug to the Irish, leaving our women dead. If they miss Remus that much we'll send a few more of them to keep him company.' The rumbling voices turned to laughter. 'There's going be a great deal of blood spilt until I'm satisfied these threats have been dealt with. I won't tolerate any more shit from anyone. *Do I make myself clear?*'

There was a brief pause, after which the smirking man got to his feet with reckless confidence. 'Jack, don't you think you're getting out of line? I mean, killing an MI5 boss, its lunacy. And as for a turf war in South London, why don't we just talk to them? I'm sure we could work something out.'

The room fell silent. All eyes focussed on the boss who had dropped his gaze towards the floor, considering his response.

The man searched around for some sign of support. It didn't come. His insolent smile vanished as Jack stood up and started to walk towards him.

'Look, friend,' Jack reasoned, laying a hand lightly on his critic's shoulder, 'the only person getting out of line here is you.'

Without warning, he brought his knee up savagely into the man's crotch. The mobster yelped with pain and crumpled to the floor, clutching his groin.

'Any more questions?' Jack asked in a quiet voice, barely audible above the groaning. 'Good, then let's put out the rubbish and we'll discuss our plans.'

Two minders moved in to drag the injured man from the room. A few minutes later, the crack of a distant gunshot caused the conversation to dip momentarily: a salutary reminder of Jack Bronson's merciless authority.

*

Robson's long legs made it difficult for Peter McCann to keep up as they climbed a succession of steep stairs and marched purposefully along the labyrinth of grey painted corridors to reach the 6th floor of MI5 HQ. It had been an early start and McCann was hungry, but despite his rumbling stomach the prospect of a late breakfast was fading fast thanks to this latest development.

The Controller had been assisting his agents in completing a report ordered by the government as a result of the failed operation carried out in Germany. True to character, the Director General had insisted that Robson take full responsibility for the whole affair. Robson managed to lay most of the blame on the German Secret Service, successfully putting an end to the matter, until a message had been received from Jan Stevens to meet in his office.

'Just when I thought we'd put that Hamburg business behind us,' Robson grumbled.

'Bronson must be mad making threats against you, sir,' McCann called out, as they wheeled round the last corner.

'It's not unexpected, comes with the job I'm afraid,' said Robson, slowing down outside his office.

As he reached for the handle the door disintegrated in front of him with a roaring explosion, throwing both men off their feet. A scorching heat flared down the corridor, setting alight tiny fires across the thinly carpeted floor. Robson's ears drummed painfully. He propped himself up against the charred walls, wiping a hand across his watering eyes to search out his colleague through the black smoke belching from the doorway.

'Are you alright, McCann?'

He could just make out a raised thumb from the prostrate figure. The Controller pulled his lean body from the floor and grabbed a fire extinguisher off the wall. Stumbling into his office, he released a powerful stream of foam into the blazing room. Within seconds the intensity of the flames had died away to reveal the blackened form of a woman lying close to the smouldering desk.

She had been critically injured by the blast. Her right leg had been blown off below the knee, and what was left of her attractive face had been transformed into a mass of raw, reddened skin. Robson dropped the extinguisher and fell to his knees. He yanked off his tie to form a makeshift tourniquet around the severed limb, before gently gathering her in to his arms. The sickly smell of burnt flesh rose into his nostrils.

'Stevens...*Jan!*' he whispered urgently. 'Can you hear me? Talk to me, you *must* stay awake.'

Her eyelids flickered open to reveal a flash of beauty hidden beneath the appalling wounds. Robson ached with compassion, helpless to relieve her suffering. He was old school, and had never been comfortable with the progressive policies that allowed women to be involved in dangerous occupations. It was fundamentally wrong: morally wrong. She was trying to speak. He cursed his lingering deafness, lowering his ear to her lips.

'The bastards missed you eh, sir...didn't think they'd have the balls... must have been some kind of rocket...or grenade. I've got the note from Bronson.' Her scorched fingers fell open to reveal a crumpled piece of paper. 'Don't think I'll be drawing that pension...'

He forced a smile. 'Nonsense, you'll be fine. Just rest easy.'

She made one painful attempt at a grin, and closed her eyes.

Distant shouting could be heard above the jangling fire bells. There was nothing he could do except hold her, and pray that help would arrive soon.

McCann staggered into the smoke-filled room. He picked up the extinguisher and sprayed more foam onto the dying flames.

'How is she?' he asked, dropping down beside the young woman.

Robson shook his head slowly.

It seemed like an eternity before the medical crew finally bundled through the doorway. The Controller looked up from the floor.

'I'm afraid you're too late. Thank God, she died quickly.'

*

A white van blasted its horn. The doors to the warehouse swung open, allowing it to enter. Three men dressed in brown boiler suits left the vehicle and walked swiftly to the office where Jack was waiting at his desk.

'It's been on the news already. Is he dead?' he demanded, clutching a full glass of whisky. His aides had become concerned by his excessive drinking, but none would dare question it.

'Our contact confirmed that the note was delivered, and Robson had definitely gone to his office,' the man replied confidently. 'Yeah, he's dead. We could see a figure moving about in there before we fired. We made a bloody mess of the building. That grenade launcher is a serious piece of kit.'

Jack imagined his friend standing in front of him, wearing one of his slick Italian suits. 'That one was for you, Doug,' he said, flinging a shot of neat whisky into his mouth, clamping his teeth together as the fiery liquid burnt its way down.

'It's time to cross the river. Is everything ready?'

'It is, Mr Bronson,' one of the minders said, stepping forward with his boss's coat. 'Six cars are waiting outside, and all the men are armed, just as you ordered.'

'Good. Now we'll show those black bastards what a war is all about.' Jack allowed the coat to be slipped over his shoulders and drained his glass.

'Let's go.'

*

The driver tapped his fingers impatiently on the wheel, waiting for the thousand tonne road sections to settle back into place. He was soon accelerating across the Gothic structure of Tower Bridge, leading a small convoy of cars south of the river. When they reached Bermondsey, Jack looked through the rear window to see the other vehicles begin to peel off in different directions, heading towards their appointed destinations. He sunk back in the luxury of the Rolls-Royce, closing his eyes to compose himself in readiness for the violence that was about to take place.

Remus's mob owned many different interests in South London: pubs, clubs, bookmakers and restaurants, mostly situated within six suburbs: Lambeth, Kennington, Balham, Mitcham, Brixton and Streatham. Each place would be hit with a ferocity deserving of Jack's brutal reputation. He had chosen to attack Streatham, the black gang leader's hometown, making it the perfect place to exact his personal revenge. These people had betrayed him to the IRA, and they were about to pay for their treachery: Sandra would be avenged.

It was early afternoon and Streatham High Road was alive with activity. A few heads turned in mild interest as a white Rolls-Royce crept to a halt alongside the redbrick pub. A man leapt from the car and ran straight into the saloon bar, carrying two bottles with a burning rag stuffed in each neck. He reappeared in seconds to jump back in beside the driver, leaving behind a flash of flames that sent screaming customers tumbling out on to the pavement.

Not content with the outcome, Jack stepped from the vehicle armed with an ex-military Sten MK2. He braced himself, standing feet apart, and raked the submachine gun across the front of the pub, gunning down those trying to flee the inferno.

'For you, Sandra...this is for you!' he yelled above the clatter of gunfire.

His men waited anxiously while he stood, clutching the smoking weapon, taking time to survey the results of his handiwork. He then calmly climbed back into the car, leaving behind a groaning mass of tangled bodies, to drive away in search of a fresh target.

*

The audacious attack on a government building, followed by the gang's violent onslaught south of the river, shook the British capital; London now feared him. The gangster's brazen disregard for the law, and his cruel indifference to the sanctity of life, had been established beyond doubt. And such was the man's arrogance that he insisted on throwing a celebratory party at the Pink Pelican that evening.

*

Once it had been revealed that the death threat found in Jan Stevens' hand was from the gangster, Jack Bronson, an insatiable thirst for revenge raged within the department, making it difficult for Robson to maintain discipline.

How Bronson had so nearly achieved his objective still remained a mystery. And despite rigorous investigations, it was generally suspected that the informant had been some low paid, expendable employee: possibly a cleaner, or office boy.

The attempt on Robson's life, and the killing of an MI5 officer, together with bulletins that had been flooding in all afternoon following the South London shootings, had officially elevated Jack Bronson to public enemy number one.

The Controller leant beside the window of his temporary office, staring grimly into the evening sky. Beneath his inflamed skin he bore the appearance of a man struggling to remain focussed under extreme provocation. The Director General had infuriated him by daring to suggest that he should be mindful of his position, and not allow personal feelings to cloud his judgement.

It was easy for him to say that. He hadn't been there to hold the woman's charred body and smell the burning flesh. He hadn't been there to watch a beautiful, vibrant life expire in his arms. He was the one who had prevented Robson from hunting down Bronson when he had returned from Germany.

Peter McCann appeared to be in good shape apart from a few minor cuts across his face. After examining a handful of recently submitted police statements, he placed them into a filing cabinet and slammed the drawer shut.

'Bronson's a raving lunatic. He's got to be stopped. What are we going to do about him, sir?'

'The short answer is we kill him,' Robson replied, turning to face the younger man. 'But we have to take great care. This man's an arrogant psychopath, and extremely dangerous. He must be taken out with careful planning. We can't afford to lose any more of our people.'

'But surely, after this afternoon's bloodbath the Commissioner has every justification to deploy his armed officers and finish him.'

'Not that simple I'm afraid,' said the Controller. 'The police can't just wander up to the man and shoot him. The law demands they need witnesses, and witnesses are useless unless they're willing to testify. People are terrified of Bronson. And he knows that. He's not stupid.'

'Well okay, to hell with witnesses, I'll just kill the bastard. We don't function like the police.'

Robson lapsed into a tired smile. 'You know as well as I do that is not the official line. Theoretically, we're bound by the same lawful restrictions as any other public bodies. However, if we obeyed that ruling our agency couldn't function. It's all bullshit, a game if you like. We have to appear squeaky clean while carrying out our government's dirty work. Great job isn't it.'

McCann kept grudgingly silent. Jan Stevens'

death had hit him hard.

Robson softened, sympathising with his officer. 'Peter, you have to trust me, and you *will* obey orders,' he said sternly. 'I'm receiving continual updates on Bronson's movements, and I promise we will have him before the night is through. Fair enough?'

*

Andrei was sitting in the living room with his mother and sister watching the evening news. Pictures of a badly damaged government building, and sickening images of dead people strewn across London's pavements, filled the screen. Occasionally, references were made to the gangster, Jack Bronson, with allegations of his involvement in the outrage that had hit the British capital. Desperate appeals for witnesses were being made. Marta Wolenski rose from the sofa and moved across to turn off the television.

'I think we've seen enough,' she said in a subdued voice.

Maria glanced at her brother who was still staring at the blank screen: his face set like a stone mask. She got up to sit on the arm of his chair, laying a comforting arm across his shoulders.

'Remember what he told you, Andrei,' she said, her voice choked with emotion. 'Yakov left us many years ago. Jack Bronson is not worth fretting about.'

Andrei turned away to hide the tears that had begun to fill his eyes.

*

The celebration was in full swing, leaving the bar staff hard pressed to keep up with the insatiable demand for free drinks. Grovelling well-wishers shouted their flattery above the booming music as Jack moved among them. His minders had become disillusioned, weaving their way through the crowded club, wondering how far they would be prepared to go in protecting a reckless drunkard whose life must now be under a growing threat.

One man sat unnoticed at the bar, watching the evening's developments. After a while he slipped away, leaving his drink untouched.

*

In the early hours of the morning gunfire erupted outside the Pink Pelican, causing the drunken revelry to trail into a sobering silence. One of the doormen stumbled in from the foyer clutching a bloodied arm and collapsed to the floor. Women started to scream.

A white-faced Steven Bradley appeared behind the wounded man. 'Everyone get out! A bunch of guys just pulled up outside. They've started shooting…it looks like they're coming into the club.'

A group of people sitting at Jack's table leapt from their chairs and scattered towards the exits. Jack got to his feet, the alcoholic haze blown away as if a freezing blast of wind had struck his face.

'It's got to be that Remus mob. I thought we'd taken the bastards out. Get out there and finish the job, *now!*' he yelled above the mayhem.

His bodyguards had no stomach for a gunfight. Jack glared at them as they backed away in defiance: their loyalty finally spent.

The dependable manager battled his way through the jostling crowd, waving a set of keys above his head. 'Your car's parked out back,' he cried, tossing them at Jack who managed to snatch them from the air.

'Thanks, Steve. Coming with me?'

'No, you go, Mr Bronson, I'll take my chances here.'

The plucky manager had decided to remain in the club with a few members of his staff who were simply too frightened to run.

Jack rammed open a *Fire Exit* and ran to the waiting vehicle. He jumped behind the wheel, steadied his hand, and inserted the ignition key. It was time to lay low for a while; there was one place he might be safe.

Driving across London he reflected on his good fortune at having survived so many attempts on his life. He was clearly not fated to die. With his abundant wealth he would soon recruit new thugs to punish those who had betrayed him, and his vengeance would be terrible.

*

'Well done, McCann. For God's sake don't lose him.'

The car's crackling radio couldn't disguise the relief in Mike Robson's voice. His plan was working better than he had hoped. A group of his agents, posing as gangsters, had wounded one of Bronson's men at the club, successfully flushing out their target, leaving him alone and dangerously exposed. Peter McCann's driver was tailing the Rolls-Royce towards the East End of London, keeping a safe distance between the cars.

'So far, so good, sir,' McCann replied, gripping the handset. 'I'll report back when he reaches his destination. My guess is the warehouse down by the docks.'

'You could be right, and remember, *no* witnesses.' The order was cold and business-like as it closed the conversation.

Chapter 47

Mrs Hurwitz was rudely awakened by an insistent banging from the depths of the empty café. She slipped into her dressing gown, switched on the landing light, and picked up the shop keys. It took a moment for her eyes to adjust before making her way down the stairs.

'Rachel. It's me…let me in.'

There was no mistaking her son's muted voice. The old lady's first instinct was to leave him outside. Her hatred for him had intensified after Sandra's death. The girl had been like a daughter to her. But she was drawn towards the door; it was something she had to do.

He stumbled into the café swathed in a sweet stench of alcohol. His mother locked the door and invited him up to the flat for a coffee.

Jack took off his coat and threw it across the kitchen table, dragging out a chair to sit down. 'Thanks for letting me in, Mum. I need somewhere to stay for a while. Hope you don't mind?'

She made no comment and reached for a mug, while the kettle started to whistle softly.

'Look, I know we've had our differences. And I want to make it up to you, I really do. We can't go on behaving like this,' he said, trying to start a conversation.

Mrs Hurwitz shrugged in despair. 'I begged you to stop this madness, but would you listen?'

'Come on, Mum. It's not that easy to just walk away from things. You must realise that,' he argued.

'All I realise is that you killed Sandra as surely as if you had pulled the trigger yourself. Your own child is without a mother. Tell me, Jack, was it worth it?'

'That's not true,' he shot back, his temper rising. 'I would have died for that girl. You have no idea what I'm going through. My life is nothing without her.'

'At least you have a life. It's more than she has,' his mother replied in a chilling voice.

'Oh it's easy to throw insults and accusations,' Jack protested. 'You and Dad were happy enough to reap the benefits in the early days. And don't tell me you didn't know what was going on.'

His mother was incensed. 'How dare you! We trusted you, Jack. Your father thought the world of you. We rescued you from a miserable life in Poland, and you repaid us by becoming a gangster...a killer!'

'A gangster, yeah that's right,' he jeered, the alcohol firing his temper. 'Meanwhile, we didn't do badly out of it. We lived a great life, remember?'

'Didn't do *badly?*' the old woman yelled. 'Have you no shame, no pity? My husband's dead. That beautiful, innocent girl, Sandra shot to death. It should have been *you*, damn it!'

A stony silence fell across the room.

'*Should have been me?*' Jack muttered.

Mrs Hurwitz stared into her son's face. Tears welled in her eyes. 'It was you and Levin that were supposed to die that night, not those poor girls,' she confessed in a whisper, falling back against the kitchen cabinet, trembling with fear.

Jack's jaw fell open. He glowered at his mother. 'It was never the black mob. It was *you* wasn't it? You betrayed your own son to the IRA. How could you do such a thing?'

'You aren't my son anymore, you've become a monster,' she cried, her cheeks wet with tears. 'Yes, it was me. I phoned the Republicans. It wasn't difficult. I found their number in the pad lying on your desk. Someone had to stop you.'

'You evil bitch!' Jack shouted, losing control. 'Well I hope you're satisfied. What a bloody turnaround. Levin was murdered by MI5, you stupid cow.'

Mrs Hurwitz wasn't listening anymore. She was groping frantically behind her back for a drawer handle, keeping her eyes fixed on her son.

He started to laugh wickedly. 'All you managed to do was kill my Sandra, and her friend, Lucy. All that dying for nothing, and *I'm* still here.'

'Not for much longer,' Mrs Hurwitz sobbed, swinging both hands up in front of her, levelling a gun at the enraged man. 'Something else I found in your desk.'

Jack turned pale. He held up his hand, rising slowly to his feet. '*Steady*, Rachel, put the gun down, this has gone far enough…*Rachel!*'

The gun exploded, arching Jack's torso

backwards over the chair. He was dead before he hit the floor, but his body still continued to jerk as the old lady kept squeezing at the trigger, with tears streaming from her eyes, until the deafening shots turned to the hollow click of an empty chamber.

The sound of smashing glass was followed by a stampede of footsteps on the stairs. Three armed men stormed into the kitchen. She seemed unaware of their presence as they carefully relieved her of the weapon, and led her gently from the building.

*

Jack's death had come as no surprise, but Andrei had still been heartbroken at the loss of his childhood friend, and the circumstances of his killing simply deepened the tragedy. The first thing he did after the news was to contact Mrs Hurwitz. As expected, there was little he could say by way of comfort, but he was encouraged to find her fully supportive of his plans to adopt young Marek. It was as if fate had decreed that it should be his responsibility to shelter the child. Having lost the opportunity of fulfilling his childhood promise to Mr and Mrs Bronovitch to protect their son, Yakov, he felt a strong obligation to give a life to the grandson they had never lived to see.

He wasted no time in instigating proceedings for adopting the five-year old orphan, and instructed estate agents to search for a substantial property in Surrey, adamant that the boy should be brought up in a similar environment to before. His mother and sister were happy to assist in raising Marek; they adored the youngster as if he were their own. He would not be deprived of a loving home.

*

Mike Robson took his time. There was no need for haste as he left his office to attend a meeting with the Director General. He knew exactly what was about to take place: a firm handshake, followed by the predictable, insincere platitudes on a job well done. He could only imagine his boss's conversation with the Home Secretary. The thought of that man basking in the success of finally eradicating the country's most wanted criminal, Jack Bronson, sickened Robson to his stomach. Such moments would often shake his resolve.

The fact that it had been brought about by a frail, seventy eight year old woman would be conveniently played down. And the death of an aspiring young officer, Jan Stevens, would be listed simply as another unfortunate statistic: fallen in the line of duty. Robson reflected on a personal observation he had long held. The higher you climbed up the ladder of command, the further you rose above the harshness of reality. It typified the Director General perfectly. But in his capacity as Operations Controller, Robson vowed that it would never happen to him

The job would always come first. He was a professional.

*

When Peter McCann and his fellow officers broke into Sam's Café on that winter's night they witnessed the end of one of the country's most notorious criminal regimes. The slaying of Jack Bronson became the final deathblow to the organisation. Turf wars erupted, fragmenting the huge crime syndicate into smaller, less effective gangs that gradually dwindled into obscurity.

The inquest into Bronson's death was carried out swiftly, with the minimum of publicity, while the case against Rachel Hurwitz was considered to be unsustainable. An elderly widow protecting herself from a ruthless gangster was considered to be an extremely brave victim rather than a murderess, and any connection she may have had with the Bronson name was conveniently overlooked and would be forgotten in the fullness of time.

Mrs Hurwitz remained in her flat, continuing to enjoy a friendly relationship with her tenants. Although rarely leaving the refuge of her modest home, she was fortunate to receive frequent visits from Andrei and his family.

Chapter 48

The sound of squeaking brakes drew the old lady to the window. A tall man wearing dark glasses, with his long fair hair tied into a ponytail, had turned to pay the cab driver. His young companion looked up from the pavement, waving excitedly. She waved back and made for the landing to welcome her guests. Today was Marek's sixth birthday and Andrei had insisted they come over to visit.

'Grandma, it's me,' the small voice cried above the sound of footsteps galloping up the stairs.

Mrs Hurwitz reached out to the bright-eyed youngster. 'Hello, darling, it's wonderful to see you.'

She took the child's hand and led him into the sitting room, followed by Andrei who gave her a tight hug before settling into a worn armchair.

'Thank you for coming, you don't know how much pleasure I get from seeing you both,' she said, easing herself into the sofa opposite.

'We do, that's why we're here,' Andrei grinned.

Mrs Hurwitz gave Marek's hand an affectionate squeeze. 'You're growing into such a handsome young man,' she beamed.

There were no mistaking Sandra's eyes and soft features. Although he did share the same slight build and shock of dark hair as his father when he had been a small boy, suggesting that he would probably grow into a big man when he reached maturity: a true Bronovitch.

'Your gift is on the kitchen table. And I've put out your favourite cakes. The ones with the little coloured beads on them,' she said with a gleam in her eye.

'Thanks, Grandma,' Marek shouted, racing from the room.

'I understand you leave for America soon?' she was quick to ask once they were alone.

'Yes, at the end of the week. I do wish you'd change your mind and come with us. I'd lay on the best of everything for you,' Andrei pleaded, longing to convince her.

'You're such a sweet man. Please don't be offended. I'm no youngster anymore and I am content to remain here.'

Following the collapse of the Diamond Agency, the Blues Knights had been inundated with offers. They eventually signed to a prestigious American agency, which meant they would be spending the next twelve months in California to honour their musical commitments. Andrei had been trying to get the old lady to accompany them. His family had also endeavoured to persuade her, but to no avail.

Shrieks of delight could be heard from the kitchen. *'I love my present! Can I have two cakes, Grandma?'*

'Whatever you want, but don't make yourself ill,' she called back.

'Won't you reconsider for Marek's sake?'

Andrei persisted. 'He'll miss you terribly.'

Mrs Hurwitz remained resolute. 'As much as I love Marek, you have no idea how difficult it is for me to be around him. Not only do I feel responsible for his mother's death, but I also *killed* his father. This torment is my curse. It's something that will haunt me for the rest of my days The only comfort I get is staying here, in this flat, where I feel close to my Samuel,' she said, gazing slowly around the room. 'I still miss him so much.'

'Of course it's difficult, Rachel. How could it be otherwise? But it's time to move on. Samuel and Yakov are no longer with us. You must stop blaming yourself for everything.' Andrei's voice was gentle, but firm.

'Little Marek is just like Yakov,' she said distantly. Then a thought struck her. There was urgency in her voice. 'Andrei, you *must* tell him the truth about his father, before others get to him.'

He reflected on the sudden request.

'I will tell him that Yakov was a good person, who was turned bad,' he answered, springing to his friend's defence. 'No child should have suffered how he did. I blame my evil father for that. And I don't care what people think, I loved Yakov as a brother, not a lover.'

'Who would say such a thing,' Mrs Hurwitz said, appalled at the suggestion. 'You're a wonderful man. No, I blame myself. It was me that insisted on bringing Yakov to England. I sometimes think we should have left him in Poland then he would never have become Jack

Bronson. Maybe the way he turned out *was* my fault.'

Andrei's handsome face dropped into an uncertain frown. He had hidden the truth for too long; it was time for a confession. 'Rachel, there's something I have to tell you, a dark secret that only my sister and I know about.'

Mrs Hurwitz was suddenly attentive, fearful of what she was about to hear.

'I believe Yakov became Jack Bronson, as you put it, when he was ten years old,' Andrei began, glancing briefly towards the kitchen to check that Marek was out of earshot. 'On Christmas Eve, back in 1946, it was Yakov who stabbed my drunken father to death, using the knife he had been given as a present that very night. The same one he carried ever since. He had no choice. My father would have killed him.'

The old lady looked astonished. 'But we thought *you* did it. The whole town followed that trial in the papers. We read about the way your father treated you. It was sickening.'

'That was the whole point. I took the blame, knowing that I could plead self-defence against the man. Yakov was already in a state of shock after the murder of his parents, and the idea of the poor kid being sent to some institution was unthinkable. Anti-Semitism was rife. Anything might have happened to him. I had to do something.'

Mrs Hurwitz remembered that fateful afternoon at Grandma Anna's cottage when the wounded youngster had acted so strangely; the pumping hand, and her husband's comments about hitting back at their enemies. Things began to make sense.

'Dear God, do you think he was mentally unstable?' she asked.

'We'll never know, Rachel. But I have to remember him as he was when we were children. I have to believe that Yakov was not born a bad person.'

Mrs Hurwitz breathed a woeful sigh. 'I did love him you know, Andrei. He was such a lonely, defenceless child. It seems that everything I've tried to do in my life has turned out badly. I don't know what to think anymore,' she said, dropping her head into her hand.

Andrei leaned forward to comfort her. 'That's simply not true. You did what you thought was right. No one could have foreseen such a tragic turn of events. We could go on blaming ourselves forever, but it won't change anything. As I said, it's time to move on.'

The old lady sat motionless for a while, gazing into her lap. Andrei maintained a respectful silence. She eventually emerged from her thoughts and looked at him with glassy eyes. 'Move on…yes, you're right.'

He offered a smile of encouragement.

'Now, where's my little ray of sunshine,' she announced in a stoical voice, rising stiffly to her feet to join her grandson in the kitchen.

*

The authorities at Heathrow Airport had obliged Andrei's party by fast-tracking them through the formalities, minimising their exposure to the pestering photographers. Their brief journey across the concourse surrounded by security staff rekindled painful memories of his arrest. So much had changed since then. It seemed like a million years ago.

Relaxing in the refuge of the VIP lounge, Andrei

made a few phone calls, mostly international conversations with his new management in Hollywood, and members of his group who had already started work in the recording studios. The last call was to Mrs Hurwitz. As expected, it proved to be emotional. Assurances were made that time would pass quickly before their return, along with the inevitable promises to keep in touch. The final moment when Marek said goodbye left them all extremely heavy hearted.

Marta Wolenski was not keen on aeroplanes. She sat beside her son on the firm couch, nursing a cup of coffee.

'Aren't young ones amazing? Everything's an adventure. They see no danger in anything do they,' she chuckled, watching Marek drag Maria alongside the panoramic window that ran the length of the departure lounge. He was pointing at a row of neatly parked Boeing 707s that lay like so many slumbering giants, waiting their turn to climb into London's summer sky.

'Certainly not for that little one,' Andrei said, amused by his sister's attempts to keep up with the lively child. 'He seems to have accepted the loss of his parents very well.'

'Oh no, not really,' his mother corrected, 'we still have the occasional tears at bedtime. I fear it will take a long time coming to terms with something like that.'

'You're right, of course,' Andrei conceded. 'I more than anyone should appreciate the misery caused by a traumatic childhood.'

Marta Wolenski looked directly at her son. 'I can't help worrying about Rachel. The poor soul seems so alone. Do you think she'll be alright?'

He shrugged uncertainly. 'I'm sure she'll be fine. She's a strong woman,'

'Pan American flight 344 to Los Angeles is now boarding at gate seven.'

A tinny, singsong voice announced suddenly through hidden speakers, stirring the VIP lounge into action. Andrei experienced a strange reluctance to leave; there were too many memories to ease his departure.

Maria walked over to them with a delighted small boy tugging impatiently at her arm, desperate to join the other passengers who were already queuing to board the plane.

'Just a moment, Marek,' Andrei said, beckoning the youngster to stand in front of him. The little boy did as he was asked, with a puzzled look on his face.

Andrei reached inside his shirt collar to retrieve the wooden talisman. 'I think it only right that you should have this,' he said, slipping it gently over the child's head. 'It was made for me a long time ago by my best friend. And I know he would have wanted you to have it.'

Marek looked up with an innocent smile. 'Is he still your best friend, Andrei?'

'Oh yes,' Andrei whispered. 'And that's how I will always remember him.'

Epilogue

Early on Monday morning, a police car and an ambulance were parked in the Whitechapel Road. Their flashing blue lights revolved solemnly outside the small café with no apparent sense of urgency. The couple had called them out soon after arriving for work. They had found the shop floor flooded, and after hurrying up to the flat discovered the body of Rachel Hurwitz lying in a bath of murky, red water.

Two ambulance men were edging around the cramped bathroom trying to set up a stretcher. They were being hindered by an insensitive police officer, leaning against the wall, irritably scribbling details of the incident into his notebook. He could have done without this at the end of a long night shift. He should have been back at the station, enjoying a fried breakfast and a hot cup of tea.

The ambulance men pulled on rubber gloves. One of them shook his head sadly as they prepared to move the body. The old lady's slashed wrist hung over the side of the bath. Her bloodied fingers were pointing limply to the floor where a picture frame's shattered glass almost obscured the faded photograph of a dark haired boy.

Beside it lay a long bladed knife, with an ornately carved handle.

Printed in Great Britain
by Amazon.co.uk, Ltd.,
Marston Gate.